IR

Praise for Daryl Wood Gerber's Cookbook Nook Mysteries

"There's a feisty new amateur sleuth in town and her name is Jenna Hart. With a bodacious cast of characters, a wrenching murder, and a collection of cookbooks to die for, Daryl Wood Gerber's *Final Sentence* is a page-turning puzzler of a mystery that I could not put down."

—Jenn McKinlay, *New York Times* bestselling author of the Cupcake Mysteries and Library Lovers Mysteries

"In *Final Sentence*, the author smartly blends crime, recipes, and an array of cookbooks that all should covet in a witty, well-plotted whodunit."

—Kate Carlisle, *New York Times* bestselling author of the Bibliophile Mysteries

"Readers will relish the extensive cookbook suggestions, the cooking primer, and the whole foodie phenomenon. Gerber's perky tone with a multigenerational cast makes this series a good match for Lorna Barrett's Booktown Mystery series . . ."

—*Library Journal*

"So pull out your cowboy boots and settle in for a delightful read. *Grilling the Subject* is a delicious new mystery that will leave you hungry for more."

—Carstairs Considers Blog

Books by Daryl Wood Gerber

The Cookbook Nook Mysteries

Final Sentence
Inherit the Word
Stirring the Plot
Fudging the Books
Grilling the Subject
Pressing the Issue
Wreath Between the Lines

The French Bistro Mysteries

A Deadly Éclair
A Soufflé of Suspicion

Writing as Avery Aames

The Long Quiche Goodbye
Lost and Fondue
Clobbered by Camembert
To Brie or Not to Brie
Days of Wine and Roquefort
As Gouda as Dead
For Cheddar or Worse

Stand-alone Suspense

Girl on the Run
Day of Secrets

WREATH BETWEEN
THE LINES

A Cookbook Nook Mystery

Daryl Wood Gerber

BEYOND THE PAGE
PUBLISHING

Wreath Between the Lines
Daryl Wood Gerber
Copyright © 2018 by Daryl Wood Gerber
Cover design and illustration by Dar Albert, Wicked Smart Designs

Beyond the Page Books
are published by
Beyond the Page Publishing
www.beyondthepagepub.com

ISBN: 978-1-946069-83-2

Acknowledgments

"Nothing can dim the light which shines from within."
~ Maya Angelou

No book comes together without the help and support of so many. Thank you to my family and friends for all your encouragement. Thank you to my talented author friends, Krista Davis and Hannah Dennison, for your words of wisdom. Thank you to my Plothatcher pals: Krista Davis, Janet (Ginger Bolton), Kaye George, Marilyn Levinson (Allison Brook), Peg Cochran, and Janet Koch (Laura Alden). It's hard to keep all your aliases straight, but you are a wonderful pool of talent and a terrific wealth of ideas, jokes, stories, and fun! I adore you. Thanks to my blog mates on Mystery Lovers Kitchen: Cleo Coyle, Krista Davis, Leslie Budewitz, Roberta Isleib (Lucy Burdette), Peg Cochran, Linda Wiken (Erika Chase), Denise Swanson, and Sheila Connolly. I love your passion for food as well as for books.

Thank you to my online groups, Cake and Daggers as well as Delicious Mysteries. You keep me on my toes. I love how willing you are to read ARCs, post reviews, and help me promote whenever possible. Authors need fans like you.

Thanks to those who have helped make this seventh book in the Cookbook Nook Mystery series come to fruition: my publisher, Bill Harris, at Beyond the Page; my agent, John Talbot; and my biggest supporter, Kimberley Greene. Without you all, I'd go haywire.

Last but not least, thank you librarians, teachers, and readers for sharing the delicious world of a cookbook nook owner in a fictional coastal town in California with your friends. I hope you enjoy this story.

Thank you to my Plothatcher pals.
You make writing and chatting about life fun!

Chapter 1

"Tigger, look!" I shouted and then whispered, "Scary." I pointed out the driver's window of my VW Beetle at the supersized blow-up Santa that towered in front of Jake Chapman's white Victorian beach house. I loved its dormer windows and wraparound porch. It was situated at the north end of the strand and had a beautiful view of the ocean.

My ginger cat, not frightened in the least, stood in my lap on his hind feet, his front paws propped on the driver's window and nose sniffing the air. For over an hour, we had been cruising the streets of Crystal Cove while listening to a variety of Christmas music on the radio. Currently, Johnny Mathis was singing one of my favorites, "It's Beginning to Look a Lot Like Christmas." After touring five neighborhoods, Tigger and I had finally made it back to our own.

"The rest of his decorations are pretty, too, aren't they, Tig-Tig?"

Old Jake—as many in town call him—had affixed twinkling lights along the eaves and around every window, as well as along all of the branches of his leafless crape myrtles. A pair of gigantic candy canes flanked the end of his walkway. Wreaths hung on every door. "It might be the prettiest we've seen."

Tigger meowed then yawned.

"Ready to call it a night, pal?"

He purred his assent.

I made a U-turn to head toward home. "Most of our neighbors do Christmas up right, don't you think?" I'd set battery-operated candles in all of my windows and hung a beautiful berry and celosia wreath on my cottage door. "Not a lot of *bah humbug* types around here," I said. Of course, a few hadn't decorated for religious reasons.

At the undecorated house across the street, I caught sight of Jake's neighbor, Emmett Atwater, peeking furtively between a break in the drapes. He reminded me of a weasel with his needle nose and beady eyes. The tip of his cigarette glowed as he inhaled. I didn't think he was gawking at me in particular. I wasn't the only one driving with headlights off to take in the festive décor. Catching me staring, he snapped the drapes closed.

1

"Can't please everyone," I murmured, recalling a time a few years ago when I'd worked at Taylor & Squibb Advertising and had championed a campaign for Laser Luminescence. The product was a type of lighting system that could be set up anywhere on the property. It would project moving holiday images on a house or garage door or even a tree: elves, snowflakes, sugar plum fairies, you name it. The owner of Laser Luminescence had a rollicking sense of humor. He thought it would be fun to make one of the actor *neighbors* carp about how bright and garish the lights were, so the actor *home owner*, purely to irk the neighbor, put out hot chocolate for all who came to admire his lights. Needless to say, the foot traffic drove the cranky neighbor nuts.

"Poor Mr. Atwater." I nuzzled Tigger under the chin. "Maybe Jake should give him a few shares of his Apple stock to appease him." Jake could afford the gesture. He was a self-made millionaire.

Tigger meowed.

I nodded. "You're right. Time for bed. No more dawdling. We have a big day ahead."

• • •

Tuesday morning, after taking a brisk walk on the beach and eating an English muffin slathered with cream cheese and home-made cranberry sauce, I donned my favorite Kelly green sweater, a pair of jeans, glittery holiday earrings, and flip-flops—yes, even in December I liked to wear sandals—and drove to the Cookbook Nook, the culinary bookstore I now owned with my aunt.

Tuesday was typically my day off, but I couldn't afford to take it this week. The Crystal Cove Christmas Festival would get under way tomorrow and run until Sunday evening. Every day shoppers would be out in droves because Christmas was two weeks away. *Tick-tock*. We were almost ready. We'd set out numerous Christmas-themed cookbooks as well as a few mysteries featuring the holiday, like *A Cajun Christmas Killing* by Ellen Byron, *The Diva Wraps it Up* by Krista Davis, and *Read and Gone: A Haunted Library Mystery* by Allison Brook. The latter didn't offer any recipes, but I adored ghost stories.

Get a move on, Jenna Hart, I urged. I needed to tweak our window display and unpack dozens of boxes of new cookbooks and gift items.

I stepped out of my car with Tigger tucked under my arm and drew in a deep breath. How I loved the crisp air in winter. I found it invigorating and hopeful, like good things were in store. Singing "Fa-la-la-la-la," I pushed open the door to the shop, weaved through the bookshelves to the children's corner, and plunked Tigger on the kitty condo my father had built for him.

After stowing my purse and turning on a music loop of Christmas instrumental music — the first in the queue was a bright version of "The First Noel" — I moved to the display window and examined what I'd created yesterday. Wreaths were the theme the mayor had designated for the festival this year. She wanted a wreath hanging on every shop door. A few days before Christmas, a panel of judges would choose a winner. All of the shops in Fisherman's Village, the charming white, two-story complex abutting the ocean where the Cookbook Nook and the Nook Café were located, had gotten on board. Beaders of Paradise, a beading and craft store, had fashioned a beautiful wreath using broaches, rhinestones, and pearls. It glistened in the morning sunlight. The surf shop had made a wreath with toy-sized surfboards. The retro movie theater on the second floor had cleverly decorated an old film reel with ribbon. Vines, the wine bar above the café, had adorned artificial vines with frosted grapes and twinkling lights.

For ours, I had commissioned a local artist to create a wreath using miniature cookbooks, tiny salt and pepper shakers, aprons, and cookie jars. A huge red bow trimmed the top. Perfect!

The window display, on the other hand, needed work. Yesterday I'd set out a white picket fence and a fake blanket of snow. Atop that, I'd positioned a number of cookbooks, including *Jamie Oliver's Christmas Cookbook: For the Best Christmas Ever.* Women were our primary customers, and over the course of the last year and a half, after leaving my advertising job to join my aunt in this venture, I'd learned that Jamie Oliver's handsome face was an instant lure to women. The recipes in the cookbook were a lure, too. I had my eye on trying either the roast goose or the turkey wellington. Granted, I was not a gourmet cook — yet. My mother had done all the cooking when I was growing up; I hadn't needed to learn until I'd moved home to Crystal Cove. I was still challenged by ten-ingredient recipes, but I was becoming bolder by the day.

"Cookies," I said aloud. "We need a plate of wreath-shaped cookies. And a set of cookie cutters. And a gingerbread house with wreaths on all its doors."

"Talking to yourself is a sign of dementia," my aunt crooned as she came into the shop, the folds of her silver caftan rustling with every step. She was carrying the matching turban.

"Hogwash. I talk to myself all the time."

"I rest my case."

"LOL," I said, using the abbreviated form for *laughing out loud*.

She strode to me and peeked at the display. "Hmm." She tapped her chin. "You need glitter. And twinkling lights. And a north star."

"A star. Of course." I kissed her cheek. "You're brilliant."

"Tosh."

My aunt was truly brilliant and she was wicked smart when it came to finance. She was top of her class and valedictorian in college. Like Jake, she had invested well over the years. In addition, she had a refined sixth sense. She enjoyed telling fortunes—hence, the caftan and turban—and she could read auras. I adored her and was thrilled she had convinced me to give up advertising and move home to Crystal Cove. I'd lost my smile. It felt good to have it back.

I hurried to the storage room, put the items my aunt had recommended into a box, and set the box on the sales counter by the antique register. Next, I raced through the breezeway that connected the shop to the Nook Café to put in an order for wreath-shaped cookies and a gingerbread house. Chef Katie Casey, one of my childhood friends, assured me she was up to the task. She would have my goodies ready in less than two hours.

Back at the shop, I plugged in my glue gun to warm it up. By that time, Aunt Vera had donned her turban and had settled onto a chair by the vintage kitchen table near the entry. She was straightening a jigsaw puzzle that featured a wintry Dickensian Christmas, complete with vendors hawking food and gifts.

She glanced up. "Where's Bailey?"

Bailey was one of my best friends and the lead salesperson at the shop.

"She asked for the day off. She and her hubby are house hunting." Bailey and Tito Martinez recently married. So far, they were doing swimmingly. His small apartment, however, wasn't going to be big enough for them in the long run. They were talking about starting a family. Yep, Bailey, who months ago had balked at the idea of kids, had been won over by her husband's zeal. To get a jump on motherhood, she was reading every book she could find on the subject. I reminded her that her mother was one of the best role models in the world. Even so, she wanted to bone up so she wouldn't screw up.

"And Tina?" Aunt Vera rose to her feet, righted her turban, and grabbed a feather duster, which she began swishing back and forth across the bookshelves.

"I'm here!" Tina Gump, a svelte young woman who was working for us while she took culinary classes at night—she hoped to become a chef—waltzed in. "Merry almost Christmas."

"Why are you here?" I asked. "It's your day off."

"In December? Are you nuts? I'll take a few extra days in January when we're slow." She lifted a candy cane apron off a hook, pressed it to her chest, and twirled like she was dancing with an imaginary partner. Tendrils from her casual updo wafted in the breeze.

"Aren't you chipper?" I said. "What's up?"

"I had a date."

"With the poetry guy?"

"Yes."

During the Renaissance Festival a few months ago, she'd fallen for a young man who delivered scrolls of poetry. His real day job was teaching at the junior college.

"He's so dreamy. Did I tell you his specialty is marine biology? He owns dozens of fish. He has a huge aquarium at his place."

"You've visited his apartment?" I waggled my eyebrows at her.

"No, not yet. *Pfft.*" Tina flicked a tendril of hair off her face. "We're taking it slow. But I've seen pictures. He has dozens of pictures. By the way . . ." She didn't continue. She rehung the apron, fixed the sales tag, flung her purse on a shelf beneath the cash register, and started in on sorting money into the register drawers.

"Go on. You said, 'By the way.'" I returned to the display case with my box of decorations and trusty glue gun.

"Right. Sorry. I got distracted. Anyway, when I was at Latte Luck Café this morning, I saw Jake with a guy who looks just like him. He was really tan and scrawny. But he wasn't dressed very nicely. I think Jake was treating him to coffee."

"And . . ." I asked leadingly.

"They were talking in muffled voices, like they had a secret."

"Okay."

"A bad secret." She gazed earnestly at me. "The other guy seemed frightened."

• • •

Ever since Tina told me about seeing Jake and his friend, a worrisome knot had taken up residence in my stomach. No amount of Christmas music was easing it. Decorating my three-foot-high Douglas fir wasn't helping, either. So when someone began frantically knocking on my cottage door, my sensors went on high alert.

Heart racing, I called, "Who's there?" I knew it wasn't my boyfriend, Rhett, or my aunt. Rhett was in Napa Valley visiting his family. My aunt was having dinner with Deputy Appleby.

"Jenna, open up!" a woman with a low-pitched voice shouted. Not Bailey. Her voice was higher in tone, plus she and Tito were making candy cane cookies to donate to the homeless shelter.

"Jenna!" More knocking.

I rose to my feet. The woman knew my name. It wasn't posted on my mailbox or the door of my cottage. Wiping my hands on my jeans, I stole to the door. "Who is it?"

"Me," the woman replied.

"And me!" a girl trilled, giving me a hint as to who might be assaulting my door.

Tigger scampered to my side and batted my leg with his tail.

"Don't worry, buddy." I peeked through the peephole and

confirmed my guess. "This is friend, not foe." But not someone I was expecting. Whitney. Winsome, willful Whitney. My older sister. Light to my dark and curvier all over. And her eldest daughter, Lacy.

I finger-combed my hair, shook out my shoulders to loosen any kinks—I hated looking tense around my sister—and whipped open the door. The pretty wreath I'd hung on the door swung to and fro. "What a surprise."

My sister hugged me briefly, the top of her head barely reaching my chin, after which she breezed into my cottage. The tails of her mohair cardigan flapped backward like wings. *New and homemade,* I supposed. Whitney was a whiz with knitting needles.

"Nice wreath," Whitney said. "Did you make it?"

"I bought it." I was an artist, and in my spare time I painted, but during the holiday season I barely had time to breathe.

Lacy, a fourteen-year-old who roamed the earth under a dark cloud, slogged inside after her. She matched her mother in skin tone and hair color, but she was taller than Whitney by at least four inches and apparently didn't like her mother's neutral color palette. Her attire consisted of black leggings, black army-style boots, black tank top, and black scarf knotted at the neck. A silver ring adorned her nose. Black orchid tattoos graced her shoulders. Wasn't she cold? She offered me a slim smile—no hug—and instantly scooped up Tigger. "Hey, kitty, kitty."

"Tigger," I said. "His name is Tigger."

"Tigger," Lacy cooed. "You are so cute."

I peered outside searching for more of Whitney's family. I didn't see a car. The merry Christmas lights illuminating the roof on my aunt's house would have revealed one. "Where's Spencer?" Her husband.

"He's dropping our stuff at Dad's house and then has an errand to run."

"Dad's house?"

"That's where we're staying while he's on the cruise. Didn't he tell you?"

My father and his significant other, Lola, Bailey's mother, were on a river cruise along the Danube. I was so excited for them. He and my mother, rest her soul, hadn't traveled as much as they would have liked. Lola had renewed his spirit to explore. They would be back on Christmas Eve.

"Why are you here?" I asked.

"Geez!" Whitney huffed. "I told Dad to tell you. Lacy is competing in the Christmas a cappella event at the festival in Azure Park. Twenty groups from up and down California have qualified for it."

"Congratulations, Lacy."

She grunted.

"Of course, Lacy's group isn't like typical a cappella groups," my sister went on. "It's very edgy. They do a lot of hard rock." Her disdain was evident.

Lacy threw her mother a vile look. "We're good."

"Where's Lily?" I asked, referring to my other niece, a twelve-year-old tomboy who resembled me more than she did her mother. Dark shoulder-length hair. Cute turned-up nose. No curves.

"She begged to stay with her friend in Los Angeles. She hates going to competitions with her sister. She wants to practice her pitching." Lily was an ace softball player. "You know kids."

Actually, I didn't. Other than the ones that frequented the Cookbook Nook, I was at a loss. Oh, sure, I'd done a little baby-sitting growing up, but I'd never spent lengths of time with children. Did I want them? Rhett and I hadn't broached the subject yet. We'd recently started talking about tying the knot. After my husband's death, I'd been gun shy about committing to a relationship.

Whitney shrugged out of her sweater, revealing a pretty cream blouse tucked into coffee-colored trousers. She always dressed picture perfect. She fluffed her honey blonde tresses and eyed my place. It was the first time she'd visited since I'd moved home to Crystal Cove. "It's tiny."

"It's perfect," I countered.

"Small tree."

"In scale with the cottage," I said in singsong fashion, one of my coping mechanisms with my sister. Over the years, I had learned to deflect her dismissals. I turned to Lacy. "Are you excited about the competition?"

"Sure." Her single word lacked conviction.

I tilted my head. Was she singing for her enjoyment or for her mother's?

"Got anything to eat?" Whitney asked, making a beeline for my refrigerator.

"I was getting ready to make Mom's meat loaf. Want to join me?"

"Why don't I throw it together?" she offered.

"I can handle it. I've been practicing."

Whitney wrinkled her nose. I scrunched mine in response. *Sisters.*

"Should you let Spencer know you're staying for dinner?" I asked.

"He'll figure it out."

I grabbed her arm. "Hold it. What's with the attitude? What's going on?" My sister liked to have tabs on her family at all times.

Whitney glanced at Lacy, who was sitting cross-legged on the floor in front of the fireplace taunting Tigger with a piece of string, and then hooked her index finger at me to follow her to the front porch.

I did and closed the door. "Spill."

Whitney blinked back tears. "I think Spencer is having an affair."

Chapter 2

Over the course of the next half hour, as I made turkey meat loaf and Whitney sipped wine—Lacy had retreated to my bedroom, earbuds in place, so she could vocalize and warm up her voice—I learned why Whitney felt her husband was straying.

"He goes out almost every night and offers feeble explanations. An errand here. An errand there."

"He's a contractor. Maybe he has to pick up supplies."

"Whenever he's away, he doesn't answer his cell phone."

My mouth formed an O. I didn't let the word escape my lips.

"Whenever I confront him—"

"You've confronted him?"

"Not directly. Sort of." She pressed a hand to her chest. "He assures me he loves me and only me, but I don't believe it. I think . . ." She drew in a deep breath. "I think he might be jealous of how my home business is thriving. I told you he's been in and out of work. It's not steady."

"Is it possible he's taking on other jobs to boost his income and is embarrassed to tell you?"

"Why would he be embarrassed?"

"Because he's a man."

"No, that's not what's going on." She flipped her hair over her shoulder. "Besides, he always comes home teeming with energy. Another job would sap him of get-up-and-go."

"Not necessarily. Perhaps the job is creative." Painting was an outlet for me that brought me emotional comfort and restored my energy.

"He's not creative," she murmured.

The timer on the stove chimed. We tabled the discussion.

Over dinner, I tried to get Lacy to talk. She didn't.

Around ten, as they were waiting for an Uber driver to pick them up, Whitney pulled me aside again and asked me to take Lacy shopping for a dress tomorrow so she could have it out with Spencer.

"I have a shop to run," was my response.

But my sister was relentless. She wore me down with her *pretty pleases*, and after she cajoled me into admitting that I'd completed the window display, shelved all the new books, and set out plenty of gift items—she was a shark when it came to grilling me—she said Bailey, Tina, and Aunt Vera could manage the shop for a few hours. At ten in the morning, I would pick up Lacy.

I agreed, but only if she consented to lead a wreath-making clinic on Thursday. Tit for tat, right?

• • •

At noon on Wednesday, I stood in the dressing room at the Gossip Parlor waiting for the typical teen rant from Lacy about being too fat or too tall as she adjusted the halter strap of the dark red dress that she was trying on, but it didn't come.

For five long minutes, she assessed herself in the body-length oval mirror, turning this way and that. And then, to my surprise, she said, "Aunt Jenna, is it terrible to wish a truly evil person dead?"

I gulped. "Um, wishing and doing are two entirely different things."

"How different?"

She shot me a wicked glance, and something flipped in the pit of my stomach. I remembered the day she was born. Whitney had expected a perfect child with perfect manners and perfect brains; what she had gotten was entirely different. By the age of five, Lacy had shown signs of being a handful. *Time,* my father had told Whitney, *would soften the edges.* Right about now, I wasn't so sure.

I tugged the hem of my snow-white sweater over my hunter green corduroys and tried to lighten the mood with a fake conspiratorial smile. "Who's your target? Veronica Devereaux?" Veronica was the hottest girl in Lacy's school and a fellow singer. The one time I'd seen a photograph of Veronica, she was wearing an exercise outfit only a sausage could appreciate.

"Not her. My mom!"

I gulped again. Harder.

Crocodile tears pooled in the corners of Lacy's Dutch blue eyes. Seconds later they spilled down her pale cheeks. "She's so . . . mean! 'Be home by ten. Call when you get there.'" Lacy pitched her voice to match my sister's. Not a bad imitation. "'Do your homework. Cover your tattoos.'"

Ah, yes, I mused. *A mother's work is never done.*

"And now she's making me get a dress? I might as well shrivel up and die. I can wear black jeans and sing, can't I? The others in the group are wearing black. We want to look like a team."

Oh my. I braced myself for an even longer-than-expected day. Whitney had said to find a dress that would make Lacy look feminine and well mannered, no small feat with her ragged hair — did she cut it herself? — and chewed-to-the-nub fingernails. "I'm sure your mom means well," I said.

"No, she doesn't. She never does."

Up until now, Lacy and I had had a fairly good time, the teenaged version of a Las Vegas moment. *What happens in Crystal Cove stays in Crystal Cove.* Over the course of a few hours, she hadn't had any meltdowns, and we'd shared a few secrets, like where she stashed her candy at home — she adored Milky Way bars — and which rock stars she liked. Her favorite was Dilettante, of course. At the first dress shop we'd visited, Lacy had insisted on trying on some dreadful dresses that included a slinky leopard-print sheath and a mini black velvet number that barely reached her you-know-what, all of which, to my horror, she had gushed over. Afterward, I'd steered her to our present location, a new boutique located in Artiste Arcade, the cluster of high-end shops across the street from Fisherman's Village. The Gossip Parlor catered to the arty and youthful, but it didn't have quite the *edge* of the first shop. Its primary-color décor reminded me of a Mondrian painting.

"Mom says if I wear a dress to this competition, everyone will think I'm normal." Her voice rose in typical teenaged hysteria. "I don't want to be normal!"

I leaped off the blue velvet dressing room bench and threw an arm around her. The gesture felt a little awkward. We hadn't hugged since she was little.

She wriggled free and riveted me with her overly made-up eyes, now raccoon-like, thanks to the tears. "You've got to help me."

All my senses went on alert as I flashed on her initial question. Did she wish her mother dead? What did she want me to do, knock off my sister? Definitely not included on today's agenda.

I stayed cool and jutted a finger. "Hold on, young lady. I'm merely helping you shop for a dress, not abetting you in murder, got me?"

"*As if.*" Her mouth twisted up on one side, an indication that she had a personality worth salvaging, and I breathed easier.

"Back to the task at hand." I clipped her chin with my knuckles. "This dress. What do you think? I like you in red."

"It's blood-red."

"I stand corrected."

She twirled in front of the mirror. The knee-length skirt fluted around her thighs. She gazed at her backside.

"You look beautiful." I wasn't lying. She had a cute little figure, and red — *blood*-red — suited her pale coloring. If only I could get her to rethink the fake nose ring.

"It's okay."

"Good enough for me." I pulled my to-do list from my purse and crossed off the first item. One of the things I'd learned when I was at Taylor & Squibb was that I should never go anywhere without a pen, a pad, and a to-do list. Owning a special set of tools, like a gold pen and gilt-edged paper, made the list making that much easier.

"And the shoes?" I asked.

The saleslady had handed Lacy a pair of rhinestone-studded silver sandals.

"I can't stomp in these."

"Stomp?"

"We stomp in our routine. But I like these shoes."

Lacy needed a pedicure, but I'd tackle that issue later. Maybe if the rest of the day went well, I'd offer her a shopping spree in San Francisco during the summer. I'd fly her up.

In addition to the sandals, we picked out a pair of sensible heels that she could stomp in. Afterward, I paid for our purchases and we walked back to the Nook Café for a snack.

I loved our intimate café with its white tablecloths and view of the ocean. And the food? Excellent, if I did say so myself.

As a waitress ushered us to a table by the window, Lacy said, "Hey, did I tell you about my boyfriend? He's a musician." She snickered, as if *musician* said it all.

I could only imagine. More tattoos than Lacy? Shaggier hair? Maybe he was a sensitive kid who lived beneath an equally dark cloud.

"Mom says—"

My cell phone chirped, and I scanned the caller ID. Speak of the devil.

"It's her, isn't it?" Lacy started to gnaw on the cuticle around her thumb.

My heart wrenched at the sight. Most girls didn't show such overt dread of their mother. Whitney and I needed to talk. How critical was she of her daughter? Would she listen to me since I'd never been a mother?

Later. I let the call roll into voice mail.

Before I sat, Lacy threw herself at me and squeezed hard. "Aunt Jenna, thank you. I know I'm a pain in the neck, but . . . well, I couldn't have done this without you. Listen, if Mom goes ballistic about the tattoos on my shoulders showing—"

"She won't. I promise." I held her at arms' length. "The dress we bought is exactly what your mother wants to see you in." Seeing the black orchid tattoos were the least of her worries. "As for your boyfriend—"

"Oh, he's not my boyfriend. Not technically."

Not *technically.* I grinned. How many times had I said that when I was Lacy's age? My father was an FBI man and *technically* mattered to him. No lying. No obfuscating the truth. I'd toed the line—barely.

I tweaked Lacy's cheek. "Let's forge a plan for how to get your *not technically* boyfriend approved by your mom. Now, how about some iced tea?"

We ordered two mint teas and a plate of peppermint cookies.

As we waited for our order to be served, Lacy peered out the window. "Ew, who's that? And what's he doing?" She was pointing toward the beach below.

"That's Old Jake, a friend of your grandfather's, and he's cleaning the sand with his sandboni."

"His what?"

"It's like the machine they use to clean ice rinks—you know, a *Zamboni*—but this is for sand. That big fork thing at the back sifts through the sand and collects all the litter. He does it out of the goodness of his heart."

"It's not his job?"

"Nope. He doesn't need to work. He's a millionaire."

Lacy's eyes widened. "What did he do to make a million bucks?"

"He invested in the stock market."

"If he's that rich, why is he dressed in tattered clothes and that ratty old hat?"

"Because you don't wear your Sunday finest when you're dealing with trash and sand." I laughed. "Sometime this week, I'll take you to see the Christmas lights, and we'll drive by Jake's house. His are the most elaborate in town."

A waitress returned with our cookies and a pair of crystal flutes filled to the rim with tea and fresh mint. She set the drinks on cocktail napkins and asked if we needed anything else. We didn't.

Lacy dove into the cookies. I bit into one and hummed my appreciation. If only I could bake as well as our illustrious chef. I was getting pretty good at making candy—not the difficult kind that required using a candy thermometer, but I could throw together a pan of fudge that made Rhett swoon.

Between bites, Lacy told me everything about her *not technically* boyfriend. When she'd exhausted every synonym for *fabulous*, she sighed and said, "Isn't it a beautiful day?"

The weather did seem to be mirroring her good mood. The sky was an exquisite blue with orange sherbet-swirled clouds.

After wiping her mouth with a napkin, Lacy said, "How's your life?" as if we were now best friends.

"Good, thanks for asking."

She leaned forward on both elbows. "So why aren't you married?"

I nearly spurted my tea.

"My mother says you and your boyfriend are perfect for each other."

"She does?" I'd never said a word to my sister about Rhett. Maybe our father had talked to her. He adored Rhett. They fished together and swapped stories.

"Is it because Uncle David died?"

"No." My heart wrenched as I remembered what my husband and I once had, but all the lies and sadness he'd caused had tainted the good memories.

"If you got married, I'm sure your boyfriend would let you work."

"*Let* me?" I chortled. "In today's day and age, men don't have a say in what women do. At least, they shouldn't. Women should do what they want."

"If you say so." Lacy tugged at her ragged hair.

I reached for her hand. "How about we swing by the hair salon and have my hairdresser tweak your hair?"

"Do I have a say?" she jibed.

I grinned. "Of course."

"Okay. Let's go."

The hour at the salon was well worth it. Lacy loved her new hairdo so much that she'd even allowed the makeup artist to apply fresh eye makeup. On the way back to the Cookbook Nook, she kept checking herself out in store windows. She seemed happy until we reached the edge of Fisherman's Village parking lot.

She halted and glanced right and left before saying, "Mom and Dad aren't happy."

"What makes you say that?"

"Mom cries a lot. Dad's got a secret. I asked him to tell me what it is, but he said I didn't need to worry my little head. Talk about dismissive." She blew a raspberry. "I can handle whatever he has to say."

"I'm sure you could, but parents rarely tell their kids what's bothering them." My mother hadn't mentioned anything when she got sick, and we were all adults. I stroked Lacy's shoulder. "Relax. I'm sure they'll work out whatever it is." She didn't seem convinced. "Hey, want to do one errand with me? I want to buy a star for my display window."

Crystal Cove was set on the coast of California, south of Santa Cruz and north of Monterey. To the west lay the ocean. To the east rose the Santa Cruz Mountains. The main street, Buena Vista Boulevard, boasted most of the shops and restaurants.

We strolled down the block and stepped inside Home Sweet Home, a delightful store filled with everything from scented candles to comforters to collectibles. Thanks to the town's wreath theme, the shop was filled with them. Flora Fairchild, the owner, didn't have to do much additional decorating during the holidays. Year round, the shop featured a Christmas tree filled with Crystal Cove-themed ornaments. Michael Bublé singing "White Christmas" played softly through speakers. The aroma of hot apple cider hung in the air.

The place was packed with people I didn't recognize. The Christmas festival was attracting a ton of tourists.

Flora, who looked fetching in a green knit dress, was helping a dapper elderly gentleman select a doll from the holiday-clothed collection. Spotting a basket filled with sparkling stars just past them, I steered Lacy in that direction.

"Is there a smudge, Adam?" Flora asked worriedly.

Using his silk tie, the man buffed the chin of a curly-haired blonde doll in a red velvet coat trimmed with fur. "Not anymore." He grinned.

Flora released the breath she'd been holding. She prided herself on making everything in the shop pristine.

I selected a glittery silver star and showed it to Lacy. She chose a gold-filigree one. We held them side by side, trying to decide.

"How old is your granddaughter, Adam?" Flora asked.

"Amy? She's eight."

"Amy. What a sweet name," Flora said in a coquettish voice that surprised me. Her twin sister was a notorious flirt; Flora was more subdued. Not to mention, the man—Adam—was a good thirty years older than she was. "She'll love this doll."

"I'd like to buy all of them."

Lacy elbowed me and mouthed: *All?*

Flora's apple cheeks turned rosy with excitement. "Honestly?"

"Yes. She's my only granddaughter. I like to spoil her rotten."

Lacy mouthed: *Rotten.*

I knuckled her arm and bit back a laugh.

Adam said, "I'm buying a vacation home in town and want to decorate a room for her."

"Ooh, I have all the items you'll need. Bedding, lamps, wall hangings." Flora toyed with the plait of hair she invariably wore in front of her shoulder. "Which house are you buying?"

Adam shook his head. "I'm keeping mum until the deal is done."

"Who's your realtor?"

"Zoey Zeller."

"Zoey? Really?" Flora tapped my arm to get my attention. "Is it true, Jenna? Zoey's a realtor now?"

"She is." Zoey Zeller, or Z.Z. as most of us called her, was Crystal Cove's mayor. "Her son decided to go back to college. She doesn't want him to have to take out loans, so she's trying to drum up extra income."

"Doesn't she—" Flora placed a hand on her chest. "I'm sorry. I'm being rude. Adam, this is Jenna Hart. Jenna, meet Adam Kittridge."

We both nodded a greeting.

"As for Zoey, I had no idea." Flora liked to be current on all the gossip. "Doesn't she know it's not good to make life too easy for children?" She wasn't speaking from experience. She had no children; she'd never been married. "Children need to carve out their own paths. If a parent isn't careful—"

"Watch out!" a woman yelled.

Too late. A basket of fragile ornaments crashed to the floor. A mother restrained her freckle-faced child by the arm and admonished him.

"Oh, my, oh, my." Flora darted to fix things.

Under her breath, Lacy said, "At least I'm not the only bad seed in town."

"Stop." I bit back a smile. "Let's go."

Quickly, I returned the star I'd been comparing to its basket, brushed the glitter off my hands, took hold of Lacy's star, and headed to the checkout register. She trailed me, doing her best to stifle a case of the giggles. The sound was music to my ears.

Sadly, when we returned to Fisherman's Village, my niece's lightheartedness disappeared. Was she worried her mother would criticize her new hairdo?

As we neared the front door of the Cookbook Nook, I wrapped an arm around her and said, "C'mon, young lady. Stand tall. Big smile. You look gorgeous."

Before we crossed the threshold, she pulled me back. "Can I stay with you tonight, Aunt Jenna?"

"Don't you have a rehearsal on the event stage?"

"Afterward. Please? Mom and Dad can work things out if I'm not around." Her eyes pooled with tears. Her lower lip quivered. "Pretty please?"

I cocked my head and gave her a wry look. How could I refuse? She had learned how to beg from the best.

Chapter 3

The remainder of the afternoon at the Cookbook Nook went off without a hitch. The star that Lacy had chosen for the display was perfect. After placing it in position, she asked if there was anything else she could do. Seeing as her mother was arriving at that exact moment to set out items for tomorrow's wreath-making clinic, I said, "Yes, indeed."

For two full hours, Lacy worked alongside Whitney. After covering the craft table with a pretty tablecloth, they set out tiny pinecones, colorful beads, and an assortment of petite Christmas ornaments, everything from miniature instruments to elves to "Nutcracker Suite" characters. Neither exchanged a harsh word. Whitney even complimented Lacy on her new hairdo. I didn't see family counseling in my future, but I felt a small twinge of pride that I'd found a way to help them communicate. To my dismay, however, because business picked up in the shop, I couldn't find time to pull my sister aside and ask how the heart-to-heart with Spencer had gone.

At six, as Bailey, Tina, and I were counting the day's take and discussing the schedule for tomorrow, Whitney whisked past the sales counter.

"My, how times flies," she said. "Lacy, let's go. You've got rehearsal in an hour." She tapped her watch and bustled toward the door.

Lacy jogged after her mother and grabbed her shoulder. "Mom, wait. Um, I've been meaning to ask, can I spend the night at Aunt Jenna's?"

Bailey whispered in my ear, "Aw, sweet. You're having a sleepover? Are you going to paint each other's fingernails? Remember the trouble we used to get into?" She snickered.

I elbowed her to hush.

"Please say yes," Lacy pleaded.

Whitney turned to me. I nodded.

"That way, after rehearsal, you and Daddy can have a date night," Lacy added. "Won't that be fun?"

Whitney winced but quickly covered the kneejerk reaction. "Of course."

Lacy let out a chirp of glee.

After enduring a little more playful teasing from Bailey, I took Tigger home and assured him I wouldn't be late. I donned my puffy ecru jacket and headed to the festival to catch the rehearsal.

Azure Park was the town's largest park and featured live music monthly. As I arrived, an all-brass version of "Joy to the World" was playing through speakers. White tents circled the perimeter of the park, each outlined with tracer lights, many of them featuring handmade crafts, while others offered food and beverages. All the trees were lit, too. The park glistened like a fairyland.

At the north end of the park stood the event stage. A huge arced tent protected the stage, and gigantic klieg lights illuminated it. Dozens of teenagers were huddled near the apron. A few were stamping their feet to keep warm.

When I caught the aroma of hot cocoa and mulled spices, my stomach growled. Wanting something substantial, I sought out the Soup Meister and purchased a cup of puréed squash-apple soup topped with crispy bacon. Man, did it hit the spot. I downed every morsel in a matter of minutes.

"Jenna, over here!" Whitney yelled. She and Spencer were standing near a coffee vendor. She looked quite petite next to her husband, given his height and broad shoulders.

I tossed out my empty soup cup and joined them.

Spencer leaned in for a hug. "Good to see you, Jenna. You look great, as always."

I couldn't say the same for him. His jaw was ticking with tension, heavy bags marred his usually handsome face, and his eyes were red-rimmed, as if he hadn't slept in days. His rumpled white shirt and chinos didn't do much to help the impression. Had he and Whitney fought? Were they on the brink of divorce?

"You look a tad tired," I said. "Burning the midnight oil?"

His face tinged red. He cut a look at my sister. She wasn't listening to us. She was searching the venue.

"Lacy!" Whitney waved.

My niece bounded to us, the flaps of her bomber jacket flying open. As before, she was dressed in one color—black tube top, black fashionably torn jeans, and black Doc Martens. She clasped my hand. "Come with me, Aunt Jenna. I want to show you my favorite vendor."

"You're not wearing your dress," I said.

"Well, duh. This is rehearsal."

"Lacy, that was rude," Whitney snapped.

"Sorry."

"Where are we off to?" I asked, trying to diffuse the tension. "Let me guess. One of the vendors sells Christmas-themed nose rings."

"Ha-ha. Very funny." Lacy hooked her arm through mine.

I addressed my sister. "Is it okay if we roam?"

Whitney and Spencer exchanged a look. They both gave the go-ahead sign.

"This way." Lacy tugged me. "The place features all sorts of cool musical instruments. You know I play guitar, right? Well, I also want to learn to play a zither, and this place has zithers. You know what a zither is, right? Like a mini harp but better."

We passed a number of vendors hawking delicious-smelling goodies like cinnamon pretzels and build-your-own gingerbread bear cookies.

Inside Holly and Ivy, a floral vendor, I spotted one of our regular customers, a vivacious older woman named Gran, chatting with a gaunt redhead in a boxy gray sweater dress.

"Jenna, dear," Gran called. "Join us. What perfect timing. Were your ears burning?"

I said to Lacy, "Do you mind? Just for a second. Her name is Gran. Actually it's Gracie, but she hates that. She's a hoot. She has an extensive selection of cookbooks and comes into the shop at least once a week to add to it."

"Sure, okay, but no long conversation, got me? Mom would talk the woman's ear off. Like for *hours*." Lacy rolled her eyes.

"Two shakes of a lamb's tail," I promised.

We weaved through the beautiful displays of wreaths to reach Gran.

She nudged her companion. "Olivia, this is the friend I was telling you about, the one who owns the Cookbook Nook. Jenna Hart."

"Nice to meet you." Olivia had a gravelly voice, as if she'd spent decades smoking. She fidgeted with the strap of her cross-body purse. I didn't know her, but she reminded me of someone.

With my luck, I'd remember who at two in the morning. I was a light, often restless sleeper.

"This is my niece Lacy," I said.

"What a pleasure." Gran smiled. "You've got the prettiest eyes."

"I got them from my grandmother."

"As did I." Gran chuckled. "Jenna, Olivia is quite good with a barbecue, so she tells me. Do you have any cookbooks with a barbecue theme?"

"We have loads," I said. "Stop in, Olivia, and I'll give you a tour."

"I don't use recipes," she admitted. "I wing it."

"O-oh," I stammered, a bit flummoxed. Why had she and Gran been talking about cookbooks then?

Gran gestured like a display model. "Olivia and I were admiring all the beautiful wreaths. She likes the live green ones with red bows. I happen to adore this fake one." She picked up a black wreath made of lace and beads. "Isn't it handsome?"

Lacy whispered into my ear, "It looks perfect for a funeral."

"Handsome," I said, echoing Gran, and bit back a smile. "Well, ladies, it's been lovely chatting, but my niece and I have a couple of vendors to visit before she rehearses for the songfest, so we'll say good night. Olivia, nice to meet you."

"And you."

"Hold on, Jenna." Gran clasped my hand. "A little birdie told me wedding bells might be in your future."

"Well, that birdie doesn't know squat." I laughed. "Rhett and I are talking. We've made no decisions yet."

"Don't let him slip away," she warned. "He's a keeper."

I guided Lacy out of the tent.

When she got her bearings, she pointed. "There's the zither place. See it? It's called A Christmas Note."

She released me and raced ahead. When I caught up with her, I paused in the entryway to appreciate the vendor's cleverness. Instruments stood on musical note- and clef-shaped stands. Overhead, instruments hung by wires from the tent's supporting bar.

Lacy strode to a table loaded with instruments and ran her

finger along the strings of a rosewood harp zither. The sound was melodious. "Isn't this beautiful?"

I eyeballed the price tag. "It's quite expensive."

"I'm saving up. Look at this one." She gestured to a black one that was painted with colorful flowers. "Isn't it pretty?"

I loved her enthusiasm. How I wished her mother could see this side of her.

We browsed for another few minutes, Lacy pointing out bongo drums and bells and tambourines.

As we left, I peeked inside the tent next door called Forget Me Not, named after the rare collectibles shop situated at the north end of town. I tapped Lacy on the shoulder. "Hold on. My turn to make a short stop."

"Again?"

"Yes, again. I want you to meet someone."

She groaned as only a teenager could.

The owner of the shop, Raquel Adagio, a plump, cherub-cheeked woman in her late forties, visited the Cookbook Nook with regularity on the hunt for cookbooks with easy recipes to give her youngest sister. The last time she'd ventured in, she admitted she wasn't sure her sister had even opened one of them. *Lazy*, she'd muttered. I'd countered that perhaps her sister wasn't lazy but, rather, intimidated, and suggested enrolling her in a cooking class to help her overcome her fear. I confided how lengthy recipes had overwhelmed me for a very long time. Raquel had loved the idea.

"Follow me," I said.

Raquel didn't look up as we stepped inside. She was standing at the checkout counter holding a loupe in one hand and examining a stamp affixed to an envelope for two gentlemen with their backs to us.

On either side of the checkout counter stood glass display cases, each rimmed with twinkling lights and containing stamps and other curios. A freestanding bookshelf holding leather-bound books and a few statues stood along the far wall of the tent. A foot-high blinking Christmas tree perched on top of one. A woman who I assumed was one of Raquel's older sisters—she had the telltale Adagio cherub cheeks, although she was leaner and dressed in an all-black, form-fitting outfit that a cat burglar would crave—was standing beside an antique clerk's desk flipping through an album.

"It's definitely a Blue Mauritius," Raquel said to her customers, her voice breathless with awe. "I've never seen one up close."

"You want me to meet *her*?" Lacy asked.

"No, not Raquel." I squeezed my niece's arm. "One of the men she's helping." I signaled Raquel that I was sneaking up and thumped the shoulder of the man on the left.

Jake Chapman swung around. "Hey, Jenna. What a nice surprise." His pale green eyes were bright. His silver hair gleamed in the overhead light. He was dressed in a crisp white shirt, blue jeans, and a casual but very expensive suede jacket. He swung back to Raquel, removed the envelope from her hand, and gathered a pane of stamps off the counter. Jake slipped the pane into the envelope, slotted two other items into it, and deposited the envelope into his jacket pocket.

His friend, who was as lean and old as Jake, mirrored the moves, stowing a pane of stamps and loose papers into an envelope and slotting the envelope into his jacket pocket. I sensed Raquel wanted to say something more to the men, but she held back.

Jake offered a rakish grin and reached out to me. I took hold of his hands. "You're looking well," he said. He didn't lean in for a kiss. That wasn't his style. He rubbed his thumbs gently across my knuckles, a paternal gesture my father often made.

I released him and said, "Jake, this is my niece Lacy. She saw you riding your sandboni earlier."

"This is *that* guy?" she gawped. "But he's . . ."

"Handsome in a gnarly old cowboy way?" I joked.

"Well, yeah."

"Jake, I'm afraid she thought you were pretty ratty-looking in your work clothes," I confided.

"Balderdash. I'm sure I was the epitome of handsome." He smirked, which highlighted his strong jaw. "I hope you have wonderful things planned for yourself, young lady," Jake said to Lacy. He uttered the same line to everyone new he met.

"I do." Lacy eyeballed the guy standing next to Jake. "What's your name?"

The man didn't answer.

"Geoffrey, don't gawk at the ladies," Jake said. "Say hello."

Geoffrey said, "Hiya."

When he grinned, I flinched. I couldn't help it. Every one of his front upper teeth were capped, and he was missing at least two of his lower teeth. What had happened? I recalled Tina saying Jake's friend had seemed scared. Had he been in a fight? Other than his teeth issue, he didn't appear to have any apparent bruises.

"Geoffrey and I go way back." Jake hooked his thumb. "Wa-a-ay back."

Had they known each other when Jake was a drifter, before he took the road less traveled and settled in Crystal Cove?

Jake and Geoffrey stepped outside. I waved goodbye to Raquel, and Lacy and I followed the men. A cool lick of breeze hit my face and neck and made me wish I'd worn a scarf.

"What were you and Raquel discussing, Jake?" I asked.

"We were checking the value of a few stamps," he said. "I collect them."

"Do you collect them, too, Geoffrey?" Lacy asked.

"Not really. I—"

A strident sound crackled through a loudspeaker. Some of the teenagers near the stage covered their ears.

"Oh, that's my cue," Lacy said.

"Cue for what?" Geoffrey asked.

I wrapped an arm around Lacy's shoulder. "My niece is competing in the a cappella Christmas competition."

"Congratulations," Jake said. "What song are you singing?"

"'Same Old Lang Syne.'"

"I don't know that one," I said, sorry I hadn't thought to ask her before.

"Sure you do." Jake hummed a few bars. "It's a Dan Fogelberg tune."

"Not bad, Jake," Lacy teased.

"I used to sing and play guitar." To me he said, "The song tells the story of a performer who meets up with a former lover at a grocery store on a snowy Christmas Eve. They talk about their mess-ups and their current lives and realize they'll never get together."

I gazed at Lacy. "Why are you singing that? It sounds so sad. And so adult."

"Because we don't want to sing standards. We want to be unique. You'll see. Bye." She gave me a squeeze and ran off.

"Ah, me," Jake sighed. "She reminds me of the one that got away."

"Who was that?" I asked. "Obviously not your wife. You were married for forty years."

"There was one before her. Before I came to Crystal Cove." Jake's eyes grew misty.

"What happened to her?"

"She dumped me."

"Why?"

He hesitated. "I got in trouble with the law. She split before my sentence was determined."

"Sentence? What did you do?"

"It doesn't matter. I was acquitted, but I had to do three months public service."

"I'm sorry she left you."

"Life doesn't always come wrapped up in a pretty bow." He shrugged. "You of all people know that, Jenna."

Did I ever.

"Jake, hold up!" Mayor Zeller called from a distance. "We need to talk. It's urgent!"

Chapter 4

Z.Z. chugged toward us, her red cape swirling about her. Whenever I saw her, I was reminded of a supersonic train, or like tonight, a whirling dervish. She never seemed to run out of energy.

Geoffrey said, "Jake, I'm going in there." He pointed to a tent featuring handmade Christmas ornaments. Odd. Was he really interested in ornaments, or was he trying to duck the mayor? Maybe he had a police record of some sort and was worried the mayor might recognize him. I flashed on that silly scene in *Romancing the Stone* when Danny DeVito tried to grab his picture off the wall in the police station in Colombia and tumbled off the counter.

"Hello, Jenna," Z.Z. said and graced my cheek with a kiss. "Jake—"

"You aren't here to ask me on a date, are you, Zoey?" Jake jibed.

Z.Z. flushed three shades of pink. "No. Heavens, whatever gave you that idea?" Although she was more than twenty years younger than he was, everybody knew she had a crush on him. I was pretty sure he liked her, too. They had yet to date. "This is business."

"You can ask me out, you know." Jake winked. "Women are allowed to do that nowadays."

"Stop." She swatted his arm. "You're a tease, but if I did, would you say yes?"

"You'll have to ask."

She scrunched up her mouth. After a moment, she said, "To business. A client of mine wants to buy your house."

"It's not for sale."

"I know that, but he's determined to change your mind. He saw it and desperately wants to own it."

I said, "Is he about yea high"—I measured above my head—"fairly attractive with salt-and-pepper hair and a hook nose?"

Z.Z. nodded. "How did you know?"

"I saw him at Home Sweet Home purchasing a passel of dolls for his granddaughter. He said he wanted to buy a vacation home here."

"That's him. Adam Kittridge. He's a prominent businessman from San Francisco."

28

"Well, you'll have to find him another one," Jake said. "I'm not selling. Where else can I step outside each morning to commune with the beach?"

"He's offering ten million."

"No way."

"He'll double that offer."

"I don't care if he quadruples it. Find him someplace else."

"Aren't you tired of living next to that crackpot Emmett Atwater?" Z.Z. asked. "He's always filing complaints about you and your flagpole." Daily, Jake hoisted an enormous American flag on a fifty-foot flagpole. "And now with the Christmas décor . . ." She waved her hand.

"Emmett is Emmett," Jake said. "Some people feel the need to grouse. He's got the right to free speech. I ignore him."

"Hello, singers!" a skinny woman with a ponytail on the stage blasted through a microphone. The noise reverberated in my ears. After an electrical adjustment, the woman said, "In two minutes, the rehearsals will begin. Make your way up here."

"That's *my* cue," Jake said. "I want to hear your niece sing." He whistled to Geoffrey. The two of them headed off.

"Well, I never," Z.Z. said.

"His mind is made up. Time to move on with this Adam fellow." I squeezed her elbow affectionately. "However, if I were you, I would ask Jake out on a date. He gave you every opportunity."

She beamed. "He did, didn't he?"

Two groups rehearsed before Lacy's. The first, an octet of young ladies dressed in matching red dresses and Santa hats, sang "We Need a Little Christmas" with cheery energy. The second, a blend of a dozen boys and girls that called themselves the Ransom Notes, all clad in red spandex, put on an exciting version of "This Is My Wish," with coordinating dance and gymnastic moves.

When it was Lacy's turn, she and her ensemble, Nothing but Treble, which consisted of eight teenaged girls, met center stage. Like Lacy, they were all wearing black tube tops, torn jeans, and Doc Martens. I spotted the curvy Veronica Devereaux in the group. What do you bet she had a say in the outfit?

As the ponytailed director had done for the two previous

introductions, she tapped her microphone and said, "Whenever you're ready, team."

Lacy crooned a beat-box tempo. Within seconds, all the girls began strutting along the stage, using their heels to emphasize the downbeat, and I understood why Lacy had wanted shoes she could stomp in. After thirty seconds of rhythm, they began their soulful and haunting song. Before each chorus, they broke into a scatting sequence that Ella Fitzgerald would have approved. When they finished, I glimpsed the ponytailed director. Her mouth was agape. Apparently Nothing but Treble had surprised her. In a good or bad way, I wasn't sure.

I applauded and searched for Lacy's parents. I didn't see them. In their stead, I rushed to greet her as she left the stage.

"Well?" she asked. "What did you think?"

"I loved it. You were great. And between us, I think you rock in black. How about adding a red scarf to the look to get in the Christmas spirit?"

"No blood-red dress?"

"Nope. Keep that for Christmas dinner and surprise your mom."

• • •

We found Whitney at the tent named A Stitch in Time, a knitting and sewing store packed with darling sewing kits and decorative knitting needles and yarn. She was carrying a handful of knitting needles to the sales counter.

"Finding what you need, Mom?" Lacy asked as she kissed her mother.

"What do you think?" She regarded Lacy with a smile. "By the way, you were good, sweetie. Very good."

"You seem surprised."

"I wasn't expecting . . ." Whitney struggled for the right words.

"Such a coordinated effort?" I suggested.

"Exactly." Whitney paid for her purchase.

I said, "I liked the costumes."

Whitney nodded. "I did, too, I have to admit."

Lacy uttered a gleeful sound.

"But what about the dress, Jenna?" Whitney said. "You and Lacy spent the whole day shopping."

"No big deal. I'll take it back." I elbowed Lacy. "We had fun."

"Where's Daddy?" Lacy asked.

"A man named Jake approached us and asked him if he could hire him to fix a snafu with his Christmas lights."

"Jake Chapman," I said.

"I believe so."

What kind of snafu could Jake have had? Did that cranky neighbor of his sabotage them?

"He said he recognized us from pictures Dad had shown him," Whitney added. "Dad had touted Spencer's skills."

"Mom . . ." Lacy gazed at me. "Is it still okay for me to stay at Aunt Jenna's?"

"Yes, of course. I'm a big girl. I can be alone at night. Don't worry. I'll wait up for your father."

There was a bite to her tone. How I hoped they could resolve whatever was going on between them.

Lacy and I drove to my father's house, picked up a few things for her one-night stay, and sped to the cottage. Tigger was ecstatic to see her. He trotted beside her like a shadow. She delighted in the attention.

"What should we cook?" I asked. "Do you like pizza?"

"I eat too much pizza, and cheese isn't good for my vocal chords. Do you have fish or vegetables?"

I gawked at her. She was a surprise a minute. "I have both."

"And lemons and honey and white wine?"

"Wine?"

"To make lemon sauce. Mom taught me how."

Huh. Well, at least my sister and her daughter could bond in the kitchen. That was a plus.

Tigger settled onto his kitty condo—yes, my father had built him a second one so he wouldn't scratch everything in my cottage—and I put on a Judy Garland CD of Christmas music. When Lacy and I started singing along with Judy, I felt a tug on my heartstrings. My mother and I used to do the same. Close to eight, we sat at the table in my tiny kitchen, and Lacy lit into her food.

"The sauce is good," I said.

"Thanks." She leaned forward, fork in hand, and set one elbow on the table. "Tell me more about that Jake guy."

"Why?"

"My dad is working for him. Call me protective." She tapped her fork on her plate. "He and his friend were sort of secretive, don't you think? I mean, like, the second we walked into Forget Me Not, they pocketed whatever they were holding."

"Because their transactions were concluded."

She clicked her tongue, not buying my explanation at all. "Oh, sure, they were checking out stamps. I got that. But Jake was stuffing other junk into that envelope, including a bankbook and birth certificate. Is he on the run?"

"What a leap in reasoning."

"He was cagey, and his friend was cagier."

I gawped at her, astonished by how much she'd taken in. "Why did you notice all that?"

"Because I save everything like ticket stubs, playbills, and report cards so I can fill up my diary. I want to recreate my life story. To get started, I made a copy of my birth certificate. Plus, I recently opened a bank account because I'm making some good money."

"Doing what?"

"Walking dogs at twenty bucks an hour."

I ate another bite of dinner and set my fork down. "I would imagine Jake might always travel with those items."

"Why?"

"When he first arrived in Crystal Cove, he was a nomad."

"You mean, homeless?"

"No. He was looking for somewhere to put down roots. He was on the beach one day, and he saw your grandfather in the water. Jake was about eighteen then. Dad was twelve and goofing off with some of his friends. A wave hit him hard and he caught a lungful of water. He went under. When he didn't resurface, Jake dove in and saved him. My grandfather was so thankful to Jake for saving Dad's life that he took Jake under his wing and taught him how to invest. Jake had a knack for numbers and became a millionaire."

Lacy dug into her food again. "Yeah, okay, I suppose he wouldn't run off and leave his wife with that big house."

"He's a widower."

"Geez, that's sad. Does he have kids?"

"None."

"Wow."

Around ten, as we were washing the dishes, someone knocked on my cottage door. Thinking it was Whitney and concerned that Spencer and she might have fought, I rushed to answer. Seeing Jake, his hair askew and his eyes moist with tears, sent a shiver of worry through me.

"Jake, what's wrong?"

"Come quick." He was still dressed in his suede jacket and jeans. "You've got to help me. My friend — Geoffrey — he's . . ." Jake gulped in air.

"What happened?"

"Decorations. Lights." He punctuated each word, making no sense. "Come. Please." He reached for me.

I fetched my cell phone and jacket and took hold of Jake's hand. It was clammy. I said to Lacy, "Stay with Tigger."

"Fat chance." She threw on her leather jacket and ordered Tigger to stand guard.

As we ran along the street toward the north end of the shore, I yelled, "Jake, is your friend hurt?"

"Yes."

"What happened?"

"Stabbed. With a star."

"A star?"

"A tree topper."

"Why didn't you call 911?"

"I disconnected my house phone. Too many robocalls."

"What about your cell phone?"

"I don't have one. It causes cancer."

Old school, I thought as I punched 911 into my phone.

"He's around the side, by the kitchen door." Jake let go of me and bolted ahead.

His house glowed brighter than it had when I'd driven around the neighborhood with Tigger. My brother-in-law must have amped up the Christmas décor wattage by a factor of ten.

"Geoffrey," Jake called. "I've brought help, buddy."

I followed Jake between the detached garage and house. I gasped when I saw Geoffrey lying faceup, halfway in and out of the kitchen doorway, his body trussed in Christmas lights. A boom from the surf pounding the shore punctuated my gasp.

Jake hustled to his friend and slipped a hand behind his head.

Lacy tried to pass me. I gripped her arm. "Stay back."

The 911 operator answered my call. "What's your emergency?"

"A man has been stabbed and tied up with Christmas lights." I didn't see blood on his shirt. How badly could a decorative star have injured him?

I gave the operator the address, heard her say she was sending a team, and ended the call. Geoffrey's face was tinged blue. There was no rise and fall to his chest. Upon closer inspection, I could see the string of Christmas lights were wound tightly around his neck. Too tightly. An ornate gold tree-topper star and bloody brick lay to one side of him. Open containers of Christmas lights and ornaments stood on the other side, as did a stack of loose bricks.

I knelt beside Jake. Tears streaked his weathered face. He obviously knew what I knew — Geoffrey was dead.

"Are these your Christmas lights?" I asked.

"Yeah. I was ready to return the extras to the garage."

"And the tree topper?"

"Uh-huh. From Home Sweet Home. My wife" — he sucked back a sob — "collected them."

"What are the bricks for?"

"I repaired the planter last week. I had a few leftovers."

"I don't see blood on Geoffrey's chest. Did you move him?"

"He was facedown. I was afraid he'd suffocate. The star was in his back. The brick —" Jake moaned. "Emmett must have done this."

"Emmett?"

"My neighbor." He shot a finger at Atwater's house, spittle flying from his mouth. "You heard Z.Z. He hates that I decorate for Christmas. He's constantly carping on me to take it all down. Every year, he slaps me with injunctions. He must have thought Geoffrey was me."

Looking at Geoffrey, I could see why. He and Jake looked similar: same build, same hair. Attacking from behind with a brick, the killer could have easily made the mistake.

Lacy let out a squeal. I spun around. She had inched closer. Her hand was covering her mouth. I ran to her and turned her away from the horror.

"Daddy was here helping Jake," she said. "Maybe he saw what happened."

"Jake, where's Spencer?" I asked.

"He left when I did."

"Where did you go?"

"To the store to buy a frozen pizza. Geoffrey and I didn't want to eat out, so I—" His body shuddered.

I noticed a toppled paper grocery bag from the local grocery store at the foot of the steps leading to the kitchen. I'd missed seeing it before. The corner of a box of pizza peeked from the opened end.

A siren pierced the air. Red flashing lights flared between the house and garage.

I said, "Jake, I'm going to meet the EMTs and steer them in this direction."

"There's nothing they can do."

Chapter 5

I sprinted to the front of Jake's house. Lacy ran beside me like a well-heeled puppy.

A male and female emergency medical technician clambered out of a fire truck.

"Follow me," I said, "but I'm afraid he's dead."

The female asked me questions. I shouted answers over my shoulder. I didn't know Geoffrey's last name. Jake would have to supply that.

Minutes later, the male EMT declared Geoffrey, last name Gunther, deceased. The female alerted the police.

A short while later, Chief Pritchett arrived with her team. Cinnamon and I were friends, and recently we'd met for coffee to discuss her upcoming wedding—yes, after deliberating for months, she and her intended had set a date—but tonight she was all business. She gave me a cursory glance before hitching her brown trousers and crouching to take a closer look at the victim.

I sidled to Lacy and wrapped my arm around her. I knew I should take her home, but I didn't want to leave Jake. With my father out of town, I was Jake's *family* tonight. "Are you okay?" I whispered. She was shivering. "Do you want my jacket?"

She wagged her head. "Poor Jake looks lost."

He did. His jaw was slack, his eyes red-rimmed. He was sitting on the edge of a planter filled with pansies, gazing up at Deputy Marlon Appleby, who towered over him asking questions. We were close enough to hear a few of the questions like *who, what,* and *when* and whether he'd moved the body. After that, the chatter of the police technicians wiped out all other conversation.

An eerie sensation snaked up the back of my neck. Not from the cold. From a presence. I turned and saw Jake's neighbor creeping around the garage. The police hadn't cordoned off the area yet. Dressed in a heavy army fatigue jacket and camouflage trousers, with his arms extended in front of him like paws, Emmett resembled a weasel more than ever, which disturbed me because I'd seen a weasel in a zoo enclosure wrap its body around a rat to immobilize it, and then deliver a killing bite to the back of the head.

I rasped, "Chief."

Cinnamon glowered at me.

What? I mouthed. Certainly she didn't think I had anything to do with the current situation. Okay, sure, I had some experience finding dead bodies. *Too much* experience. I wasn't happy about that, either, but this wasn't my fault. None of the incidents were my fault.

I jerked a thumb in Emmett's direction and dared to draw nearer. "Jake thinks his neighbor might have done this."

"Why?"

"Because he hates Jake's over-the-top decorations. I think Jake might be right. Yesterday, when I was driving around looking at Christmas decorations, I saw the guy peering through the break in his drapes. He was angry."

"You don't strangle someone with Christmas lights and stab them with a star if you're ticked off. You take them to court. You get an injunction."

"Mr. Atwater has filed reports."

"There, you see?"

I scowled. "Not everyone is as clearheaded as you."

I heard Deputy Appleby snicker and turned in his direction. His big moose jaw was trembling. He was doing his best not to laugh at my exchange with Cinnamon.

"Deputy," Cinnamon said, "bring Mr. Atwater to me, please."

Emmett heard the order and did an about-face, but Appleby was fast for a large, fifty-something man and nabbed him by the shoulder. The deputy said something. Emmett nodded and allowed Appleby to escort him to his boss.

Lacy and I settled on the planter next to Jake. "How are you doing?" I asked.

"Not good."

"Tell me about Geoffrey."

"He was a decent man."

"Any family?"

"No. They died in a car crash when he was sixteen. He was away at camp. It tore him up. After that, we hitchhiked together until I settled here. He never stayed in one place long enough for anyone to care. He visited every once in a while, but he didn't want to get tied down."

I recalled Tina's account of hearing Jake and Geoffrey sharing a secret. Then I remembered Lacy asking about the envelope Jake had slipped into his pocket at the festival. Geoffrey had filled an envelope with similar items. "Jake, was Geoffrey running from the law?"

"Not exactly."

"What does that mean?"

"He owed a bundle."

"To the mob?"

"To the city of Las Vegas. He didn't pay a slew of tickets."

"Speeding tickets?"

"Jaywalking tickets. He doesn't . . . *didn't* . . . own a car. He always worried that the cops would track him down and make him cough up the money."

"Maybe someone else followed him. An enemy."

He shook his head.

"Jake, he looked like he'd been in a few fights. His teeth—"

"Bad oral hygiene. No insurance." He scratched the back of his neck. "This is my fault. The killer was after me."

"If that's true and he killed Geoffrey by mistake, then you aren't safe."

"Sure I am. They'll find out Emmett did it and put him in jail. Case closed."

"What if he didn't do this? Who else might want you dead?"

A frisson of fear passed across Jake's face. "I'm on a few local committees, but I'm a listener, not an instigator. I never fooled around with anyone's wife. I never hit anyone with a car. I don't have any outstanding debts. It's Emmett, I tell you. He did this."

Across the way, nearer the corner of the garage, Emmett lurched away from Cinnamon. "No way!" he shouted. "I did not do this." He shot a scathing look at Jake. "I . . . I . . ." He gulped in air. "Yes, I hate the decorations, and I hate all the people cruising my neighborhood. They trash it. They play loud music. But I did not do this, Chief Pritchett." He glimpsed right and left, like he was searching for an escape route. "The other man who was here earlier came back. Maybe he did it."

"What other man?" Cinnamon asked.

I said, *"Psst.* Jake, does he mean my brother-in-law?"

"I suppose."

"He came back." Emmett flailed a hand. "He was angry. They argued earlier."

"Mr. Chapman." Cinnamon beckoned Jake. "Come over here, please."

Jake rose shakily to his feet. I got up, too, my legs unsteady. Spencer returned? Angry? Had he and Whitney fought? Did he take his frustration out on poor Geoffrey? No way!

Cinnamon shook her head at me and held up a hand, indicating she wanted me to remain where I was. Well, that wasn't happening. I knew my father wouldn't have, and in his absence, I was his proxy. I told Lacy to stay put and boldly followed Jake to Cinnamon.

She tipped the rim of her broad hat backward and raised an eyebrow. She meant the latter move to be intimidating. It wasn't.

"Jake is my father's friend," I said. "Whatever you say to him, you say to me so I can pass it along to my dad, since he's out of town."

During Cinnamon's high school years, when she was a handful to raise, my father had become her mentor. By the way she was staring at me, I could tell she was struggling with her decision now to have allowed him into her life. Finally she addressed Jake. "Sir, tell me who else was here."

"Spencer Westerson."

"My brother-in-law," I offered. "Jake had a situation with his lighting and asked Spencer to help. Spencer is a contractor in Los Angeles. He does odd jobs."

"How did you know he could help?" Cinnamon asked Jake.

"Cary," Jake said, referring to my father, "always brags about how handy Spencer is. He says if he didn't know better, Spencer was his son. I saw the kid at the festival and reached out to him."

Kid. Spencer was in his mid-forties. Hardly a kid.

"Did he and Geoffrey Gunther fight?" Cinnamon asked.

"No way. They hardly knew each other. Spencer left when I went to get pizza, about an hour ago."

"Mr. Atwater said he came back."

"He's lying."

"Why would he have cause to lie?"

"Because he did it and wants to pin this on someone else."

I breathed easier. Of course. That made sense.

Cinnamon pursed her lips and turned to me. "Please call your brother-in-law and tell him he's wanted for questioning."

I tapped Spencer's number on my cell phone. It rang and rolled into voice mail. My insides snagged. Whitney said that she could never reach Spencer at night. Where was he? I willed my face to remain blank and left a message for him to call me. To take the chief's focus off my brother-in-law, I jutted a finger in Emmett's direction and said, "What's his alibi?"

"We haven't gotten that far." She addressed Jake. "Mr. Chapman, one more time. You pulled out the star and rolled over the body. Why?"

I'd been wondering when she would return to that teensy but not insignificant fact.

"Like I told your deputy, he was facedown." Jake dragged his hand along his jaw. "I didn't want him to suffocate."

"But he was bleeding."

"I never took any medical classes, ma'am. I didn't know, as your deputy informed me, that he might bleed out. I didn't—"

"He didn't die from bleeding out, sir. He choked to death."

Jake swallowed hard. A wracking sob made his shoulders shudder. "Why? Who did this? Geoffrey was my lifelong friend."

Cinnamon said, "He looks as though he'd fallen on hard times."

"He was always on hard times."

"Did he ask for money? Did you refuse?" She worked her tongue inside her cheek. "Maybe Mr. Atwater heard him arguing with *you*."

"No way. If he'd asked me for money, I would've given it to him. Gladly. He didn't." Jake cut a look at Emmett. "I want to know *his* alibi."

"Deputy Appleby, please fetch Mr. Atwater and bring him to us."

The deputy did as bidden.

Up close, Emmett Atwater seemed petrified. His eyes blinked repeatedly. He wasn't small. He appeared to be about the same size as Jake. With a brick in hand, he could have easily knocked out Geoffrey and trussed him in Christmas lights. Except the area was well lit. Emmett would have known the difference between Jake and his pal, wouldn't he?

Cinnamon smoothed the front of her uniform. Though she resembled a perky camp counselor with her blunt haircut and girl-next-door face, no one in his right mind would discount her strength. She was quite athletic. She worked out with weights two hours a day. When she didn't work out, she rollerbladed great lengths along the highway. And she was a crack shot. I wouldn't care to face her in a duel.

"Mr. Atwater," she said, "let's review your testimony."

"What's your alibi?" Jake demanded.

"Mr. Chapman, be quiet," Cinnamon said. "I'll ask—"

"I was . . . at the movies," Emmett said. "I saw *It's a Wonderful Life.*"

"Then how did you hear anyone arguing with my friend?" Jake demanded. "Movies run from nine to eleven. Geoffrey died between the time I went to the store and returned."

Cinnamon drew in a sharp breath. She hated whenever she wasn't in control of a situation, especially an interrogation.

"It's a valid question, ma'am." Jake raised his chin. "He said he heard Spencer and Geoffrey going at it."

"Earlier," Emmett said. "They were in the front part of the house." Spittle flew out of his mouth. He wiped it with the back of his sleeve.

Cinnamon tilted her head. "Mr. Atwater, when did Spencer Westerson return?"

"Around ten. I left the movie early."

"Liar," Jake muttered.

"Are you sure it was him?" I asked.

Cinnamon shot me a harsh glance. "All right, that's it," she said. "Let's split up. Mr. Atwater, you stay with me. Deputy Appleby, please escort Mr. Chapman into his home and resume questioning. Jenna, please leave."

"But—"

"Leave."

I lowered my voice. "Does Jake need an attorney?"

"He'd be well advised to secure one."

Chapter 6

I took Lacy back to my place and fixed her a cup of tea. Then I drove her home. I told her I needed to talk to her dad and she ought to be with her mother. Looking as lifeless as a ragdoll, she didn't fight me. In my VW, she leaned against the passenger door with Tigger crooked under her arm. Poor kid.

On the drive, I called Zoey Zeller. She was flabbergasted by my news and said she'd find an attorney for Jake lickety-split. I didn't have to ask whether she would accompany the attorney to Jake's house. I knew she would. Before hanging up, I urged her to make Jake reconnect his home phone—in case someone needed to reach him.

My father's house was a beauty of a Mediterranean villa set in the hills. My mother had designed the interior with the beach in mind—white furniture, blue-and-green throw pillows, and sleek silver accents. From the porch, there was a spectacular view of the ocean. Even at this elevation, we could hear the ocean's steady ebb and flow.

Whitney brought out a tray set with three steaming mugs of tea and a platter of green wreath cookies decorated with red bows that she'd baked for the a cappella group's rehearsal tomorrow. She set the tray on the coffee table and nestled beside her daughter on the love seat. Lacy inched away and picked up Tigger.

Whitney didn't address the snub. "Jenna, do you think your friend is guilty?"

"He didn't do it!" Lacy bleated. "He was torn up."

Whitney grimaced. "I can't believe his neighbor would attack the friend simply because of Christmas lights."

"The guy is slightly off," I said.

"You should see him, Mom. He looks like one of those coyotes that prowl our street." Lacy attempted to mimic Emmett's face. Tigger flipped up his tail.

"Lacy, sweetheart, I'm talking to your aunt, not you."

Lacy threw her a sour look and nabbed two more cookies.

The front door opened and slammed shut.

"That must be Daddy." With Tigger in tow, Lacy ran to the foyer.

Whitney stared anxiously toward the interior of the house. Tears pressed at the corners of her eyes. "What time did you say Spencer left Jake's house?"

"After eight."

"He didn't come home."

"Jake's neighbor said Spencer came back later. Perhaps he went to get something to eat."

"Or maybe he met someone."

"Stop. You're jumping to conclusions." I rested a hand on my sister's knee. "You don't live here. How would he have hooked up with someone so quickly?"

Spencer strolled onto the patio, his arm wrapped around his daughter's back. She had slung Tigger over her shoulder. He was sniffing Spencer's neck. "Lacy told me what happened. How horrible. From what I could tell, Geoffrey was a nice guy."

I said, "Jake thinks he might have been the target, not Geoffrey."

"Why?" Spencer's gaze swung from me to Whitney.

"Forget that," she said. "Where were you when it happened? Why didn't you come home? We were supposed to go to dinner."

I sighed. Sometimes my sister could be a bear.

Spencer's face tinged pink. He kissed Lacy on the forehead and said, "Sweetheart, why don't you go to your room? Mom and I need to talk."

Lacy didn't hesitate. She took two more cookies and trudged away with Tigger. He glanced expectantly at me. I twitched a finger, signaling he would be fine.

Whitney waited until she heard the guest room door slam and then said in a low growl, "The police want to question you. You could be a person of interest."

"Why?" Spencer scratched his neck, looking totally at sea.

"Because Jake's neighbor heard you arguing with this Geoffrey person." Whitney crossed her arms over her chest.

"That's a lie. We didn't argue."

"He heard you."

"Maybe he heard me telling Geoffrey that joke about the guy in the canyon. You know the one I mean, where I yodel. You love that joke."

Whitney frowned. "So where did you go after you left Jake's house?"

"I went to the beach. I needed to think."

"Spencer North Westerson, why are you lying?" My sister's voice was raspy with anger. "I can tell you are. Your face always gives you away."

"Why would I want to kill that guy?" Spencer splayed his hands. "I have no motive. None. Zero."

"Should I leave?" I asked.

Both squawked, "Stay!"

Deafening silence consumed us. By now, I hoped Lacy was listening to music with her earbuds. At the very least, I prayed Tigger was consoling her.

Spencer said, "I went for a walk because I wanted to figure out what to do about our marriage. I know you're disappointed in me. I know I'm not earning enough money. I want to make you proud."

"You—" Whitney jammed her lips together. Obviously she couldn't say *You do make me proud* with conviction. "Did anyone see you?"

"I don't know. I didn't see anybody. It was dark. There's only a crescent moon."

"Weak," Whitney muttered.

I knew she meant it was a weak alibi, but Spencer flinched, obviously taking it to mean he was *weak*.

After a long tense moment, Whitney said, "Are you having an affair?"

Spencer gasped. "What? No!"

"You're hiding something."

When he didn't respond, tears pooled in her eyes. I couldn't remember her ever looking so vulnerable. My sister was formidable and always right. Witty, wondrous Whitney.

The wind knocked out of her sails, she said, "I'm going to bed," and fled into the house.

Spencer chased after her. "Whitney, wait."

A door slammed. Like daughter like mother.

"Open up, babe." Spencer rapped on the door. "Please. Babe . . ."

She didn't respond.

A short while later, my brother-in-law returned to the patio and gazed at me with a hangdog expression. He opened his mouth but no words came out.

A sickening feeling clawed my throat. He *was* hiding something. "Spencer," I said. "Talk to me."

Staring at the floor, he raked his fingers through his hair.

"I won't tell Whitney if you want me to keep a secret." I knew that wasn't right of me to promise, but I had to pry the truth out of him some way.

He sighed as if the weight of the world hung in the balance. "I didn't go to the beach. I went to Nuts and Bolts."

When my father retired from the FBI, he wanted to do something with his hands, so he bought a hardware store and named it Nuts and Bolts. It was a small but well-stocked shop on Buena Vista Boulevard.

"Why wouldn't you tell Whitney—"

Spencer held up a hand to silence me. "Let me explain. I went there to pick out a few things I need for an invention I'm designing. I'm building a prototype. I didn't want to admit it to Whitney for two reasons: one, I broke in and stole from your father."

"You used his keys to enter the shop, I presume. The ones that hang in his kitchen?"

"Yes."

"Then you didn't break in, and honestly, he would give you the shirt off his back so you weren't stealing. What's number two?"

"Whitney will put the kibosh on what I'm doing."

"No, she won't."

"She has before."

I gripped his shoulder. "Spencer, you heard her. She's worried you're having an affair and scared that you'll leave her. She'll be thrilled to learn—"

"I can't, Jenna. Not until it's finished. I want to see pride in her eyes, not regret."

"But—"

"No."

"What are you inventing? I won't blab." I crossed my heart.

With a grin he said, "A game for schoolyards."

"Game?"

"Tetherball and jump rope all in one. It's very cool. I'm using a friend's garage in Los Angeles to build it. While we were in town, I decided to pick up a few things to perfect it. When it's finished, I'll get the copyright or whatever is required."

"It sounds great, but don't you think—"

"No." Spencer's eyes flickered with a mixture of hope and angst. "Please, Jenna, you can't tell her. Let her think the other for a bit. She's pretty hard on me. Perhaps she'll come to realize how much she loves me."

Or you'll tick her off further, I thought.

"Hey," I said as an idea dawned on me. "The good news is the security tapes from Dad's shop will prove you weren't at the crime scene."

"Oh, my gosh, you're right. Should I contact the police? Should I go to Jake's right now?"

"I'm not sure. Call Chief Pritchett and ask her." I gave him Cinnamon's cell phone number. "Before you do that, one last question. Why did you return to Jake's?"

"I didn't."

"Jake's neighbor said he saw you."

"He lied."

• • •

When I returned home, I could see police down the street staking out Jake's house. There were three or four patrol cars plus a food truck, and someone had placed floodlights in the driveway. I wondered how Emmett Atwater liked that setup? I also wondered whether Spencer had contacted Cinnamon yet and, based on his testimony, whether she'd determined that Emmett Atwater, the liar, should be her primary suspect.

I spotted Mayor Zeller locking her car near the floodlights. A stately gentleman accompanied her. The two proceeded toward the house.

"What's going on, sweetie?" My neighbor with the blue-streaked hair popped onto her porch. We'd never introduced ourselves, even though she had visited Aunt Vera for a few tarot readings.

"A man was murdered."

"Heavens. Not Jake. How horrible." She rocked herself with her arms. "What is this world coming to? Did that crazy Emmett kill him?"

"Jake didn't die. His friend did. Why would you think Emmett murdered him?"

"That man never has a kind word for anyone. I've warned him to clean his chakras. Twenty minutes a day around water will do the trick." Aha! That was why she visited Aunt Vera so often. She was into spiritual healing. "He needs to get rid of that emotional gunk inside him." She jutted a thumb at her abdomen. "A stroll along the ocean would do him a world of good, but will he do it? No. He's a bitter, miserable man."

Before she returned inside her house, I yelled, "My name is Jenna, by the way."

"I know." She closed the door.

Certain that my father would want me to touch base with Jake and knowing he'd disconnected his home telephone, I called Cinnamon, but she didn't pick up. What would Jake do after the police finished questioning him? I couldn't imagine he'd want to sleep in his house after the murder. Would Z.Z. invite him to her place? Would he stay at an inn?

Unwilling to contact my father given the nine-hour time difference, I sent him an email to bring him up to speed, after which I called Rhett in Napa. I wanted him to assure me that all would be right with the world . . . someday.

He answered on the third ring. "Hey," he said warmly but groggily.

"Did I wake you?" I nestled into the corner of my sofa.

"Just fell asleep."

"I'm sorry. Are you having a good time with family?"

"Yes. No. It's complicated. But we'll talk about that another time. What's up?"

The words spilled out of me. Jake. Geoffrey. My sister and brother-in-law's situation. His refusal to tell her the truth.

Rhett said, "They'll work it out. They're grown-ups."

"Sometimes."

"How are you holding up? I'm worried that you saw —"

"Another dead body?"

"Yeah."

"Maybe I should move back to San Francisco. I'm bad luck for Crystal Cove."

"Don't even talk like that," he said. "You're the best thing that ever happened to the place. Your father and aunt would be bereft. Bailey would have a hissy fit. And I—" He let the word hang in the air. "I would be lost without you, my love."

"I'd be lost without you, too."

For a bit, he whispered sweet nothings to me. I let the tenderness of his words wash over me, until another notion hit me.

"Jake!" I blurted. "If Emmett Atwater isn't the killer, Jake will be the main suspect."

"You said he has an alibi."

"He does, but what if the cameras at the grocery store weren't working? Or the clerk doesn't remember him? Or the time frame doesn't match? What am I going to do? Dad's not here. I'll need to—"

"No, you don't."

"No, I don't what?"

"You don't need to solve the case."

I clicked my tongue. "I wasn't going to say that."

"Of course you weren't."

I bit back a smile. How well he knew me.

"I'm driving home tomorrow," he said. "We'll figure out the next step together."

Chapter 7

On Thursday morning when we opened the Cookbook Nook, customers were chattering about the murder. Hearing I had insider knowledge, Bailey, Tina, and my aunt wanted details, so I steered them into the storage room and filled them in.

When I finished, Bailey tugged on the Santa-style hat that didn't quite go with her turquoise blouse and jeans, and muttered, "Not so merry, ho-ho-ho."

"Definitely not."

"How's Jake coping?" my aunt asked.

"I don't know. I'm hoping his alibi stood up."

"You mean he might be in jail?" Tina asked.

"The chief considered him a person of interest."

Because our business thrived on happy news, we all agreed to discourage any discussion of the sad event and returned to work.

Around midmorning, over a dozen students assembled for the wreath-making clinic that my sister was leading. In an effort of self-promotion, the local Christmas tree vendor had supplied pine boughs, and Home Sweet Home had provided ribbon. Both would serve as the basis for what Whitney and Lacy had arranged Wednesday. Earlier, I had set out twenty copies of *Deck the Halls: How to Make a Christmas Wreath*, written by a YouTube sensation who encouraged everyone to find his or her unique talent. All but two had sold.

Ten minutes into the clinic, Tigger was the life of the party. He scampered beneath the table, dodging pieces of pine bough while picking up scraps of ribbon. The children making wreaths were encouraging him. The adults were tolerating him.

When I realized he was becoming a distraction to my sister, who was, in the interest of safety, manning the glue gun, I scooped him up, kissed his nose, and set him on his kitty condo. "Play here, you rascal."

"Weaving the pine boughs together is the hardest part," Whitney said as she toured the table. She had yet to smile since setting foot in the shop.

I'd done all I could to turn that frown upside down. I'd told a joke. I'd raved about her cheery outfit, which consisted of a

Christmas-themed sweater over silver pants and silver ballet slippers. I'd even brought her one of Katie's magnificent Santa sugar cookies. Katie was an ace at icing sugar cookies. Me? I could paint; I couldn't ice. Did Whitney's attitude change an iota? No, it did not. She was upset with her husband. Why, oh, why had I made a vow not to tell her anything until he chose to reveal it? *Dumb.*

When I tried one more time to cajole her out of her mood by bringing her tea with honey and lemon—exactly the way she liked it—I suggested that she and Spencer should consider marriage counseling. If looks could kill . . .

Aunt Vera, who was sitting at the vintage kitchen table, shuffled tarot cards noisily and pressed her lips together as if she was fighting hard not to laugh.

What? I mouthed.

She jerked her head, signaling I should chat with her.

I moseyed over and bent down so she could whisper in my ear.

She adjusted the sleeves of her pearl-white caftan and tucked a loose hair behind her ear. "I think your sister needs a visit from the Sugar Plum Fairy."

I giggled.

Whitney marched to us. "I heard that."

"You were meant to," Aunt Vera admitted. "Whatever is eating at you doesn't belong in this fun environment."

"My husband is a suspect in a murder."

"No, he's not. He has an—" I bit my tongue before saying *alibi.* "You know he's not guilty."

"Do I?" Whitney waggled the glue gun.

"Yes, you do," our aunt said. "He's one of the sweetest men alive. He wouldn't hurt a fly."

"Sure he would," Whitney jeered. "And spiders and cockroaches and—"

"Stop." Aunt Vera rubbed the phoenix amulet that hung around her neck and chanted, "Sugar Plum Fairy, rise and shine. Bring a smile to ours and thine."

As if truly under our aunt's spell, Whitney took a deep breath. "You're right. Spencer's not guilty of *murder,* but he's guilty of *something.*"

My aunt rolled her eyes. "We need you to smile, dear."

Whitney flipped her hair over her shoulders and shimmied down the hem of her sweater. "Fine. I'll play nice." She returned to the table of students. "Everyone, I apologize. Who needs a sourpuss for a teacher?"

"Not me," a towheaded girl said.

Whitney chuckled. *About time*. She inspected a few of the wreaths that students had made. "Nicely done. Now, let me teach you how to whip up a bow"—she set aside the glue gun—"and after that, you can decorate to your heart's content. Six yards of ribbon will make a twelve inch bow with eight loops."

"Six yards!" the girl exclaimed. "That's enough ribbon to go around me like ten times."

I flashed on Geoffrey, hit with a brick, stabbed with a star, and bound with Christmas lights, and my stomach wrenched. What kind of rage had driven the killer to do all three? Was Emmett that angry?

"Here we are," Whitney said. In a matter of minutes, she fashioned a bow that would have made Martha Stewart envious. As she tied it off with wire, the students applauded.

When that brought another smile to my sister's lips, I moved to the sales counter. Bailey was ringing up sales for a line of customers. Out of the side of her mouth, she said, "I've done as you asked, boss. No discussion of the murder."

"Good."

Bailey peered past me. "Hi, Gran."

"Hello, ladies." Gran looked as lovely as ever in a winter white suit and red blouse. A chic Tory Burch cross-body purse completed the ensemble. She never skimped on her clothing. The first time I met her she'd been wearing one of the costliest shawls I had ever seen.

I said, "Don't you look nice today."

"I have a date." A widow, Gran had moved to town to live with her daughter-in-law and granddaughters.

"With whom?"

"Flora fixed me up with a handsome widower. His name is Adam."

"Kittridge?" I said. "From San Francisco?"

"Yes." She set a stack of cookbooks on the counter. "How do you know him?"

"I met him at Home Sweet Home."

"Isn't he lovely? We've already gone for coffee and found out we have so much in common."

As Gran inspected a few of the colorful bookmarks we had for sale, Bailey whispered to me, "Is he a fortune hunter?"

"No," I said, matching her conspiratorial tone. "He's wealthy in his own right."

"Phew."

I smiled. Funny how protective we could be of those we loved.

"Today we're having lunch." Gran placed two bookmarks on her stack of books.

I said, "I hear he wants to buy a vacation home in Crystal Cove."

"Yes. Jake Chapman's house."

"It isn't for sale."

"Adam intends to persuade him. He says he can sell refrigerators to Eskimos." Gran blanched and pressed a hand to her chest. "Listen to me, making light of things. You must think I'm awful. What a shame about Jake's friend. Do the police know—"

I shook my head. "Not yet. They're investigating."

Bailey said, "That'll put the kibosh on this Kittridge guy purchasing the house, don't you think, Jenna?"

I nodded.

Bailey slotted Gran's books and bookmarks into one of our decorative bags, tied the bag's handles with raffia, and handed the bag to her. "Thanks for being such a great customer."

"Thank you for being my favorite store." Gran headed to the vintage table, where my aunt was waiting to give her a tarot card reading. Gran didn't believe in all that *hokum*, as she called it, but once a week she loved hearing whatever my aunt was ready to reveal.

While Bailey rang up the next two customers, I checked our reports that tracked shipments online. An order of aprons covered with snowflakes hadn't shown up. I didn't want customers who had pre-ordered them to be dissatisfied.

"Whew," Bailey said as she sat on the stool facing me. "Busy morning. We sold out of *Christmas Crafts: Festive things to make and do!* I bought a copy for myself. Did you know there's a list of everything needed for each craft included in the book?"

"That's why I stocked it."

"You're so clever." She knuckled my arm. "The other big seller today is *The Great Christmas Cookie Swap Cookbook.*"

The official name was *Good Housekeeping The Great Christmas Cookie Swap Cookbook: 60 Large-Batch Recipes to Bake and Share.* Like other cookbook titles, it was lengthy and a mouthful!

"I'll bet all the people getting ready for our cookie swap contest purchased it."

We'd advertised the heck out of the event. Only adults were invited. Each was to dress up like Santa or an elf and bring a dozen of his or her favorite homemade cookies. Whoever won the contest would receive a hundred-dollar gift certificate from the Cookbook Nook. Tito and Jake, if he wasn't in jail, would be the official taste-testing judges — Tito, because he was an eminent newspaper reporter and would write up the event, and Jake because he was considered one of the town's bastions of goodwill.

"I've bought a copy so I can look at the pictures, hopeful I can learn how to pipe icing using a pastry bag someday."

Bailey hooted. "You're pathetic. Ask Katie to teach you."

After Christmas and the brouhaha of the season calmed down, I would. I really did want to learn.

"By the way" — Bailey stood and brushed flecks of raffia off her pants — "Tito and I might have found a house to rent."

"Where?"

"In the hills. Not far from your father's. It costs a little more than we wanted to spend, but the view is incredible, and it has a nice-sized yard and a patio with lots of potted plants. Tito loves to garden."

"I learn something new about him every day."

"So do I." She smiled dreamily. "We agreed that if we can get used to spending this amount on rent, then when we're ready to buy . . ."

"You won't feel the pinch so much."

"Right."

"About that. Aunt Vera and I have been talking, and we'd like to make you and Katie limited partners in the shop and the café but with no liability." My aunt had made me a full partner a few months ago.

"With no liability?" Bailey clapped a hand to her chest. "Are you for real?"

"The shop and café are thriving. It has a lot to do with the two of you. You're a great salesperson with a real sense of marketing. She's an extraordinary chef. You both deserve some of the profits."

"That's so generous."

"Aunt Vera has way too much money for her own good. She saw that movie about J. Paul Getty and decided she doesn't want to hang on to it. She wants to create a few blessings. First for the people she loves, which includes you and Katie, and then for some of the charities around town."

Bailey's eyes filled with tears. She snatched a Kleenex from a nearby box and dabbed the tears before they could dribble down her cheeks. "I don't know what to say."

"Say yes."

"Of course *yes*." She threw her arms around me. "Wait a second. She's not dying, is she?"

"She's as healthy as an ox."

"But you—"

"Also healthy."

"No, I meant *you*. *Your* inheritance. If we become limited partners, then that will cut into your portion."

"I have plenty of money. Promise." After the fiasco with David, I had saved every cent I could. It didn't hurt that Aunt Vera had started to teach me how to invest. My portfolio, which was stocks as well as bonds, was growing nicely.

"What if you have kids?" she asked.

I grinned. "I'll teach them how to manage with whatever they get."

Her stomach rumbled. She rubbed her abdomen. "I'm starved. I'm going to the Nook for a snack. Want anything?"

"One of Katie's sugar cookies, please." I'd had a protein shake for breakfast. I could afford to have a sweet.

"Have you told Katie yet?"

"Aunt Vera did earlier."

"Hallelujah!" As she scooted from behind the counter, she nearly ran into Tina, who threw up her hands to avoid the collision. "Sorry." Bailey disappeared down the breezeway.

"I'm back, boss." Tina tossed her purse into the cubby beneath the register.

"What are you wearing?" She had changed from her cropped winter gray sweater and pencil skirt into a voluminous royal blue dress.

"A new designer moved into that vacant shop in Artiste Arcade. It's called Très Vogue."

"That dress is très huge on you."

"I know, but I love it. The texture is so cool. And isn't the color fabulous?"

"You look, um, like you're hiding a pregnancy, if you want my honest opinion."

"Really? *Harrumph.*" She peered down, which made the fabric over her abdomen pooch even more. "I haven't cut off the price tag yet. I'll take it back. Speaking of pregnant, I think Bailey is."

"What?" I shrieked.

Tigger sprang off his perch and galloped to me. Whitney and the crafters gawked in our direction.

I signaled that I was okay and hugged Tigger to my chest. His heart was revving. "I'm okay, fella. Go play." I set him on the floor, nudged his behind, and rose to meet Tina's gaze. In an inside voice, I said, "Why do you think that?"

"She's rubbing her belly all the time. Haven't you noticed?"

"It's possible she's hungry . . . or she has a stomachache."

Tina's mouth quirked up on one side. "Ask her. See what she says."

"Yeah, right. She might be the best secret keeper in the history of the universe."

"Well, some secrets can't be kept forever, you know what I mean?" She drew an imaginary baby tummy in front of herself.

The two of us laughed.

Tina poked me and said, "Go ask your aunt to do a third-party tarot reading. You know, sans Bailey."

"Aunt Vera won't do that. She believes reading for someone who hasn't given permission is an invasion of privacy."

"C'mon." Tina prodded me.

As eager as my assistant to learn the truth, I hustled to the vintage table where Aunt Vera was doing a reading for Gran.

"Just a minute, dear," my aunt said without looking up.

Gran smiled and patted the chair beside her. "Sit, Jenna. Listen in. I always like to share my good news." My aunt never told Gran any bad news. No warnings. No vibes. She knew Gran purely wanted to hear something fun to pass the time. Gran tapped a finger on the table. "See what we have here?"

For her *past*, the Fool card was turned up. When upright, the Fool signified a free, spontaneous spirit. That suited Gran to a tee. The second card, which stood for her *present*, was the Lovers. When turned upright, that card signified love and relationships.

Gran ran her finger along the bottom edge of the card. "Perhaps I might find happiness with Adam."

"Perhaps," Aunt Vera said, her hand poised to turn up the third card.

Gran tapped my aunt's hand. "Hold on, Vera. May I dedicate the reading of my *future* card to a new friend?"

Aunt Vera snorted. "Gracie, you know that's not how this works."

"Don't call me Gracie," she warned.

Aunt Vera snickered. She knew exactly which of Gran's buttons to push.

"Who do you want to know about?" I asked. "Adam Kittridge?"

"No, not him." Gran flapped a hand. "He doesn't need help. I'm curious about the woman I introduced you to at the festival last night. Olivia."

"The barbecue whiz?"

Gran nodded. "She worries her hands all the time and she fidgets, which has me concerned."

My aunt muttered under her breath. Was she picking up something negative about this Olivia person?

"She makes quilts," Gran went on. "So I told her to go to Flora and see if she'd let her sell the quilts on consignment. I'd like you to tell me if she's going to find a bit of success, Vera."

"Have you seen her work?" I asked.

"No, but she showed me photographs. They're quite lovely quilts." Gran tapped my aunt's arm. "Please, Vera, turn over the third card for Olivia."

Aunt Vera did as bidden and flinched. The card she revealed was the Hermit, upside down. Even I knew what the card meant when reversed: *isolation and loneliness.* I couldn't see that being Gran's future, not with her bountiful family. So the Fates must have decided the card was, indeed, for Olivia. Poor thing.

"Why the sad face, Jenna?" Gran asked.

"Sad? I'm not sad." I searched for an answer. "I was thinking that Olivia reminded me of someone."

"Olivia de Havilland, perhaps. That's who she reminds *me* of." Gran circled her face with a finger. "She has that lovely bone structure."

I shook my head.

"I'll bet it's something about her eyes," Gran went on. "They're the window to the soul, after all."

"That's it!" I snapped my fingers as an image formed in my mind. "She looks like Jake."

"Chapman?" Aunt Vera asked.

"Mm-hm." I gazed between my aunt and Gran. "Is it possible they're related?"

"I wouldn't have a clue," Gran said. "She wouldn't give me any details of her life."

Aunt Vera said, "Has Jake ever mentioned having a sister?"

"Not to me. Maybe to Dad."

My aunt tapped the Hermit card. "It's possible they're estranged."

"If you locate her, Jenna," Gran suggested, "you could encourage her to reunite with him. She's staying at the Crystal Cove Inn."

"Me? Why me?"

"Because I'm going on a date."

Chapter 8

At noon, I decided to follow Gran's lead and visit the Crystal Cove Inn, a charming bed-and-breakfast and one of the original establishments in town. Like many of the buildings in town, the inn was painted white and its roof was made of red tiles. The sprawling lush grounds brought to mind an estate right out of a Jane Austen novel. The gardens teemed with azaleas and hydrangeas, though none were in bloom in December.

I pushed through the quaint front door and paused for a moment to drink in the ambiance. Tracer lights twinkled around the huge plate glass window. A large flocked Christmas tree decorated with ornate gold balls stood near the lobby fireplace. A young couple sat by the fire enjoying tea. A man was nestled in a wing-backed chair reading by the light of a standing lamp.

I crossed the peg-and-groove floor to the registration counter.

"Help you?" a curly-haired clerk with ultra-white teeth asked.

"Yes. I'd like to locate Olivia . . ." My face warmed with embarrassment; I didn't know the woman's last name. "Chapman," I tried, not knowing whether she was married or if she was even Jake's sister.

The clerk searched on a computer. "I'm sorry. We don't have anyone by that name staying with us."

Earlier, before letting Gran leave the shop, I'd been savvy enough to have her forward me a photograph of Olivia from the night they'd met at the festival. The two of them were beaming in front of Holly and Ivy. I showed the photo to the clerk.

"Oh, her. Yes, I've seen her. Such a sweet woman. She's not a guest, though. She reviewed the rate card"—she gestured to an acrylic card holder packed with rate cards and *What to do in Crystal Cove* brochures—"but she decided to look elsewhere. Between you and me, I don't think she was able to afford us, even though we're quite reasonably priced. After deliberating, she asked if she could tour the grounds. She sat on the bench by the pond for over an hour." The clerk motioned toward the rear garden. "I didn't have the heart to say the bench was reserved for guests. When she left, she climbed into a beaten-up Honda Civic. It appeared to be packed with clothes and whatnot." She lowered her voice. "I think she might be homeless."

Not everyone who packed a car with worldly goods was homeless. A coworker at Taylor & Squibb, a compulsive hoarder, had kept everything she owned in her car because she didn't want to be away from her *stuff*, as she called it, for too long.

"Did you happen to notice the license plate?"

"I think the letters were *LPO* or *LPQ*. I'm nearsighted. That little thing on the *Q* can be hard to tell, you know?" The clerk clucked her tongue. "It's horrible what's happening in the world today, isn't it? So many people displaced. Luckily, I have a good-paying job." She rapped the wooden counter with her knuckles. "Say, I did tell her about the low-rate motel at the north edge of town. It costs about half of what we charge. Maybe she went there. Is she a friend of yours?"

"No, but—"

Someone started tapping a foot. I peeked over my shoulder. The peevish woman behind me snarled. I thanked the clerk and, as I left, offered a broad smile to the woman. Apparently she didn't know that she was supposed to *chill* in Crystal Cove.

"Where will I find a dry cleaner?" a man said to my right. I knew the voice. Adam Kittridge, the man Gran was meeting for lunch, was standing at the concierge desk. If I wasn't mistaken, the navy blue suit he was wearing was Armani.

The bald-headed young man who was attending to Adam scribbled something on a pad and handed it to him. Adam thanked him, popped a piece of gum into his mouth, slipped the orange packet and the note the concierge had given him into his jacket pocket, and turned in my direction. His eyes blinked in recognition as he straightened his Hermès tie. "Hey, I know you."

"You do, Mr. Kittridge." I placed my hand on my chest. "We met briefly at Home Sweet Home. I'm Jenna Hart."

He nodded. "After you left, Flora told me about your culinary bookshop. I've been meaning to stop in. My daughter-in-law is a master cook, and my granddaughter is determined to take after her. She loves making cookies."

"Too bad your daughter-in-law isn't in town. We're having a cookie competition and swap at the shop Sunday. Why don't you come? Check it out. We have a lot of cookie cookbooks that are perfect for young girls, too."

"Sounds fun, but I'll be returning to San Francisco for the day to see my granddaughter in a recital." He donned a pair of leather gloves. "Flora told me you used to work at Taylor & Squibb in the city."

"I did."

"Small world. I own Kittridge LLC."

I shook my head. "I'm not familiar."

"We invest in numerous strip malls along the West Coast. Your firm did a number of advertisements for us."

"Who handled the account?"

"John Taylor."

I whistled. "Wow, you must rate." John solely worked on campaigns that were in the millions of dollars' range. Adam Kittridge's limited corporation had to be extremely high-end. "I hear you're having lunch with a friend of mine."

"Gracie."

I chuckled. "She allows you to call her that?"

"It's her name."

"She hates it."

"I'll make a note of that, but" — he winked — "I think it would be weird if I called her Gran."

"She told me you still have your heart set on buying Jake Chapman's house."

"I do."

"Even after the, um, tragedy?"

"I'm afraid I've seen my fill of tragedy over the years. San Francisco is not known for its docile nature. Plenty of houses go up for sale after something dire has occurred. There are even a few homes with resident ghosts, so I'm told. Ultimately tragedy reduces the price. I would imagine Mr. Chapman will be eager to sell."

A notion flitted through my mind. Was it possible that this man killed Geoffrey to scare Jake into selling? No. Ridiculous.

"I can be quite persuasive," he added.

"Jake can be quite stubborn," I countered. "I think you should look for another house."

"Perhaps I should. By the way" — he lowered his voice — "I couldn't help overhearing your conversation with the clerk about this person you're seeking. Mayor Zeller confided that a number of vagrants have moved into the area. She said it's due to the mild climate, but assured me they're harmless. I told her I wasn't worried. We have plenty of homeless in the city. But if you're intent on finding this woman, you might check out the nearby wooded areas. That's where they camp out up north."

• • •

On my way back to the Cookbook Nook, I couldn't shake the image of the Hermit tarot card that my aunt had turned over for Olivia. If she was Jake's sister and destitute, he'd want to know, right?

When I walked into the shop, my aunt stopped me. "Well? What did you learn?"

"Olivia is not at the inn." I explained that the clerk thought she was homeless.

"Poor dear." She rubbed the amulet and murmured a quick prayer. "How will you find her?"

"It's not up to me."

"Your father would say otherwise."

"No, he wouldn't. He would tell me to inform the police."

"Whatever." Her sigh was filled with a world of concern. As she headed for the storage room, she said over her shoulder, "We received a new shipment of books. I'll unpack them."

Bailey beckoned me to the register. On a plate beside her lay two huge Santa cookies. I also spied a glass of milk.

"Eating for two?" I teased.

"Huh?" Her eyes widened with realization. "Get out of here. How could I be pregnant?"

"You and Tito have had S-E-X, haven't you?"

"Protected S-E-X. I'm not PG. Promise." She eyed the cookies. "I simply can't resist. They're so good. But I guess I'd better watch out or I'll start putting on weight."

She offered me a cookie. I declined.

Needing protein, I went to the café and asked Katie to throw together a chopped salad with some of her savory vinaigrette dressing. She topped it with cranberries, chunks of buffalo mozzarella cheese, cubes of chicken, and green onions to give it a festive look. I enjoyed every bite.

When I returned to the shop, I set to work on our displays. The latest onslaught of customers had made a disaster of things. All the magnetic Santa and reindeer ceramic salt and pepper shakers on the kitchenware shelves had been pulled apart. All the aprons were twisted; I preferred them hanging with their designs facing front. And all the copies of *Holiday Cookies: Showstopping Recipes to Sweeten the Season* were lying flat on the front display table. While standing the cookbooks, I inspected a few of them. No accidentally dog-eared pages. No rips or tears. The covers of the books, which bore a beautiful picture of white-themed cookies linked in a wreath design, were in mint condition, too. Hooray.

Next, I tackled the bookshelves to make sure all the volumes were in the correct order before I started shelving new ones from the stockroom.

Bailey wandered over and said, "I heard you went searching for a woman you thought might be Jake's sister."

"I did."

"But you didn't locate her."

"No."

"Should you let Jake know?"

I squinted at her. Had my aunt put her up to this line of questioning?

"And tell him what?" I said. "Gee, Jake, I *think* there's a woman in town who bears a remarkable resemblance to you." I paused. "Well, not *remarkable*. They sort of have the same eyes." I fanned the air.

"First of all"—Bailey sorted books on the shelves next to mine—"you should find out if he has a sister. If he doesn't, it's a moot point."

"I like your logic."

"Next, ask whether he wishes to have any contact with that sister. He's never mentioned her, has he?"

"Not that I'm aware of, but I don't have lengthy conversations with him like my dad."

"You have a gut feeling, don't you?" She nodded, not waiting for a response. "Yeah, you do. Trust yourself. Call him."

"He disconnected his telephone. I asked Z.Z. to have him reconnect it, but who knows if he did?"

"Do it."

I pulled my cell phone from my pants pocket and punched in Jake's home number. Busy.

Bailey raised an eyebrow.

"Busy," I said.

"Try again."

This time Jake answered after the first ring.

"Jake, it's Jenna. How are you? What's going on with the investigation?"

"I was just talking to my attorney." He sounded weary.

"Your attorney. Are you in trouble?"

"No. At least I don't think so. I was caught on camera at the grocery store. The video was time-stamped. But the police are waiting until all the tests come back to confirm time of death."

"Are the police still at your place?" I asked.

"No, they've been gone for a while. They did their crime scene thing and cleared away the tape."

"Did you stay the night at your house with the murderer at large?"

"You bet I did. Geoffrey . . ." He halted. "Geoffrey wouldn't have wanted me to be scared off by anything. He slept on beaches and bus benches. I'm standing my ground in honor of his memory." Something jangled in the background. "Sorry, Jenna, I've got to go. My cell phone is ringing."

"You don't have a cell phone."

"I do now. Z.Z. can be a force, and she's the one who's calling. I'd better answer."

"Wait, Jake. I need to ask you a question. A *delicate* question."

"Hold on." I heard him answer his cell phone and tell the mayor he'd call her right back. "Okay, shoot, Jenna."

"Do you have a sister?"

Jake breathed low and slow, as if trying to form an answer. Finally he said, "Yes, but I haven't seen her in over sixty years."

"Sixty?" I couldn't hide my surprise.

"When I left my family, I left *all* of my family. I wrote her often, but she never wrote back. I'm sure she hated me for leaving her in that cesspool."

Cesspool? My heart wrenched. My father had never filled me in on the details of Jake's youth other than he'd been born in Arizona.

"My mother and father were alcoholics. My father beat me. My mother let him. I had to get out. I asked my sister to come with me. She refused. They didn't beat her. She was smart. She'd set her sights on joining NASA. She'd fallen in love with the idea of flying to the moon. Why do you ask?"

"I could be wrong, but I think she might be in town. There's a woman who looks remarkably like you. She's about your age and lean, and her eyes are similar. Her name is Olivia."

He gasped. "Livy's here? Where?"

"I don't know. She might have fallen on hard times. I presumed she might be staying at the Crystal Cove Inn, but when I searched for her, the clerk said she believed Olivia was living out of her car."

"Out of her—" He sucked back a sob. "How would she have found me here?"

"Maybe she migrated to California, too, and reads the newspaper. To drum up enthusiasm for the Santa-themed cookie competition, we posted notices in the *San Francisco Chronicle*. You and Tito were mentioned as judges. Your pictures were included."

"Oh, man." Jake moaned. "You don't think . . ."

He didn't finish.

"Don't think what?" I asked.

"You don't think she killed Geoffrey, mistaking him for me, do you?"

"Why would she do that?"

"Maybe she thought she'd inherit my estate."

His leap in reasoning sent a seismic tremor through me.

Chapter 9

After I found my breath, I said, "How would that be possible, Jake?"

"I don't have a will. With my wife dead and no kids" — his voice cracked — "why would I write one?"

"You need to call your attorney and set one up ASAP."

"Okay."

"And you should call Chief Pritchett. Tell her about your sister. If anyone can track her down, Cinnamon can. She'll bring her in for questioning and find out if she had anything to do with Geoffrey's murder."

"Got it."

He sounded like he was pacing a tile floor.

"Jake, I wish my dad was here."

"Me, too."

"Call me after you speak with the police."

"Will do."

The rest of the day passed in a blur. I waited until closing to hear back from Jake. When I didn't, worry buzzed inside me, but I forced it aside. He was fine, I told myself. The murderer, whoever it was, would be stupid to try again, right?

When Tigger and I arrived at my cottage, I was not surprised to see dozens of cars and strangers driving slowly along our street, no doubt checking out the *murder* house. Like passing a car accident on the road, people found it hard to look away from horror.

I was pleased to spot Rhett's Ford F-250 parked in my driveway. I hopped out of my VW with Tigger and rushed to him. He was sitting in the driver's seat, staring at the ocean. I tapped on the window. He startled and quickly climbed out.

I threw my arms around him and kissed him. "Didn't mean to scare you."

"I was lost in thought."

"Is everything okay?"

"Yeah. No." He shook his head. "My sister is sick." Surf crashed on the beach, punctuating his announcement.

"Ashley?"

"Scarlet."

Yes, his mother had named his sisters after characters from *Gone with the Wind.* Her name was Melanie. She was a huge fan of the book—not of the Civil War or the issues about slavery but of the passions that drove the characters.

"We think she might have an immunodeficiency," he added. "Lupus."

"Is there a treatment for it?"

"NSAIDs and steroids. We'll see how that goes. She was thinking about starting a family. Now she's holding off." He escorted me to the front door. "But enough about that sadness. Let's focus on you. And Jake. What's going on?"

The moment we went inside, Tigger jumped onto his kitty condo and began playing with the sisal ball on a rope. While I stowed my purse and jacket, I shared every detail about the murder that I could remember, including Jake's angry neighbor Emmett and how he'd tried to pin the murder on my brother-in-law.

"Is Spencer off the hook?" Rhett asked.

"I think so. I'm not sure." I mentioned Jake's sister Olivia and their estrangement. "I recommended he put a will in place. I don't know if he has. He hasn't touched base with me. Dad would want me to follow up—"

"Relax. Jake will take care of things. He's one of the savviest guys I know. Right now, he has to be feeling like a fish in a fishbowl with all the lookie-loos out there." He hooked a thumb. "You, too." He kissed my forehead. "Why don't you come to my place tonight? I'll throw some steaks on the barbecue. We'll take a walk, drink in the fresh air, and clear our heads."

He didn't need to ask me twice. Before opening Bait and Switch Fishing and Sport Supply Store, he had been a chef.

I changed out of my silk sweater, chinos, and flip-flops—I never wore flip-flops for our walks; too dangerous—and I threw on a pair of jeans, a nubby sweater, hiking boots, and a faux shearling jacket. The temperature had fallen a good five degrees since I'd left the Cookbook Nook.

On the drive to his cabin, the temperature dropped a few more degrees. We went in through the rear door, as we always did, passing by the vegetable garden. December was typically a cool month, but hardier vegetables like chard and spinach were doing nicely. Rhett plucked some chard as he passed by. Once inside, he directed me to sit at the granite counter that divided the kitchen from the living room. It wasn't that he didn't trust me in the kitchen—he knew I was getting more adept every day—but he liked to spoil me.

"Nice decorations," I said as I set Tigger on the floor.

"Thanks. They're simple but festive." He'd hung a wreath adorned with red berries over the fireplace. A fake, pre-lit tree stood in front of the living room's plate glass window.

Tigger dashed across the room to explore, beginning by sniffing every corner in the very male surroundings. Rhett used to own a dog, Rufus, a Great Dane that I'd never met. He wasn't ready to replace him yet.

After opening a bottle of Frank Family cabernet and using an aerator to decant it, he poured a glass for each of us. "I think you'll enjoy this," he said, handing me my glass.

I tilted the glass to my nose and inhaled.

"Do you detect the aroma of cassis and figs?" he asked.

I did.

"The palate is lush with savory fruit and a hint of black pepper."

I took a sip. "Mm, flavorful."

He turned on music—the jazzy holiday strains of the Beegie Adair Trio filled the air—and quickly put together a plate of sliced cheese and olives for me to nibble. Then he set to work on dinner. I loved how comfortable he was in his kitchen. Copper pots hung from a rack overhead. Utensils and oven mitts were plentiful. A floor-to-ceiling bookcase beside the Wolfe double oven was jam-packed with autographed, first-edition celebrity cookbooks that any collector would covet.

When the meal was ready, we sat at the rustic table, both of us facing the tree. The steak was perfect with a warm center, and the wilted chard with red pepper flakes was savory.

After I washed the dishes and Rhett put them away, he kissed me tenderly and said, "Feel like talking about us?"

"*Us?*"

"Don't be coy. Last time I asked you to discuss our future, you shied away from the conversation. Are you ready to tackle it head-on?" He ran a finger along my arm. "I love you, but I don't want to pressure you. I'd like you to spend the rest of your life with me, but I won't ask you to marry me unless I know you're going to say yes. I can't handle the rejection." His eyes twinkled with sass.

"Let's take a walk."

He handed me my coat, donned his own, and fetched a flashlight.

"Tigger, we'll be back in a bit," I said.

As if he could care. He was curled into a ball on Rhett's reading chair and snoring like a champ.

The scent of pine was heady, but a cool breeze made me shiver. Rhett put his arm around me, and we strode along the dirt path that led to the lake.

"David hurt me deeply," I whispered as we passed a stand of pine trees and weaved right.

"I won't."

"He made me gun-shy about trusting any man again."

"No weapons in my arsenal."

I elbowed him. "I love you and your wit and, well, everything about you, but . . . How can I say this nicely?"

He pulled to a stop. "Do I have bad breath?"

"No, you goon. It's . . ." I licked my lips. "I can't live in the cabin. It's too far away from everything."

"Okay."

"And—" I clenched his arm and signaled him to halt. The aroma of a campfire wafted toward us. I heard voices. "Who would be camping in December?"

"The homeless."

I recalled what the man Gran was dating had said about indigents moving into the woods up in San Francisco. "Is that allowed?"

"There are a lot of public grounds around here that don't belong to me or my neighbors."

"Has anyone bothered you?"

"Nope." He shrugged. "In fact, one guy, Zeke, weeds my garden for free if I let him pick something fresh each week."

"You know them?"

"Not all. A few, like Zeke and his friends. They're harmless."

"Can we talk to them?"

Rhett's eyes widened in understanding. "You want to find out if Jake's sister is among them."

I nodded.

He frowned. "You told Jake to contact Cinnamon and have her look into it."

"What if he didn't? He'd sounded resistant." I tugged his hand to move forward.

He held me back. "Jenna, stop. I don't want you involved in this."

"What will my father say if I don't at least ask?"

He turned me toward him and lifted my chin with a finger. His eyes were dusky with passion. "This will not stop me from talking about us."

I winked. "Gotcha."

"This way." He ducked beneath the bough of a tree and forged ahead. I matched his brisk pace. We zigzagged through the forest until we came to an area where three men and a woman were sitting on camp chairs around a foldable, portable barbecue. The aroma of spicy sausage hung in the air.

"Hey, Zeke," Rhett said.

The largest of the men stood up. "Rhett, my man." A grin spread across his craggy face. Judging by the wrinkles around his eyes, I figured him to be in his sixties. I couldn't see the rest of his face because a bushy beard covered it. His flak jacket, jeans, and boots were dirty. A ratty ski hat covered his hair. He jutted out a hand. His fingerless mittens had seen better days. "Why are you here?"

"Taking a late-night stroll." Rhett shook hands with him. "My girlfriend, Jenna, has a question for you."

"Fiancée," I said and instantly felt my cheeks warm because my reflex response revealed how I'd wanted to answer that pesky question.

Rhett grinned, pleased with my answer.

"What's the question, beautiful?" Zeke asked.

"I think there's a homeless woman in Crystal Cove who might be the sister of somebody I know."

"What's her name?"

"Olivia. Her last name—"

"We don't use last names around here." Zeke regarded his camp mates. "We like anonymity."

"She's about five eight and lean." I raised a hand to the top of my head. "In her early seventies with dyed red hair."

"Gray roots?" the woman asked.

"Yes," I said, recalling how I'd thought Olivia needed to refresh her color. "And deep lines in her face."

"Smoker?" Zeke asked.

"Probably." She'd had a gravelly voice, as if she'd spent her whole life smoking.

"Drive's a Honda Civic?"

"That's her."

"She's not here."

"Was she ever?" I asked.

"Passed through," the woman replied. "She ate dinner with the wicked witch down the lane."

"Wicked witch?"

Zeke chortled. "A month ago, we booted out one of our camp mates. The woman had a mouth on her. We like to consider ourselves refined. She set up camp on the other side of the lake, but I don't think your Olivia stayed with her."

"Why not?"

"Because she doesn't need a campsite. She lives out of her car. I think she wanted conversation."

Rhett exhaled. "If she's living out of her car, Jenna, she's mobile. We might never find her."

Tears dripped down my cheeks as sadness overwhelmed me. How horrible to be faced with such a desolate existence. Rhett thanked Zeke and we returned to his cabin in silence.

When we stepped inside, however, the mood changed because Rhett dropped to one knee and, grinning, pulled a small box from the pocket of his jacket. He flipped the top open and presented the contents—a gleaming petite solitaire diamond ring. "Jenna Hart, will you marry me?"

This time, I cried tears of joy.

Chapter 10

We woke early Friday morning. Real early. Rhett brushed my cheek with his lips. "I'm sorry I've got to do this gig."

"Me, too."

He was taking a group of tourists sport fishing before opening Bait and Switch, the colloquial name of his sporting supply store. He did similar junkets two or three times a week, all leaving from the Pier, which was where the store was located. The Pier, which marked the south end of town, featured a carousel and a number of shops and restaurants. An age-old lighthouse stood at the north end.

When he dropped me at home, he planted another kiss on my lips. "Thank you for saying yes."

"Thank you for asking."

Tigger and I sped inside. I skipped breakfast but fed the cat. While he dined, I showered and then threw on a pair of black cigarette-style pants, a sassy red sweater, and black sandals. A dash of red lipstick completed the ensemble. I ran a brush through my hair, but it was too tired and lackluster to perk up.

"Grin and bear it," I said to my reflection in the mirror. "Nothing is going to spoil your mood today, not your hair or even silence from Jake." I caught sight of the gleaming diamond ring on my finger and delight burbled up inside of me. "Nothing."

Despite my declaration, however, I felt the urge to check on Jake. As I left for work, I drove to his end of the street. Jake's car was in the driveway. I spied him moving about his kitchen. That made me breathe easier. He was alive. I tapped in his home number on my cell phone and caught him looking toward the telephone, but he didn't answer.

Ruing the fact that I hadn't asked for his new cell phone number, I left a voice mail asking him to touch base with me, and I continued to the shop.

After setting my purse under the counter and Tigger on his kitty condo, my stomach grumbled. "Tina, I've got to get something to eat. Are you okay on your own?"

"Fine."

"Are you sure?" In her snow-white knit dress and matching

boots, she looked a little pale. "Are your culinary night classes running you down?"

"Are you kidding? I'm supercharged." To prove it, she started rearranging our mobile bookshelves on her own to make room for the folding chairs needed for this afternoon's event.

"I'll be right back."

I hurried to the Nook Café and begged Katie for one of her specialty breakfast muffins. They were a perfect blend of eggs, bacon, cheese, and chives, just right for a simple Christmas brunch. In exchange, I promised to help her with her Yule log demonstration later in the day. We had twenty reservations from customers eager to see how she would put together the challenging cake without fear. Me? I scanned how many steps the recipe required and nearly had a panic attack.

By the time I returned to the shop, Bailey and my aunt had arrived. Bailey was filling the cash register with change. Aunt Vera was on her way to the storage room to check inventory.

At ten to nine, as Tina and I were setting up the chairs for the Yule log event, Pepper Pritchett opened the front door and poked her head inside.

"Is it too early, Jenna?"

"No, come in."

Pepper was a beading pro who owned Beaders of Paradise, a charming shop kitty-corner from ours. She was wearing what I assumed was one of her latest creations, a green sweater with gold beads around the collar, cuffs, and hem.

"How long did that take you to make, Pepper?" Tina asked.

"About a week." She plucked cat hair off her sleeve but didn't seem perturbed by it, which surprised me. Before adopting the stray ginger cat that had crashed Bailey's wedding, she was a no-pets-wanted-ever person.

"How is Mr. Cat?" I asked. Yes, that was what she'd named him. Not original, but quite cute.

"He's doing well. He likes my new beau." Her *beau* was the haberdashery guy she'd started seeing a few months ago. "Can I help you with the chairs?"

"Sure." I never said no to an extra pair of hands. "How are the plans for your daughter's wedding coming along?"

"At first Cinnamon didn't want me involved, but I convinced her to let me arrange the venue." Pepper set out a folding chair and went to fetch another. "I've found the most fabulous place." She drew out the word *fabulous*.

"Where?"

She waggled her eyebrows. "It's a secret until I get it booked. There's a long waiting list, but I've asked Z.Z. to help me finagle something."

"Have you clued in Cinnamon?"

"Not yet, but she'll love it."

I exchanged an amused look with Tina. I would bet dimes to dollars Cinnamon would want to have her say about the venue. What if it turned out to be a roller skating rink? Pepper might think that was *fabulous*. Cinnamon, most likely not.

As I reached for another folding chair, Pepper grabbed my hand. "Jenna Hart! Is that a new ring?"

"What?" Aunt Vera sailed through the storage room drapes carrying a stack of books. She dumped them on the sales counter and strode to me, the folds of her emerald green caftan swishing noisily.

"Ring?" Tina echoed. "I missed seeing a ring? What am I, blind?"

Bailey scooted to me, the flaps of her bolero jacket flying open in her haste. "You're engaged?"

I extended my hand. "Rhett asked me to marry him last night . . . and I said yes."

Aunt Vera squeezed me like a boa constrictor. "I'm so happy for you."

Bailey followed with a mighty hug of her own—mighty for someone her size. Pepper and Tina *ooh*ed their approval and tugged my hand to get a better look.

I pulled free, and over a flurry of questions said, "No, we haven't set a date. No, we don't have a venue. No, we don't know any details. I'm not sure when we will. This will take time. I promise all of you will be the first to know. Now, no more questions. Back to work. We open in a few minutes."

Aunt Vera saluted. So did Tina.

"Oh, my, time flies." Pepper fluttered her fingers. "I'm going to grab one of those muffins in the breezeway, and then I've got to run. Congratulations!" She bustled to where Katie was setting a three-tiered tray of breakfast muffins cleverly set in holiday cupcake holders.

Bailey swept past me and crooned, "Love is in the air."

"It sure is."

I plucked the topmost books from the stack my aunt had set on the sales counter and moved to the front display table. I shifted a few books to one side and added *The Perfect Cake: Your Ultimate Guide to Classic, Modern, and Whimsical Cakes* by America's Test Kitchen, which included some easy crowd-pleasers, sky-high stunners, holiday cakes, and adorable miniature cakes. I'd already taken a copy home and had my eye on making one of the easy recipes. Maybe I'd surprise Rhett on the first-week anniversary of our engagement. Was that too mushy?

A handful of customers bustled in right after Tina flipped over the *Open* sign. Most flocked to the display table. A few browsed the collection of cookie jars I'd stocked for Christmas. My personal favorite was the *Ho-ho-ho* one with Santa's feet sticking out of a snow-covered chimney.

"Jenna?" Cinnamon strode into the store with Deputy Appleby at her heels. Both were in uniform. "Is my mother here? She left a voice mail saying she had something vital to tell me."

"She's in the breezeway, helping herself to a treat." I lowered my voice. "I think she wants to tell you that she found a venue for your wedding."

"That's vital?" Cinnamon rolled her eyes.

"To her."

"Argh. What am I going to do with her?"

"Didn't you give her the task?"

"Under duress."

"She said it's the most *fabulous* place."

Cinnamon moaned. "It had better not be a karaoke bar."

"I was thinking skating rink."

That brought a smile to the chief of police's face. Appleby's, too.

"Excuse me," he said and slipped past us to greet my aunt. They had been dating for quite a while and both had agreed that marriage was not in their future, but I believed, despite the gap in their ages, they were lifelong mates.

Cinnamon seized my hand. "Is this an—"

"Engagement ring. Yep."

"When?"

"Last night."

"About time. Congratulations. Have you set a date?"

I skewered her with a look. "As if."

She chuckled. It had taken her and her hunky fireman a long time to pick a year, let alone a month.

"Walk with me," I said and fetched a copy of *How to Catch an Elf*. For fun, I set it next to *The Perfect Cake* book. Children needed something to read when their parents were browsing cookbooks. The elf book was a tad quirky but had adorable artwork. "I hope you don't mind me asking about the investigation."

"You know I do, but that doesn't seem to deter you." She smirked.

"Have you looked further into Emmett Atwater? He lied about seeing my brother-in-law return to Jake's house. Does Emmett really have an alibi? Was he at the theater like he claimed?"

"No one remembers seeing him there, but that doesn't mean anything. Over the years I've discovered that people rarely take notice of their surroundings. He did buy a ticket."

"He could have done that earlier in the day."

"Honestly, why would he kill Geoffrey Gunther?"

"Because he meant to kill Jake."

"He would've recognized him."

"I'd thought the same thing, but maybe rage blurred his vision."

"Relax, Jenna. We've got this. I will have my people question Emmett again, okay?" She put a hand on my arm.

Feeling patronized, I jerked away. The sudden move made my elbow fly back. It connected with the elf books. *Splat, splat, splat.*

"Temper, temper," Cinnamon teased.

Scowling, I reset the books. "If my father was in town, he would be all over this, pressing you for answers. He loves Jake like a brother."

"Have you spoken to your dad?"

"I wrote him an email, but he hasn't responded. With the nine-hour difference, I've been loath to call him. If I don't hear from him today, I'll reach out to Lola. C'mon, bring me up to speed."

"Fine." Ticking off her fingertips, she said, "I've interviewed neighbors. Nobody saw anything. Many were at the festival. Some were at church. I've —"

"I was at church that night, sweetheart." Pepper emerged from the breezeway carrying a half-eaten breakfast muffin. "I saw Flora there."

"Flora's always there on Wednesdays," I said. "She sings with the choir."

"That's why I was there," Pepper said. "To listen to them go through a repertoire of carols. They have voices like angels. As always, Flora did a remarkable solo in Handel's 'Messiah.'"

"We're not talking about church, Mother," Cinnamon said curtly.

"I know what you're talking about. I wasn't born yesterday. You're talking about where people were on the night that vagrant was murdered." She took another bite of her muffin.

"He wasn't a vagrant," I said.

Pepper swallowed and licked her lips. "Yes, he was. Jake told me so."

"When did you talk to Jake?" Cinnamon asked.

"When we bumped into each other outside Latte Luck Café earlier this morning. He said his friend was a drifter, riding trains all over the country and going from job to job. That's a vagrant."

"Not if he paid for his roving lifestyle, Mother. A vagrant . . ." Cinnamon clicked her tongue. "Never mind."

"Darling" — Pepper patted her daughter's cheek — "when you're done with Jenna, stop into Beaders. We need to talk about the wedding venue."

"Can't we talk now?"

"No. In private." Pepper sniggered and left the shop.

"I hate when she laughs like that," Cinnamon muttered and started toward the door.

I raced after her. "Hold up. Did Jake Chapman call you?"

"I haven't spoken to him since I released him on his own recognizance."

Shoot. So much for Rhett being right about Jake following through. "He was supposed to —"

"I have to admit I've got my doubts about having released him," Cinnamon interrupted.

"Why?"

Her face turned grave. "Jake told me he was arrested at seventeen."

"He was acquitted."

"He was, but perhaps he shouldn't have been."

I gulped. "What did he do?"

"He didn't tell you?"

"No," I said, sorry I hadn't pressed.

"He beat his sister's boyfriend to a pulp."

I flinched. "Did Jake tell you why?"

"Because the boyfriend warned the girl Jake loved about the family's drinking problem, and the girl dumped him."

"The one that got away," I murmured.

"We all have one that slipped through our fingers, don't we?" Cinnamon said. Years ago, Rhett and she had been an item until the restaurant where he'd worked as a chef was torched. She'd had to investigate the arson; he had been a person of interest. After he was exonerated, they became friends again, but by then he and I were a couple.

"But Jake's alibi of being at the store proved to be true, right?"

"Yes."

"Let me tell you about Jake's sister," I said. "I believe she's in town. I suggested he call you and tell you. Her name is Olivia. Last name, Chapman, unless she got married. She might be homeless and living out of her car." I recited the three letters the clerk at the Crystal Cove Inn had gleaned from the license plate. "You could find her with the help of the DMV."

"Jenna—"

I held up a hand. "Please hear me out. I have not been nosing into your investigation."

She listened attentively as I told her how I'd met Olivia at the festival and how Gran had encouraged me to find her. I reiterated Jake's theory that his sister might have wanted to kill him in order to inherit his estate.

"She'd have recognized her brother," Cinnamon stated.

"Not necessarily. They haven't seen each other in sixty years.

Coming at him from behind, she could have easily mistaken Geoffrey for Jake. They were the same height, build, and approximate age, and they both had silver hair. You've got to track her down."

Chapter 11

After Cinnamon left, I was determined to reach my father and bring him up to speed. I settled at the computer behind the sales counter and wrote Lola an email. Ten minutes later, she sent a response. She and my father were looking at the glimmering city of Vienna from their terrace on the boat, enjoying a glass of wine.

Lola: What do you need?

Me: I wrote Dad an email, but he didn't respond.

Lola: Your father isn't reading any email. He made a pact to relax. What's wrong?

Me: Jake Chapman is in trouble. His friend was killed. We think Jake might be the target.

Lola: Heavens. What is Cinnamon doing?

Me: Everything she can, but being Cinnamon . . .

My cell phone chimed. I fetched it from my purse, read the screen, and swiped it to answer. "Hi, Lola. Hold on." I covered the speaker with my palm. "Tina, handle these customers, would you?" A pair of women had approached the counter with armloads of books and gifts.

"Sure thing, boss." She abandoned straightening aprons adorned with jingle bells and approached the customers. "Oh, good selections, ladies," she said, indicating their purchases. "I love *The Christmas Cookie Book*. Did you see the recipe for the ones that you can hang on the tree?"

I lifted the cell phone to my ear. "Lola—"

"Jenna, it's Dad. You tell Cinnamon she's to inform me every step of the way."

Heart be still. He wanted me to deliberately insert myself into an investigation?

"I want this killer brought to justice, do you hear me?" he went on. "I want—"

"Gee, Dad, you've always told me to keep my nose out of things. How the tables turn."

"Don't be a smart aleck."

"Never. I'm a soothsayer. Now you understand why I care so much, right?"

My father sighed. "Yes."

"I'm on it, and Cinnamon has been forthcoming." I filled him in on our recent discussion.

"That's good," he said. "The two of you make a great team."

Heart be still a second time. "Ahem. Dad, we're not a team. She's the police. I'm an innocent bystander."

"Innocent, my foot." He snorted. "Tell Jake I'm sorry about his friend."

"Yeah. He's taking it hard."

"Jenna!" Bailey cried as she scurried through the breezeway.

"Give my love to Lola," I said and ended the call.

"Was that your dad?" Bailey skirted the sales counter and skidded to a stop. "Is everything okay? Is my mom—"

"She's fine. They're both fine. I contacted them to bring them up to date about Jake's situation."

"Phew. Traveling is dangerous these days. I've been worried sick ever since they left." She caressed her abdomen.

I glanced in that direction and bit back a smile.

"Stop it. I'm not pregnant."

"Have you done the home pregnancy test?" I asked.

"No." She blew a hair off her face. "And I'm not going to. I'd *know*."

"Ha! My mother once told me that after I came along she would always *know*—guess I was feisty in the womb—but she didn't realize she was carrying my brother until she was four months along."

"No way."

"Way." I crossed my heart.

Bailey grimaced.

"Relax. You're probably right. You'd *know*." I petted her shoulder. "Why were you racing through the breezeway?"

"Your sister is in the Nook Café with her husband."

"Man the fort," I said. "I'll return in time for the Yule log demonstration."

Bailey cracked an imaginary whip. "On Dasher, on Dancer . . ."

The café was jam-packed. Kenny G's instrumental "Jingle Bell Rock" was playing softly through speakers. Tables were set with vases filled with colorful sprigs of holly. A joyous, electric energy pulsed in the room. Most of these people didn't know about the murder. They weren't pondering death. How lucky they were.

Whitney and Spencer were sitting by a window with a view of the ocean. A feeling of hope soared through me as I drew near. Spencer was running a finger along the top of my sister's hand.

"Hey, you two. How are things?"

Whitney's eyes were misty, but they were bright with joy, not anger. "Wonderful. Spencer is in the clear. The police verified his alibi. And now he's told me everything."

"Everything?"

Spencer proudly ticked off a list: "The invention. The late nights. No affair."

I bumped him on the shoulder with my fist. "Way to go, bro."

"It was time. Thanks for the nudge. I still have to talk to your dad about filching stuff from his store."

"He'll understand."

"I hope so. Babe, I'll be right back." Spencer stood and excused himself to the restroom.

I perched on his chair and gazed at my sister. "So . . ."

"I don't know why he felt he couldn't tell me the truth."

"Because he's scared of you."

"Of me?"

"So is Lacy." I tapped the table. "So am I for that matter."

"Get out of here."

"Truly. All my life."

She lowered her chin. "Because I'm judgmental?"

"Because you're a perfectionist. You don't suffer fools lightly." I knew I was putting a twist on St. Paul's message, but it seemed to have the right effect.

Whitney's eyes pooled with tears of shame. Two leaked down her cheeks. She brushed them away with a forefinger. "I suggested to Spencer that we see a marriage counselor."

"Great. Let him vent. You, too. Find the things you love about each other and find the things you don't. I wish I had with David. It breaks my heart how little I knew about him."

"I hate secrecy."

"Me, too. Secrecy breeds contempt." I stood and kissed her on the cheek. "Where is Lacy?"

"We dropped her at the festival for a run-through. The concert is tomorrow night. You'll be there, won't you?"

"I wouldn't miss it. Why don't I pick her up after rehearsal so you and Spencer can have a night by yourselves?"

"Would you? Oh, that would be lovely." Whitney brushed my shoulder fondly. "Why have I ever been mean to you?"

"Good question." I smirked. "What time will Lacy be finished?"

"Seven-ish."

Spencer returned to the table, sat in his chair, and snapped his napkin onto his lap. "What did I miss?"

"Nothing," Whitney and I chimed together.

Feeling lighter knowing my sister's marriage wasn't on the rocks and that my brother-in-law was in the clear with the police, I returned to the shop. While Tina attended to a few customers and Bailey took apart the completed jigsaw puzzle on the vintage table, I slipped into the storage room and queued up more instrumental Christmas music. Customers seemed to be enjoying it; many were mouthing the words or whistling along.

In midafternoon, Katie wheeled her mobile cooking cart into the shop. She did so many demonstrations nowadays that we had invested in high-end carts. She bent to retrieve a rectangular box from the lower shelf and her toque nearly fell off. In the nick of time, Bailey ran to her and set it upright.

I joined them and noted the fixings for the Yule log: flour, sugar, cocoa, eggs, butter, parchment paper, rolling pin, piping bag with tips, and more. Katie had previously prepared a beautiful cake. She had set the cake on a foil-lined sheet and decorated it with plastic pine boughs, small forest creatures, and meringue mushrooms dusted with cocoa.

"Nice job, Katie," Bailey said.

"These mushrooms . . ." I pointed to them. "I've always wondered about the reason for them. I mean, they look so harmless in this setting, but aren't forest mushrooms poisonous?"

"There are thousands of edible mushrooms in the wild," Katie assured me. "However, the consequences of making a bad guess or misidentifying a mushroom can be, like, yikes. A careless person might even require a liver transplant or worse."

"You mean death?"

She bobbed her head. "Take the green-spored parasol, for example. When it's young, it looks like the common white button mushroom."

"Like this cute one on your cake."

"Yep. It often comes up in grass after a good rain. It's called a toxic look-alike."

I gulped. "Are we sending a bad message to children who will watch the demonstration?"

"I'll make sure they know. Hey!" Katie grabbed my hand. "Is that an engagement ring? Jenna Hart, how could you not tell me?" She stared daggers at Bailey. "And you!"

"Slipped my mind." Bailey threw up her hands in defense.

"When, how, got a date?" Katie blathered, throwing out the typical questions.

I gave her the same answers I'd given the others. "When I know, you'll know."

"You'd better, or there will be heck to pay." She swooped me into a congratulatory hug.

A half hour later, the crowd arrived. I'd set out more festive cake cookbooks, including *2016 Southern Living Christmas Cookbook.* As my aunt said, *One can never go wrong with a Southern Living book.* The recipes were beautiful; many were easy enough for me to tackle.

For the next hour, Katie wowed the audience as she took them through a step-by-step demonstration of how to make the cake. Many *ooh*ed when she showed them how to roll it up jelly roll style, using clean tea towels. For each phase of her presentation she had a finished product.

When it came time to form the meringue mushrooms, her cheeks were florid and the crowd's attention was waning. Making a Yule log was not for the faint of heart. To keep them enthralled, she pulled two children from the audience and taught them how to wield a piping tool. As they squeezed out tops and bottoms of mushrooms, the crowd watched via the angled mirror attached to the top of the demonstration cart.

"Now, meringue mushrooms take time to dry out in the oven, so you can make them in advance," Katie said. "Also"—she addressed the children—"there's no need for perfection. Remember, no two mushrooms are alike." That was where she threw in the spiel about toxic mushrooms. "Last but not least, make sure you're making the meringue on a dry day. Humidity can ruin them. Got it?"

The children bobbed their heads.

When Katie concluded and revealed a finished product, the audience cheered. Afterward, they purchased lots of holiday gifts. What a win-win.

• • •

After work, I dropped Tigger at home and headed to Azure Park. On the way, I telephoned Rhett and asked him to join Lacy and me later at the cottage for dinner.

The Christmas festival crowd was twice the size it had been on Wednesday. There were roving carolers in full Dickensian costumes—the women in tightly fitted jackets with pagoda sleeves, bell-shaped skirts, bonnets, and hand-warming muffs; the men in waistcoats, pants held up by suspenders, and top hats. Also, at a North Pole setting in the center of the park tonight, there was a Santa greeting children, and there were female elves with glittery cheeks handing out candy canes. The twinkling lights on the tents and in the trees cast a warm glow on all the faces. Seeing Santa made me think about the shop's cookie swap contest on Sunday. Pretty much everyone who was attending the event had rented a Santa costume or Santa's helper costume through Flora. A supplier in San Francisco had given her a great deal.

On the stage, Lacy and her fellow a capella competitors were standing in a line receiving guidance from the ponytailed director. The vision reminded me of the opening of *A Chorus Line*, the teens slumped in a pose, many attentive, others lost in thought.

With ten or so minutes before Lacy finished her run-through, I roamed the grounds. Based on the customers who were wearing their purchases out of Christmas Sweater Depot, the kitschy Rudolf the Reindeer and Frosty the Snowman sweaters were hot-ticket items.

My heart snagged when I neared Forget Me Not, the memory of meeting Geoffrey still fresh. I poked my head inside. Raquel, dressed in an attractive ice-white outfit, an elf's hat atilt on her head, was so busy answering a customer's questions she didn't look up. Her older sister, who was decked out in a red silk blouse and black linen slacks, was reorganizing the items on the antique clerk's desk. She caught sight of me and waved. I returned the gesture and moved on.

I peeked into the Christmas Palace venue to see what it was selling and realized it was jammed with items that Flora might peddle in her store: darling holiday-themed ornaments, candles, and home decorating goods. I'd bet she was ruing the fact that she hadn't rented a tent like Raquel had. Enchanted Gifts, which catered to people who loved whimsical things like fairies and talking Christmas trees, was doing a booming business, as well. I slipped into Sweet Envy, which offered boxes of homemade candies, and purchased a selection of six truffles for tonight's dessert.

When I left, the aroma of hot mulled cider lured me to Warm Your Heart. I purchased a mug and took a sip. *Divine.* After I tossed my empty cup, I made my way toward the stage. A line of customers was feeding into Keller's Kool Desserts venue, which pleased me. Keller, Katie's fiancé, was an eccentric entrepreneur who pedaled around town selling delicious homemade ice cream. If we lived in the chilly northeast, business might be bad for him, but in temperate Crystal Cove, it was great.

Outside the Holly and Ivy wreath tent, I spied Gran with another elderly woman. Gran was laughing at some story her friend was telling. In stark contrast, I spotted Lacy standing at the foot of the stage with her friend Veronica Devereaux, who was stabbing the air with her finger. Lacy responded by gesticulating broadly, as if saying, *What did I do?*

Concerned, I drew nearer.

"I was not flirting with him," Lacy said.

"I saw you!" Veronica shouted. "You hitched up your top to get his attention."

"You're full of it."

"I told you from the outset I wanted him."

"And I told you you could have him. He's not my type. I like musicians, not stuck-up singers who think they can write music." Lacy caught sight of me and signaled *one second.* "Honestly, Veronica, get over yourself. He's yours. If you'd like, I'll wrap him in a Christmas bow for you."

The other girl muttered something I couldn't make out. Lacy stomped away.

When she reached me, I said, "Everything okay?"

"Yeah, fine."

Clearly it wasn't.

She was mute until we reached my VW. Slipping into the passenger seat, she said, "You saw Mom and Dad today."

"I did."

"And . . ."

"They're working things out."

"How long will that last?"

I cut her a look. "Don't be negative."

"Comes with the territory. Geez."

I tilted my head and gave her the stink eye. "Would you like to try that again?"

"Why?"

"I don't deserve the attitude."

"Sorry." In typical teenager shutdown mode, she folded her arms and curled into herself.

Driving home, I worked my lip between my teeth, wondering how or *if* I would be able to raise a child. I had no skills. Rhett and I hadn't discussed that part of our future yet. We needed to.

Chapter 12

After fetching overnight items from my father's house, Lacy finally opened up about the set-to at the festival. Her friend Veronica was mad because the others in the group had started to turn to Lacy as their leader, mainly because Veronica was boy crazy and couldn't focus on the music.

"She made up that thing about me flirting with the guy in the Ransom Notes to get under my skin. I think she figured if I'd get angry in public, then the others would think I was hot-tempered and not worthy." Lacy made air quotation marks as she dragged out the word *worthy*. "Well, ha! I showed her. I kept my cool. She can be such a diva." A teensy sob escaped her lips, revealing how much the incident had upset her. Droplets of tears clung to her eyelashes. She said, "She and I used to be best friends. Like sisters. Not anymore."

"Friends can make up. Bailey and I had a fight way back when."

"About boys?"

"About how to run an ad campaign."

"Grown-up stuff. It's not the same."

"You and Veronica will be friends again, too."

"Whatever."

When we sauntered into the cottage, Tigger bounded to Lacy. He jumped back and forth over her feet until she bent to rub him.

"Hey, Tig-Tig," she said. "I missed you, too. Yes, I did." She sat cross-legged on the floor and made silly cooing sounds.

I hung my jacket on the hook by the door and stowed my purse on the kitchen counter. "Lacy, I hope it's all right. I've asked my boyfriend to dinner."

"Cool. I can't wait to meet him."

As I was closing the door, I spotted a black Mercedes heading down the street. I couldn't make out the driver, but I'd bet it was Jake. He drove a swanky S-Class. Had Cinnamon found his sister yet? Had Jake spoken with her?

"What are you staring at?" Lacy asked.

"I think Jake just drove by."

"I can't imagine how he's feeling."

"Not good."

"You should ask him to dinner, too." Lacy raked her spiky hair with her fingers. "What are we having?"

"What I call a layered Christmas casserole. It's made with eggs and potatoes and all sorts of good stuff."

"Perfect. Mom always serves a huge five-course meal when we have guests. There are so many leftovers. It's a waste."

"Don't tell her that."

"As if."

We both laughed.

"I like your idea," I said. "I'm calling Jake. He could use a home-cooked meal." I crossed to the landline telephone that my aunt had installed. She believed every home needed a *real* telephone. She admitted it was an old-fashioned idea, but one time, using it had saved my life. I dialed Jake's number. He picked up after two rings. It didn't take much persuading. He said he'd love to dine with us.

An hour later, as I was taking the casserole out of the oven, Rhett arrived with a bottle of Beringer Private Reserve chardonnay in hand.

I set it on the counter and introduced him to Lacy.

"Well, it's about time," he said. "I've heard great things about you."

"You have?"

"Over dinner the other night, your aunt told me all about your singing and your shopping spree. I like your hairdo, by the way. It suits you."

She blushed. As she fetched the mats and silverware to set the table, she leaned in to me and said, "He's handsome."

"As all get-out."

"And his voice? It's like a really rich baritone."

I grinned. "A singer would notice something like that."

As Rhett opened the chardonnay and poured me a glass, there was a knock on the door. I opened it. Jake stood on the porch. His eyes were bloodshot, his skin wan, and his hair windblown. The shirt and slacks he was wearing were clean and pressed, however, which helped him look livelier than he obviously felt.

"Welcome." I guided him inside. Rhett offered him a drink.

"I don't drink. Water will be fine." Jake acknowledged Lacy with a nod. "Hello, little lady."

"Lady." She snorted.

"Nice cat."

Lacy held Tigger up to him. "Do you like cats?"

"I do." He scratched Tigger under the chin. "But I've never owned one."

"Me, either. Mom says she's allergic to dander."

"She might be," I said. "Our mother was."

"Nah." Lacy shook her head and tucked Tigger into her lap. "Mom just doesn't want cat hair around the house."

I said, "Jake, I heard you ran into Pepper Pritchett at Latte Luck today."

He rolled his eyes. "That woman can talk an ear off."

"She said you told her Geoffrey was a drifter."

"That's what he liked to call himself. He went from job to job. Couldn't sit still. Hated being in one place. Sad to say, but nobody will miss him other than me."

Jake roamed my cottage, glancing at the few items I cared to display: a bookshelf filled with classics, mysteries, and cookbooks, and the repaired lucky cat statue that occupied a shelf by itself. He paused by the Ching two-door cabinet and fingered the brass handles. It was one of the gems David and I had purchased in Chinatown. I stored my art supplies inside.

"I have a few of these kinds of pieces," he said. "I was never much into furniture, but my wife had very eclectic taste. Did you do this?" He jutted a finger at a painting featuring a girl dancing on the beach.

"Yes." I'd finished it last year.

"It's good."

"Don't tell her that." Rhett ran a hand along my back. "She'll get a swelled head."

I swatted him.

Lacy said, "I think she's a really good artist, too."

I blew her a kiss.

Lacy stared unashamedly at Jake. "You remind me of someone."

He smiled. "I think we established the other night that I remind you of an old cowboy. Possibly Clint Eastwood."

"I don't know who that is."

Jake groaned. So did Rhett.

Lacy continued to stare. "It's that guy who was in the movie with the actor who looks like Gramps." She turned to me for help.

"Gramps looks like Cary Grant," I said. My father was almost the spitting image of the actor when he was in his sixties. Lean build, silver hair, dashing smile. It didn't hurt that his name was also Cary, although he couldn't deliver a line with a British accent to save his life.

"Yeah, him. He and this guy were in the movie. Another guy had a claw for a hand." Lacy shook Tigger's paw. "What's the name of it?"

Rhett said, "*Charade?*"

"Yeah, that one." Lacy shot out a finger as if she were playing twenty questions. "This guy was a cowboy. Tex."

"Played by James Coburn," Rhett said.

Jake stood a little taller. "Whoa. He was a dashing fellow."

"Not in that movie," Lacy said. "He was mean."

"So you're saying I'm mean?"

"No, I . . . You're good-looking in a . . ." She faltered.

"An old cowboy way. Got it." Jake smiled.

A shiver skittered down my spine as I recalled how Tex died in *Charade*. It wasn't pretty. Eager to change the topic, I said, "Dinner is served. Jake, you sit there." I pointed to the far end of the tiny kitchen table. "Lacy, by the bay window."

Rhett helped me prepare the plates. "Smells good."

"It's just a casserole."

"Casseroles have their place, my parents would say."

His mother and father owned Intime, a chic restaurant in Napa Valley. I doubted either had ever cooked a casserole, except perhaps *cassoulet*, a sumptuous French-style meat and bean dish.

"More wine, sweetheart?" he asked.

I nodded and took my place at the table.

Lacy dug in to her dinner and hummed her approval. "I like this. Can you teach me to make it?"

"Yes," I said, thrilled to be considered the teacher and not the student.

Lacy shook her knife at Jake. "About that night when you were talking to that stamp lady . . ."

"What about it?" he asked.

I gawked. "Lacy. Not now."

"It's important. Jake reminded me of that actor in the movie because remember how they went to the stamp fair at the end? The stamp on the envelope wasn't an ordinary stamp. It was worth tons of money." She eyed Jake. "Was yours an ordinary stamp?"

"Lacy." I set my fork down. "Honestly, it's rude to talk about that night. Jake's friend—"

Jake shook his head. "It's okay, Jenna. She might be on to something."

"I might?" My niece's voice skated upward.

"She might?" Rhett and I said in unison.

Jake pushed his food around his plate with his fork but didn't take a bite. "I collect stamps. I have for years. They've always fascinated me. They can tell the tale of where someone has been, what life that person has led. Before I moved to California, I was like Geoffrey, going from job to job. I sent postcards to my sister, trying to make amends for leaving her behind. Each time, I tried to select the most unique stamp at the post office. When I settled here and I had a little extra cash, I used to go into Forget Me Not, back when Raquel's father owned the place. We'd talk about stamps and coins and all sorts of things. He was really knowledgeable. I listened. I learned."

The same way he'd picked up investing from my grandfather.

"What stamp were you showing the lady that night?" Lacy asked. "I heard her call it a blue something."

"A Blue Mauritius," Jake said.

"I've heard of that." Rhett thumped the table.

My eyes widened. "You have?"

"A guy who frequents Bait and Switch is a philatelist."

"What's a philatelist?" Lacy stumbled over the word.

"A stamp collector," Rhett said. "The Blue Mauritius Post Office stamps were issued in 1847."

I grinned. "Show off."

"That's as much as I know." Rhett leaned back in his chair and folded his hands behind his head. "Take it away, Jake."

"The name comes from the wording on the stamps that say *Post Office*, which changed in the next issue to *Post Paid*. The Blue Mauritius is one of the rarest stamps in the world."

"Maybe . . ." Lacy rolled her lower lip between her teeth. "Maybe whoever killed your friend was hoping to steal that stamp out of his pocket."

"Impossible. He didn't have it. I did."

"Right," I said, seizing on Lacy's theory. "But if the killer mistook him for you —"

Jake jumped to his feet and headed to the front door.

"Where are you going?" I asked.

"Sorry to eat and run. I've got to check on something."

I bounded out of my chair and followed him.

Rhett said, "C'mon, Lacy. Your aunt won't be deterred, and you're not staying here alone."

The three of us trailed after Jake.

"Jake, wait up," I cried, but he didn't slow his pace.

He pulled out a keychain and opened his front door. He deactivated the alarm system and forged ahead. Rhett closed the door after us.

I'd never been inside Jake's home. He wasn't kidding about his wife having eclectic taste. She had decorated with any piece of furniture that had struck her fancy. Nothing was cheap. There were nineteenth-century antiques as well as art deco pieces. I caught a glimpse of the dining room as we flew past. The Chippendale dinette set was dark mahogany and must have cost a small fortune.

Jake opened a door beneath the staircase and switched on a light. He trotted downstairs and turned on another light in the unfinished basement.

We followed. The air was cool but not dank. I caught the whirr of a hidden fan. Boxes upon boxes lined one of the walls. Shelves along another wall were stacked with paint cans. There were piles of ceramic tiles and slats of wood matching the flooring I'd seen running throughout the house, plus a few chairs and small tables that apparently hadn't found a home upstairs.

"Cool," Lacy murmured, her eyes gleaming with intrigue.

"Jake, why did you come down here?" For some reason I felt the need to whisper.

He slid a section of boxes away from the wall, revealing a precut square in the cement floor with a ring embedded in it. He bent down and pulled on the ring. The square came loose. Jake set the heavy block aside and peered into the hole below. All I could see over his shoulder was the top of a safe fitted with a crank handle and a dial. Jake spun the dial a number of times—left, right, and left—and then twisted the crank handle and lifted the lid. It hinged open. He reached down and pulled out a legal folder. He unspooled the tie that held the folder together.

"As I thought," he said. "The Blue Mauritius is here. All my stamps are. My coins, too."

Rhett and I let out a collective breath.

Lacy said, "What about Geoffrey's envelope?"

"What envelope?" Jake swiveled to face her.

"You both put envelopes into your pockets that night. Remember, Aunt Jenna, when I asked if Jake was on the run because of the passport and birth certificate—"

I held up a hand, not needing further details. "Jake, Geoffrey wasn't wearing a jacket when we found him. Where did he put his things when you came home from the festival?"

"In the guest room where he was staying."

"Did you or the police check his jacket after he was killed?"

"He didn't have anything of value."

"No stamp?" Lacy asked.

"Well, yeah, he had a stamp," Jake said. "One I'd given him. But it wasn't worth much. A used two-cent, red-and-pink Washington stamp."

"Used?" Lacy asked.

"Canceled by the post office."

"What would it go for?" I asked.

Jake rubbed his chin. "Three thousand or so."

Rhett whistled. "That's a bunch of cash to a lot of people, Jake."

I agreed. "Jake, maybe the killer went searching for it. Did the police check to see if anything was disturbed inside?"

"The police made a tour of the house. I led the way. The living room and study were empty. All the silver was in the cabinet in the dining room. We searched the basement. Nothing looked disturbed. I didn't reveal where my safe was."

"Smart," Rhett said.

"We checked my room and the guest rooms. Nothing appeared to have been rooted through. We even searched the attic."

"You have an attic?" Lacy asked, eyes wide, clearly curious to explore. "What's in it?"

"Antiques, books, toys."

"Why toys?"

"My wife got pregnant." He hesitated; his eyes wavered. "*We* got pregnant. She nested like crazy, stocking the house with all things *baby*. But at childbirth—" His voice caught. "She lost the baby. She couldn't conceive again."

Lacy sucked back a sob. "I'm so sorry."

I caressed Jake's arm. "I had no idea."

"We managed. That's why I never wrote a will, Jenna."

"But you have one now?"

"Yeah. I'm leaving everything to a children's foundation that your father suggested a few months ago."

My father was that kind of guy. He offered his help at Habitat for Humanity and found special projects that needed volunteers.

Rhett said, "We should take a look at the guest room."

Jake returned the legal folder to the safe, secured the lock, pushed the boxes into position, and trudged upstairs.

The guest room was located on the second floor to the left. The door was ajar. Jake pushed it open and flipped a switch. Lamplight illuminated the space. "See?" he said. "Everything looks normal. Nothing was touched."

The grand size of the room made me gasp. "Wow, this is big." In any other house, it would have been considered a master bedroom.

"All the bedrooms are the same size," Jake said. "My wife wanted anyone who stayed with us to feel equal."

"So the killer might have assumed this was your room."

"I suppose."

The room was decorated with beautiful ebony furniture. An elegant quilt and pillows with shams adorned the bed. The leather jacket Geoffrey had worn on Wednesday night hung on the back of a chair by a small Louis XVI writing desk.

"Did the police search the pockets of his jacket?" I asked.

Jake shook his head. "I don't know. Probably. It didn't occur to me." He rummaged through the jacket pockets. When he came up empty, his face went pale. "The envelope is gone."

Lacy whispered, "Raquel."

Chapter 13

I contacted Cinnamon and quickly recapped what we had discovered: a stamp, albeit not the most expensive, was missing. She arrived at Jake's house within minutes, dressed in a long-sleeved blue dress and heels and looking ticked to have been called out on a Friday night. Her sense of duty to my father, and thereby his extended family, must have compelled her to see to this matter personally.

"Did I interrupt a date?" I asked.

"Yes, and Bucky is not happy about finishing dinner alone at the Pelican Brief Diner." She addressed Jake, who was standing at the foot of the stairs with Rhett and Lacy, and asked him to confirm what I had told her.

He did.

"The stamp is really unique!" Lacy blurted.

Gently, Rhett invited Lacy to go with him to the kitchen so he could make her a hot chocolate.

"You're coddling me," she muttered.

He winked. "You could call it that."

Grudgingly, she accepted the invitation, but I could tell she wanted to stick around and hear whatever Jake discussed with the chief of police. Rhett assured her I'd fill her in later.

Jake led Cinnamon upstairs to the guest room. I followed. He recounted the sequence of events on the night of the murder: meeting Raquel at her Forget Me Not booth; Raquel's interest in the Blue Mauritius stamp; Geoffrey mirroring Jake's move with his envelope.

"Lacy was the one to notice they both put the envelopes in their coat pockets," I said.

"Jake"—Cinnamon turned to face him—"I don't think Raquel would kill someone to get her hands on an ordinary stamp."

"It wasn't ordinary," I said. "It's valued at three thousand dollars."

"That's chump change to Raquel," Cinnamon countered. "Her shop does extremely well. Investors come from all over to purchase collectibles. Right, Jake?"

"I wouldn't know."

"I've seen you visit the shop. Seen you chatting with her father on multiple occasions, may he rest in peace."

"You have?" His eyes widened.

"It's my job to check in on the locals. You and Raquel are friendly."

"We're business acquaintances."

Cinnamon's eyes narrowed. "Do you believe she's strong enough to have strangled Geoffrey Gunther?"

"How would I know?"

Changing tack, I said, "Have you found Jake's sister yet, Chief?"

"Not yet. We're looking."

"What if she killed Geoffrey and stole the stamp? Three thousand dollars could mean a lot to her."

Cinnamon shifted feet. "Now you're asking me to assume that a woman in her seventies—a *homeless* woman in her seventies—killed Mr. Gunther?"

"Homeless people aren't weaklings," I said.

"How would she have known about the stamp?"

"She was at the festival that night. Gran—Gracie Goldsmith—introduced us. I didn't realize at the time who she was. She could have shadowed Jake and seen him asking Raquel about the stamp."

Cinnamon raised an eyebrow. "You're tilting at windmills, Jenna."

"I don't believe I am."

"Fine." She worked her tongue inside her mouth. "I'll question Raquel, and with some luck, Jake, I'll track down your sister." She acknowledged me with a nod. "Happy?"

"Ecstatic," I said. "We're merely trying to assist the police in any way we can, right, Jake?"

"Yes, Chief, any way we can."

After Cinnamon left and after making sure that Jake felt safe in his house alone, Rhett, Lacy, and I went home. Rhett didn't stay the night. That would have been inappropriate with Lacy sleeping over. He kissed me sweetly on the porch, told me to double-check all my locks, and said he'd call me first thing in the morning.

I slept fitfully listening to Lacy toss and turn. She talked in her sleep about Jake and the stamp and the toys in the attic and the boxes in the basement. At one point, she mumbled a string of *no*'s. I could only imagine what she was dreaming. At two, I heaved off the couch and tiptoed into the bedroom to make sure she was covered with the comforter.

Tigger, who was nestled at her feet, mewled at me. I tickled his chin and whispered, "She'll be okay, pal. She's simply seen too much in recent days for someone her age."

He meowed again and gazed at me mournfully.

I sighed. "Yeah, I've seen too much, too."

• • •

The next morning, on the way to drop off Lacy at my father's house, I telephoned Whitney to update her on last night's events. When we arrived, she was on the doorstep waiting for her daughter with open arms. As she clutched Lacy to her chest and stroked her spiky hair, Lacy gave me the evil eye. I bit back a smile. She could accept being babied by Rhett, but clearly she hated her mother fussing over her.

"I'm okay, Mom." Lacy pressed apart. "The one who's suffering is Jake."

"Yes, of course."

"I've got to go to rehearsal. Can you drive me?"

"You bet. Are you nervous about tonight?"

"I'm nervous that Veronica will do something weird."

"Why would she?"

"Because she's Veronica." She waved at Tigger, who was standing on his hind legs in the driver's seat, front paws on the door's rim. "Bye, fella. Aunt Jenna, if you learn anything, text me."

By the time I arrived at the Cookbook Nook, Tina, who looked festive in a fire engine red sweater over a flirty skirt, her cheeks spritzed with glitter, had received and signed for a new shipment of books. Most of them had nothing to do with food. Once the Christmas festival concluded, we would gear up for the annual antique car festival. Hundreds of cars would arrive in town to participate in events, including a parade that would originate at the Pier. Owners would adorn their cars with wreaths, streamers, and other fun decorations. Locals and in-the-know tourists would gather with flags to cheer them on along the boulevard. I'd purchased quite a few antique car books, including *The Art of the*

Automobile: The 100 Greatest Cars, which one reviewer touted as the perfect Father's Day gift. I figured if it were ideal for that, it would be an even better Christmas present.

"Jenna, get a load of this one," Tina said, offering me a copy of *Classic Car: The Definitive Visual History.*

I flipped through it and nearly swooned. Any car lover would adore the professional photographs. "This is terrific. Would you set a few of these on the display table by the salt and pepper shakers?" I handed the book back to her. "We'll move them to the front table after the festival concludes."

"On it." Tina swooped up a handful and zigzagged through the aisles to her destination. She seemed perkier today, as if whatever had tired her yesterday was a thing of the past. Perhaps she didn't have a culinary class on Friday nights and had gotten a decent amount of sleep. Unlike me. I yawned and covered my mouth with the back of my hand.

Bailey strolled into the shop with her beloved husband in tow. When I'd first met Tito Martinez, I hadn't liked him. He'd acted like a gruff bulldog. Reporters could be like that. Truth be told, he resembled a bulldog—broad face, broad shoulders, short legs. Over the past year, I'd grown quite fond of him. After he wooed Bailey and won her heart, I realized he was dogged in all the right ways. It thrilled me to know she was happy.

On the other hand, she didn't appear very joyful this morning. Her eyes were pinpoints of angst and her makeup was a tad off. Tito didn't look so good, either.

"Morning," I said.

"Hi," Bailey replied, her tone lackluster. She pulled alongside the vintage kitchen table. "Where's your aunt?"

"Right here," Aunt Vera chimed as she pushed through the storage room drapes, a box of tissues in hand. She set the tissues on the sales counter and crossed to Bailey, the folds of her crimson caftan rustling. "Is everything all right, dear?" She began to caress the amulet around her neck.

A frisson of worry skated up my spine.

Tito said, "Bailey has been feeling sad lately and doesn't know what's up. She wants to make sure everything is okay with her mother."

I drew closer. "Your mom is fine. I spoke with her and Dad earlier." After dropping off Lacy, I'd called my father. "Your mom sounds like she's in seventh heaven. The weather has been sublime. She's enjoying all of their excursions. Text her. I'm sure she'll set your mind at ease."

"She fibs when she doesn't want me to worry," Bailey said and turned to my aunt. "Vera, could you please do a reading for us?"

"Us?" Tito raised an eyebrow.

"Okay, me. Tito's a nonbeliever."

"A skeptic." He kissed her cheek and hooked his thumb in the direction of the café. "I'm going to get a coffee. Want one?"

She shook her head and perched on a chair at the table.

I leaned down and whispered, "You're pregnant. Admit it."

"I am not. We did the test."

"Tests can be wrong."

"I'm not PG. Stop it." She flicked my arm with a finger. "Go to work. Let me have your aunt's undivided attention."

"When you're done, will you please tinker with the shop's website? Spruce it up. Give it a little more holiday flair." Whereas my artistic eye was best utilized when I was painting or decorating a display window, Bailey had a keen eye for digital design. "Can you add a welcoming jingle, too?"

"Sure." She shooed me away.

"Jenna, dear"—Aunt Vera settled at the table and withdrew a pack of tarot cards from her pocket—"I almost forgot. When you're available, Katie would like you to taste test some items. There's a big party coming in this evening after the festival."

"Will do." I wasn't much of a cook, but I had a finely tuned palate. During my time at Taylor & Squibb and during my brief marriage to David, I'd done my fair share of dining at gourmet restaurants.

In less than a quarter hour, I queued up a series of orchestral Christmas music, neatened the shop, checked on Tigger's water supply in the storage room, and tweaked the window display—a few wreaths had toppled. Throughout my chores, I repeatedly took note of Bailey and Aunt Vera. The first two cards my aunt had turned over hadn't seemed to cause any alarm. Bailey was nodding. A smile graced her lips. When my aunt turned over the third card and stiffened, concern shot through me. I hurried over.

"What's wrong?" I asked.

"Nothing," Aunt Vera said.

"Don't kid a kidder." I pointed at the Two of Pentacles, in which a young man was dancing as he juggled his worldly concerns. The infinity sign looping around the two star-filled circles, or *pentacles*, suggested that he could handle unlimited problems. "I'm not a fortune-teller, but that's not a gasp-worthy card."

"No, it's not," she said.

"But you gasped."

Bailey clucked her tongue. "Out with it, Vera. I know I don't have a clue what goes on with these readings, but because you gathered up the first two cards and didn't leave them on display with the third, I'm getting goose bumps."

"Sweet girl, all this card reveals is that you might have to adapt to change."

"Ooh!" I wiggled my fingers in my friend's face. "Does that mean there's a baby in your future?"

"Cut it out," Bailey sniped. "Vera, that card does not mean I'm pregnant."

"Not exactly, no."

Bailey shot me a *gotcha* look.

"However, you must stay centered while you stay flexible," Aunt Vera said. "You must be open to change and go with the flow as best you can."

Bailey turned ashen. "'Go with the flow'?" She stabbed the tarot card. "See the ships behind the guy? Are you sure this card doesn't have to do with my mother?"

"Those ships in the background show that the young man can easily cruise life's ups and downs." Aunt Vera swooped up the card and returned it to the deck. "This has nothing to do with your mother. The reading is all about you. You are the one who must be flexible."

I hummed "Rock-a-bye Baby."

Bailey snarled and leaped to her feet. "I need a cup of hot chocolate before I tackle the website."

"And I need to taste test," I said. "Tina, I'm going with Bailey to the café. I'll be back before we open."

She gave me the thumbs-up signal.

Before leaving, I bent down and whispered to my aunt, "Am I right? Is she pregnant?"

"We'll see."

Tito passed Bailey and me on our way to the café. "Everything okay?"

"Hunky dory," she said and kissed him on the cheek. "Have fun hunting down a new story."

When Bailey and I slipped into the kitchen, Katie was arranging canapés on a platter. Reynaldo, the assistant she'd hired a few months ago, and the rest of the staff were busily preparing baked goods. The café wouldn't open for another thirty minutes.

"Oh, good, you're here." Katie squeezed my arm in thanks. "Follow me. I've set out a number of appetizers and desserts on the captain's table." She motioned toward the table for eight that was nestled into a nook at the rear of the kitchen. Occasionally she served special dinners there. "Sit. Taste. I need three appetizers and three desserts. I've settled on the main courses." She ticked off her fingers. "Pecan crusted gulf fish, seared wild shrimp, and filet mignon with roasted root vegetables over smashed garlic potatoes."

"Yum." My mouth watered. Some days—*most* days—a power bar wasn't enough for breakfast.

"But the appetizers have me stymied," she went on. "I'd like to do something with a holiday flair." Katie pointed to the appetizers she'd set on the table. "I have shrimp and tasso over grits with *beurre blanc*. Then there's Crystal Cove succotash."

"What's that?" Bailey asked.

"Chicken and lima beans with chopped tomatoes and—"

"That's green and red," I cut in.

"True. I'm worried, though. Is it moist enough? Be honest." Katie continued pointing. "I also have a baby spinach salad with pecans and crumbled blue cheese or a strawberry salad with petite greens and goat cheese."

"The second salad is green and red, too," Bailey chirped.

"You're right." Katie tapped her temple. "I hadn't realized that."

I slid onto the bench at the table and said, "I'm digging in." I tasted the spinach salad first. The dressing was heavenly. "Is this your famous sugarcane vinaigrette?"

Katie beamed. "Good guess, and freshly made Creole mustard."

I hummed my approval and pulled a small plate of the shrimp and tasso toward me. Tasso was a spicy meat. Pairing it with the shrimp was a perfect balance—not too salty with lots of texture. "I love this," I said, pointing with my fork.

"What's for dessert?" Bailey asked.

Katie fetched three dessert plates from the walk-in refrigerator. She set them in front of Bailey. "Eggnog ice cream with white chocolate crackle. The crackle is made with saltine crackers." She patted her belly. "Very satisfying."

The gesture made me think of how Bailey had been caressing her abdomen lately. I bit back a grin and took one of the desserts. After savoring a bite of the crackle, which was yummy, I said, "Who's throwing the party?"

"Raquel Adagio."

I gawped. "She can afford a soiree like this?"

"She throws a party about three times a year, mostly for clients. Her business does very well."

I recollected what Cinnamon had said about Raquel being financially set and having no motive to steal Geoffrey's stamp.

"This one is for family," Katie went on. "A reunion of sorts. Her mother, two sisters, the older one's husband and their six children. You know Raquel's father died, right?"

"I didn't until Cinnamon mentioned it." I had never been close to the Adagio family.

"Why would she have said anything?" Katie asked.

"It pertains to the investigation. So, it sounds like you'll have a full house."

"Yes, I'm seating them at the long table by the window. Raquel told me all of them have a sweet tooth, which is why I need your opinion on these desserts." Katie pointed to a plate of cupcakes. "In addition to the ice cream and crackle, I have dark chocolate mini cupcakes with peppermint swirl icing."

"Nice." I nodded. "That's simple and appealing."

Bailey ate one in three bites. "And tasty. Kids will love them."

I said, "You could do three different flavors of cupcakes with the same icing."

Katie shot a finger at me. "I like that idea. And I could decorate them with these teensy chocolate toys I discovered on the Internet." She fetched a box and plucked three items from it: a rocking horse, a snowman, and a tin soldier, each about an inch tall. "Aren't they adorable?"

"Adorable. Speaking of toys . . ." I said as I took a bite of the succotash. "Mm-mm. Definitely moist. It might need a bit of white pepper, though."

"Already in there."

"Add more."

"Noted. You were saying about toys?"

I filled them in on what had gone down at Jake's last night and how surprised I was to learn that he and his wife had lost a child.

"What does that have to do with toys?" Bailey asked.

"His wife had been totally prepared to have a child. She'd purchased the furniture and a wealth of toys, and then, *bam*. The possibility was gone. Jake said she couldn't have any more. Isn't that sad?"

Katie's face grew grim. "I can't have children, either."

"You can't?" Bailey's eyes widened.

"I'm so sorry," I said. "Did you want to?"

"Oh, yeah. Big time. Keller and I have been talking about adopting." She and her fiancé were next in line to get married. Then Cinnamon.

"What about you, Bailey?" Katie asked. "Do you want them?"

"She's not sure." I brandished a finger at our pal. "She doesn't think she'll be a good mother."

"I might be changing my opinion on that," Bailey said and downed another cupcake.

"Really?" I fist-bumped her shoulder. "All right."

Katie turned to me. "How about you, Jenna?"

"I wanted children when I was married to David. Now I keep wondering if I'm too old, and . . ." I hesitated. "And I have to admit, I'm not sure I'll be any good at it. It's been tough handling my niece for a few days. The mood swings. The times when she shuts down. The moments when she's like a firefly, flitting all over the place in body as well as thought."

"Raising your own is different," Katie said. "Many women have assured me of that. But if you're going to have kids, you have to be ready. You have to be flexible. You have to"—she made an undulating motion with her hand—"cruise life's ups and downs."

Bailey shot her a look. "Cut it out."

"Huh?" Katie frowned.

"Vera called you, didn't she? She told you to say that."

"Say what?"

Bailey undulated her hand. "'Cruise life's ups and downs.'"

"Get real, Bailey," I chided. "Exactly when would my aunt have had time to call her?" I made an eerie *woo-woo* gesture in front of her face. "Go with the flow."

My pal didn't find my antics amusing. In fact, she looked spooked.

Chapter 14

The remainder of Saturday flew by. We didn't have any workshops or demonstrations scheduled in the shop, but we had a ton of foot traffic. We sold more cookbooks, foodie mysteries, and cookery items than we had in a month. How I loved the holiday season. Cheerily, I hummed along with "We Wish You a Merry Christmas."

When "I'll Be Home for Christmas" started playing, however, my happy mood fizzled. I thought of Jake and his sister. Had Cinnamon tracked her down yet? I also wondered about Jake's neighbor. Did Emmett have any other motive to kill Jake? Money, sex, and vengeance were typical reasons. What if Emmett had an old score he wanted to settle? Was he holding off making another attack on Jake simply because he would be the obvious suspect?

Curious to learn as much as I could from Cinnamon so I could update my father, I called the precinct. She was out and not to be disturbed via cell phone. Deputy Appleby was busy, too. I hung up and wasn't surprised when the Grinch song came up in the queue. I must have psychically summoned it. The dour tone matched my mood.

For the next few hours, I worked hard to find my smile. Far be it from me to show up to my niece's concert in a snit.

After closing the shop, I took Tigger home, changed into a hunter green sweater and jeans, threw on my faux shearling jacket, and set off for the festival. I'd asked Rhett to join me, but he was stuck doing inventory. A major shipment had arrived during the afternoon.

Whitney and Spencer had saved a seat for me in the third row. She looked radiant in red. Her makeup was perfect, and her eyes were shining with hope.

Spencer leaned over to me. "I spoke with your father today, Jenna."

"And?"

"He's cool."

"Told you he would be."

"He asked if he was now part owner of my invention."

"You told him no, I hope."

"Whitney did."

We all laughed.

"Testing, testing." The ponytailed director tapped the microphone. Realizing it was working, she cleared her throat and welcomed the audience with gushing enthusiasm. "And now, ladies and gentlemen, boys and girls, first up, the Belting Beauties."

The group was fun to watch. Each girl possessed a huge voice that would rival any of today's pop star divas. A few of them didn't move well, but when I closed my eyes, I liked their sound. The Tonic Fifths sang a little off-key. Whitney elbowed me once or twice during their performance. She, like her daughter, had a good ear. She had sung with the chorus during high school.

When Nothing but Treble took the stage, Whitney hooted.

I tapped her arm. "*Shh.* Don't make Lacy nervous."

"I just want her to know I'm pulling for her, even if you couldn't coax her to add a red scarf."

"The outfit rocks exactly the way it is." I winked.

As they had during rehearsal, Lacy and her pals stomped and scatted through their performance of "Same Old Lang Syne." The rendition made me think of what the judges on *American Idol* used to ask of their contestants—to choose a normal song and change it so much that you almost couldn't recognize it; make it *new*; make it *shine*. Nothing but Treble did exactly that.

In the end, however, the Ransom Notes' rendition of "This Is My Wish," enhanced by their gymnastics and dance prowess, won the day. Nothing but Treble came in second.

After receiving their awards, Lacy gripped her friend Veronica by the hand and dragged her to meet the other groups. The Ransom Note singer that Veronica had her eye on was quite handsome in a preppy way. Definitely not musician material. Like a true friend, Lacy made sure she introduced Veronica to him. Both girls were all smiles.

Whitney and Spencer asked me to join them and the other Nothing but Treble traveling parents along with the a capella teens for dinner at the rib place on Buena Vista Boulevard. I begged off. The notion of hanging out with fawning parents and chatty girls made my teeth ache.

Before heading home, I decided to meander through the festival to drink in the aromas, the joyous holiday music, and the happy laughter.

Like the other night, Keller's Kool Desserts was packed. A line snaked out the front of the tent and around the side. *Good for him,* I thought. I waved to a few folks who were regulars at the Cookbook Nook.

A lanky redhead said, "Hey, Jenna, can't wait until tomorrow. My cookies will win."

"We'll see about that," taunted the brunette standing next to her.

I swung by the Soup Meister and purchased a cup of smoky butternut squash soup enhanced with chipotle chiles. I downed the contents of the container in a matter of minutes, thrilled I didn't have to figure out dinner when I got home.

On my way to where I'd parked on the street, I neared Forget Me Not and noticed Raquel securing the lock on her tent. Beyond, her sister was pushing a dolly stacked with boxes. A second dolly filled with boxes stood to Raquel's right. She tilted the contraption and a box fell off. It hit the ground with a thud.

I jogged to help. My sudden movement startled her.

"Sorry if I frightened you." I picked up the fallen box. "I hear you're dining with your family at the Nook Café tonight. I don't want you to be late. Let me carry this one. Where are you parked?"

She pointed. "That way." She secured a bungee cord around the remaining boxes.

"Who all is coming to dinner?"

"My mom, my sisters, my brother-in-law, and a passel of kids. It'll be so much fun getting together. You're an only child, aren't you?"

"At times I wish I were." I laughed. "I have a sister who's also in town with her family. They live in L.A. My brother lives in Napa Valley."

"Family. What would we do without them?" She tipped the dolly on its wheels and started pushing.

I kept pace. "By the way, I did the taste testing for your dinner tonight. You're in for a feast. Don't miss the white chocolate crackle. Say, did the police talk to you?"

"About?"

"A stamp that went missing from Jake Chapman's collection."

"Yes, they did, and I told them the same as I'll tell you. I did not take that stamp. Why would I want it? It was worth a pittance."

"Three thousand dollars."

"Like I said, peanuts to me. I've sold hundreds of stamps worth ten times that much." She turned left toward the parking lot. "Visit my website. You'll see."

"Jake showed you a Blue Mauritius stamp, I heard. What did you think of it?"

"It was exquisite. Quite something to behold." Her eyes gleamed with excitement then narrowed, as if she realized she was revealing too much. "For your information, seeing as you're friends with Jake, another thing I told the police is that I was nowhere near his house that night. I was at church. I love listening to the choir sing on Wednesday nights. They do special programs, especially the few weeks before Christmas. How I love hearing 'O Holy Night,' and their rendition of Handel's 'Messiah' is, like, wow! Flora Fairchild does a solo that is amazing. Here we are."

She drew alongside a Lincoln MKX, into which her sister was stowing boxes, and set the brake on her dolly. The dashboard of her SUV was cluttered with paper, spiral notepads, a variety of atomizers, and a clipboard. The trunk was equally messy. The sight made me recall an ad campaign we did at Taylor & Squibb for Spartacus Insurance warning against loose objects in a car and how dangerous they could be in an accident. Our stunt driver, a real trouper, took a hit to the face by an atlas a dozen times without complaint.

"Sis, this is Jenna Hart," Raquel said. "Jenna, my sister Reenie."

"Maureen," her sister corrected and jutted a hand at me. "The smarter sister." Her eyes glinted with impishness.

"Smart aleck, you mean." Raquel unhooked the bungee cord. "Reenie's helping out this week."

Maureen said, "My clients don't want my services during the holidays."

"What do you do?" I asked.

"I'm a dietician in San Francisco." That explained her toned body.

"No one wants Reenie telling them to skip the cookies and bon bons until after January first," Raquel quipped.

"Guilt is highly overrated," Maureen added.

The three of us laughed.

Raquel reached for the box I was holding. "Thanks again. Nice seeing you. We've got the rest." Her sister stowed the boxes and the dolly in record time.

Watching them drive away, a niggling question cycled through my mind about Raquel's alibi. She'd offered me the same look as my brother-in-law had when he'd lied to my sister, his gaze darting left and right as if he was searching for an escape route. Was Raquel's alibi too pat? Did everyone know that Flora sang a solo? Was I the most skeptical person in the world?

I cut through the festival toward my car. I'd found a spot on the opposite side of Azure Park. Twenty yards from my destination, I felt eyes on me and spun around. Emmett Atwater was standing near the North Pole display, a lit cigarette in one hand and an ice cream cone in the other. Catching me staring at him, he dropped his cigarette to the ground, crushed it with his boot heel, and ducked out of sight. Had he meant for me to see him? Had he been tailing me?

"Jenna, is that you?" a woman called.

I pivoted. Gran sauntered toward me with two of her granddaughters in hand. All of them were wearing matching red sweaters.

"Girls, you remember Miss Hart," Gran cooed. She brought them into the Cookbook Nook with regularity. "Someday you'll be as tall as she is. You've inherited your father's genes."

"His *jeans*?" the youngest said, giggling.

"Genes," Gran repeated. "G-E-N-E-S. His DNA."

"What's DNA?" the older girl asked.

"It's . . . Oh, never mind." Gran tittered. "Why are you here, Jenna?"

"I came to listen to my niece sing."

"Oh, rats. We missed it. We've been running late all day long."

The younger of the grandchildren said, "It wasn't my fault. It was hers." She pointed at her sister, who stuck out her tongue.

"Jenna, dear, you seem puzzled," Gran said. "Is something wrong?"

"I was chatting with Raquel Adagio about what happened to Jake Chapman—" I hesitated, not wanting to talk about murder in front of the children. "About him losing his friend. I think theft might have been the motive."

"Heavens. What was stolen?"

"A stamp."

"Not the Blue Mauritius, I hope," Gran said.

"How do you know about it?"

"Jake loves to talk about his stamps and coins. He said his wife was the one who encouraged him to invest in them." Gran's gaze swung to the left. "Adam, over here."

Adam Kittridge, carrying two to-go cups from Warm Your Heart, drew near. He appeared quite hip for someone his age, in black trousers, black button-down shirt, and a red tie. He handed Gran her cider and pecked her on the cheek. The girls rolled their eyes. I almost did, too. Gran and he were sure getting serious quickly.

Don't be a killjoy, Jenna. Gracie Goldsmith is allowed to have a fling.

"Jenna, I believe you know Adam," she said.

I nodded. "Good evening."

"Evening." Adam's smile was easy. I could see why Gran was attracted to him. He sipped his cider.

Gran said, "Anyway, Jenna, back to what we were talking about before I was deliciously interrupted. Jake's wife must have been something."

"Jake?" Adam said.

"Chapman. The man whose house you want to purchase. The one whose friend, you know . . ." Gran cleared her throat and twirled a hand, as reluctant as I'd been to mention murder in front of the girls. "Jenna and I have been chatting about who might have done it. As I told you the other day, she has quite a sensibility about these things."

"You solve crimes," he said.

My cheeks warmed. "No, not exactly."

"Only when someone she cares about is involved," Gran said.

"Like Jake Chapman." Adam nodded. "Admirable."

Gran brushed his arm with her fingertips. "Jake was married to the most marvelous woman, or so I hear. I never met her, but the way his eyes light up whenever he talks about her is something extraordinary. My daughter-in-law says she was a gem."

I recalled the way Jake's eyes lit up when he'd mentioned the one that got away, too. Where had she ended up? Meeting her again, if she was alive and available, might bring him some happiness.

Keep your nose out of it, Jenna. Matchmaking is not your forte. When I'd tried to hook up a friend at Taylor & Squibb with an old college buddy of mine, let's just say it had ended disastrously with a capital *D*.

"Listen, Jenna," Gran lowered her voice, "about Raquel. No matter what she might say to the contrary, she wanted that Blue Mauritius. Badly. I overheard her talking to a vendor the other night. She said her father had searched for that stamp his whole life. You should tell Chief Pritchett."

"Me?"

"You're friends. You have her ear."

"Ha!" If Cinnamon knew I was speaking about Raquel to Gran, she'd cut off my ears and feed them to the sharks.

Adam said, "Why don't you call her, Gracie? It'll sound much better coming from an eyewitness."

"Yeah, Grandma," the girls chimed. "You do it."

"All right. I will."

Chapter 15

Because I'd barely slept a wink Friday, I crashed Saturday night. I woke Sunday morning expecting to feel refreshed. Instead, my neck ached and my temples were pounding. I downed two aspirin, fed Tigger, and drank a protein smoothie. By the time I dressed for work, the pain was minimal.

"Tigger," I said as I tickled him under the neck, "it's such a beautiful day, let's bicycle to Latte Luck for a specialty coffee first." Fresh air would do me a world of good.

My darling cat didn't argue. He loved riding in the basket of my mother's old Schwinn.

On our way into town, I clanged the hand bell whenever church bells chimed. At the café, I locked my bike to a lamppost and deposited Tigger in my tote bag. "Keep your head down," I warned.

Before stepping into the shop, I took a moment to admire the seashell-adorned wreath hanging on the café's door. It sparkled in the morning sun. At half past six, the place was pretty empty. A number of people stood in the takeout line and a few were sitting in the brown leather booths, but no one occupied any of the wooden tables. Later, after church let out, the café would be packed.

I joined the line and covertly eyed the contents of the glass display case. I wasn't hungry and we were having our cookie contest later on in the day, but I knew I wouldn't be able to resist purchasing one of the homemade goodies. The sweet aromas of cinnamon and apple and peppermint were stirring my appetite something fierce.

"Morning, Jenna," a woman said from behind. I recognized my chef's voice and turned.

Katie strolled in holding hands with Keller. Dressed in a plaid shirt and jeans—no chef's coat, no toque—she appeared as relaxed as a tourist.

"Good morning, you two," I said. "Who's manning the Nook?"

"Reynaldo took the early shift." Though Katie was a large-framed woman, she looked diminutive next to Keller, who was a lanky six and a half feet. "We wanted a little time together. Keller's been working nonstop at the festival."

"Congratulations are in order, Keller," I said. "Every time I've visited the park your booth has been packed with customers."

"With tourists as well as locals. Luckily the ice cream is all premade or my legs would be tired from pedaling." He jogged in place and coughed out an adorable yuk-yuk laugh.

His comment about the locals made me think of Jake's neighbor staring in my direction last night, and a shiver ran through me. "Hey, how well do you know your customers?"

"Pretty well. I like to chat them up."

"Do you know Emmett Atwater?"

"Yeah, sure." He swooped a thatch of unruly brown hair off his face. "He's sort of a quirky guy. I guess he can't help it, having lost his wife in that accident."

"What accident?"

"A few years ago, she fell overboard while deep sea fishing. She wasn't wearing a life preserver and couldn't swim. The current dragged her away like that." Keller snapped his fingers.

My insides wrenched as the memory of my husband's death in a boating accident scudded through my mind. The police didn't find his body . . . until he resurfaced.

"Were the authorities sure his wife's death was an accident?" Katie asked.

"You must be reading my mind, girlfriend," I said and focused on Keller. "Is it possible Emmett helped his wife over the side?" If he was capable of one murder, surely he was capable of a second.

"He wasn't on the boat," Keller said. "She was out with friends. He went downhill fast after that. He sued to prove negligence, but he didn't win. The court ruled that her death was her own fault. She'd had too much to drink. Her passing is the reason he doesn't do Christmas anymore."

"What do you mean?"

"She loved decorating, always making theirs the prettiest house in the neighborhood. After she died, he stopped putting up stuff. No lights. No tree."

I arched an eyebrow. "I thought you said you didn't know him well."

"People gossip, plus my mom, who was friends with Mrs. Atwater, talked about it a bit. She said Emmett used to smile a lot."

Keller's mother owned a dessert shop called Taste of Heaven. "Other than at the festival, he hasn't been buying my ice cream lately. Not sure why. I still sell his favorite, pecan crunch."

Katie nudged him. "Mr. Chatterbox, we've got to get a move on. I don't want Reynaldo to do a better job than me. My boss might fire me."

I grinned. "As if." I let them ahead of me in line. When it was my turn, I purchased a wreath-shaped cinnamon roll and a medium latte. Minutes later, I set the to-go bag in my basket along with Tigger and pedaled to work.

The instant I opened the front door of the Cookbook Nook, Tigger bounded to his condo. I settled behind the register, took a sip of my coffee and a bite of my wreath, and then I began to tally the cash drawer.

Half an hour before opening, Bailey came in. "Tito is so excited about this afternoon's event. He is a huge cookie fiend." She whisked off her silver scarf and matching tam, and headed to the storage room to stow her things. Over her shoulder, she said, "When I come back, I'll design some signs about how the cookie swap will be judged, okay?"

"I like your outfit," I said.

She was wearing tapered silver slacks topped with a sparkly black sweater. "Thanks. By the way, when are you putting on your Santa's helper costume?"

"After lunch." It was hanging in the storage room with the other costumes.

"I'm already dressed," Aunt Vera said as she breezed through the drapes, nearly bumping into Bailey. She was wearing a ruby red caftan and carrying an armful of books. "I'm a fortune-telling elf."

"Vera, get real," Bailey said. "You're dressed the same as always. Play along. Be a sport. Have fun."

"Dear, I don't play along. I make my own rules. You should know that by now." She set the books on the counter. "Besides, you do not want to see this old body in an elf's costume."

"You're not old," Bailey and I chimed.

"Good girls. I've taught you well." Chuckling, she headed to the café to meet with Katie about this afternoon's festivities.

For the first few hours of business, Bailey and I chatted about my niece and the concert and the beauty of marital bliss, all while selling dozens of cookie cookbooks. The most popular was *Sally's Cookie Addiction: Irresistible Cookies, Cookie Bars, Shortbread, and More from the Creator of Sally's Baking Addiction*. Not only did the cookie photographs in the book look incredible, but Sally sprinkled plenty of baking tips throughout. The way some of our customers left the shop giggling gleefully, I wondered if a few intended to race to the grocery store, purchase the required items for one of Sally's cookie recipes, and whip up a batch before returning for the afternoon's event. We hadn't stipulated that the recipes be original.

Throughout the morning I was surprised that Bailey didn't ask me how the investigation into Geoffrey's murder was going. She was usually curious about these matters. I didn't mention it. Why spoil her buoyant mood, especially since I was clueless? Did Emmett kill him thinking he was Jake? Did Jake's sister kill him for the inheritance? Did someone else in town have it in for Jake? Like Jake, I simply refused to believe that Geoffrey, a drifter, had been the intended victim, although there were a lot of tourists in town. Someone could have followed him from his last location. Were the police looking into that angle?

After a quickie lunch of Katie's specialty Christmas panini, which consisted of ham, cheddar, tomato, avocado, and a seriously spicy brown mustard, I dressed in my costume and gathered my staff. Together, we set up the shop for the party. We rolled the bookshelves to the perimeter and set out a few folding chairs. I didn't want a lot of chairs available. I wanted our guests to roam. Tina inflated silver and red balloons and tied them everywhere.

For my costume, I'd chosen a traditional red dress trimmed with white faux fur. Knee-high black boots completed the ensemble. The elf-style hat was a tad too big, but I was able to secure it with a long stickpin. Both Bailey and Tina had chosen a flirtier green-over-red dress with red-striped stockings. Their ankle-high boots featured curled-up toes. I kidded them, saying their stockings reminded me of the ones worn by the Wicked Witch of the East—the witch that Dorothy's house landed on in *The Wizard of Oz*. For the longest time, I couldn't stop laughing, which earned me a number of annoyed looks.

Tito arrived at two o'clock. Jake showed up minutes later. I marveled at how authentic their costumes were. Either could have auditioned for and won the role of Santa in *Miracle on 34th Street*. Their beards were fluffy, their cheeks rosy, their bellies plump, and the boots and black gloves free of chimney soot. The only way I could tell them apart was their eye color and the fact that Jake had a few more wrinkles.

Minutes after they showed up, Katie in her chef's coat and trousers came into the shop via the breezeway wheeling a cart set with shot glasses filled with punch. Two of the café's waitstaff set a long table against the wall near the craft area and covered it with candy-cane-themed tablecloth.

"Katie, you're not in costume," I said.

"Hoo-boy. I couldn't possibly. I have to travel between the shop and the café all day. The café is offering two seatings per meal. We're swamped. See you later." She hailed her staff, and they beat a quick retreat.

Bailey posted the contest rules sign on the wall above the table. She'd printed it in silver and red and sprinkled it with glitter. The contestants were to place their entries on the table. Each was to scrawl his or her name on the back of a folded card and write the cookie's name on the front.

A half hour later, the shop was almost full to capacity with every shape and size Santa. I recognized Deputy Appleby because of his height, but due to the beards and facial hair, most of the others were incognito. There were glittery-cheeked elves, too, plus a few Mrs. Clauses, complete with curly white wigs and round black spectacles. I neared two short Santas and realized, by their conversation, that they were Gran and Mayor Zeller.

I tapped Gran on the arm. "You look great. Where's your other half?"

"My other half?"

"Mr. Kittridge."

"He's not . . . We're not . . ." She guffawed and flapped a black-gloved hand. "He went to San Francisco today to see his granddaughter."

"Oh, that's right. He mentioned he wouldn't be here." I winked at her. "You and he seem to be getting pretty tight."

"We're just having fun."

Z.Z. said, "Fun can be long-lasting. He's intent on moving here, you know, though he's given up on purchasing Jake's house."

"It wasn't for sale," I said.

"Don't I know it!" Z.Z. honked out a laugh. "Jake has reminded me in no uncertain terms. But Adam had such hopes. He studied up on Jake, hoping to cajole him."

"Studied up?" I asked.

"He got to know all he could about Jake through articles and such. Jake might think he's low-profile, but there have been plenty of pieces written about him and his path to fortune. Adam hoped Jake might have a price. He said all men do." Z.Z. jutted her head in Jake's direction. "Doesn't he make an adorable Santa?"

Gran said, "Who? Jake? Are you two —"

"He's been a little slow picking up that I'm interested."

"Ahem." I cleared my throat. "I distinctly heard him say you could ask him out."

Z.Z. said, "Yes, you're right, but due to the investigation into his friend's death, now isn't the time."

"How is it going with the police investigation, Z.Z.?" Gran asked. "You found Jake a defense attorney. You probably have insider knowledge."

"Jake's not in jail."

"Was he ever on the chief's radar?"

"Yes," I cut in, "but he had a solid alibi, and he had no motive to kill his friend. None."

"By the way, Jenna" — Gran lowered her voice conspiratorially — "I told Deputy Appleby about Raquel and the stamp. He said he would tell Chief Pritchett. The wheels of progress can only roll so fast."

"Gracie" — Z.Z. tapped her friend on the arm — "come with me. I want to say hello to Jake before he gets too busy."

Gran winked at me and said, "Guess I'm her wingman."

"Yoo-hoo, Jenna." Flora, dressed as Mrs. Claus, approached me near the sales counter while scanning the crowd. "Ho, ho, ho. Doesn't everyone look terrific! What a boon for my business, by the way. I've never rented so many costumes . . . or *any* costumes, for that matter." She giggled. "Perhaps I'll add some to my stock for

Halloween and Pirate Week and, well, there are so many occasions, aren't there?"

Tina sashayed to us carrying a tray of punch-filled shot glasses. "Want one?"

"Don't mind if I do," Flora said. "And I must check out the cookies. Are we allowed to taste them yet, Jenna?"

"When the judges are finished." She started to move on, but I nabbed her arm. "Hold on. I heard you aced your solo in the 'Messiah' Wednesday night."

She blushed.

"Did you happen to see Raquel Adagio in the congregation?"

"Can't say as I did, but I'm unable to see long distances."

"Did the choir sing 'O Holy Night'?"

"We always do during the weeks before Christmas. It's tradition."

Even with Flora's corroboration of the evening, I wondered about Raquel's alibi. Something about the glib way she'd offered it hadn't rung true.

Tina headed off to serve more punch. Flora followed her, humming along with a jaunty version of "Santa Claus Is Coming to Town" by Michael Bolton. I had queued up a number of Christmas tunes that contained Santa in the title, like "Here Comes Santa Claus," "Boogie Woogie Santa Claus," and "Santa Baby."

A ruddy-cheeked Santa with a sequined lapel approached Tina and said something. Santa hooked a finger toward the storage room. Tina handed Santa the tray and hurried in that direction. My aunt was nowhere in sight. She must have beckoned Tina. Santa, bless his or her heart, continued distributing the beverages.

"Ho, ho, ho, my beauty." Rhett tapped me on the shoulder.

I swung around and burst into giggles. In keeping with the theme of his business, he was clad in a sporty Santa costume. His fluffy white beard was very Santa-like, but the duck vest made his belly huge, and the bass fisherman's hat with dangling lures looked ridiculous.

"Uh-uh, not fair," he said.

"I'm sorry. I didn't mean to laugh."

"No, I meant unfair that Santa has to be old and you are young and beautiful."

"FYI, I like older men," I teased.

"Good to know." He pecked my cheek.

Though his beard tickled, a deliciously warm sensation ran from my head to my toes. Yes, this man had truly stolen my heart. I was glad I'd said yes to his proposal. Now we needed to make plans. "The guests may taste the cookies in a sec. Meanwhile, there's punch if you're thirsty."

"Jenna" — Flora came back and wedged between us — "did your fiancé tell you I put his ensemble together?"

I gaped at Rhett. "You've officially announced us?"

"Haven't you?"

"I was waiting until my father returned to town."

"You haven't told him yet?"

"Nope."

Flora twisted an imaginary lock in front of her lips. "I'll keep your secret. Promise."

I tilted my head.

"I'll do my best," she revised, knowing she'd blow it. She loved to share a scoop. "By the way, did you see your sister and your niece? They make adorable Santas."

I hadn't. I scanned the shop for them.

"They're over by the cookie table. Hey, that's Pepper Pritchett." Flora pointed to a Santa that resembled all the others except this Santa was wearing a strand of green and red beads. "And there's my sister. The skinny one with the rhinestone belt buckle." Flora jutted a finger. Her twin, who was sort of flashy, was flirting with a tall, slender Santa that I was pretty sure worked in the surf shop upstairs. "Say" — Flora nodded in the direction of a ragtag Santa clad in Groucho Marx gag glasses and Groucho's iconic black tie who was cutting through the crowd — "who's that?"

"You don't know?"

"I didn't outfit that one. The hair and beard are too scraggly. I prefer fluffier beards."

Earlier, Keller had suggested that Emmett Atwater might have fallen on hard times. Was this an old costume he used to wear to humor his Christmas-loving wife? Maybe he'd donned the getup to hide his identity or to insinuate that our soiree was ludicrous.

Rhett said, "Whoever he is, you can't turn him away. He's brought cookies. I'll steer him in the right direction." He crossed to

Santa, who was shorter than he was, and gestured toward the cookie swap table. Santa gave him the thumbs-up. When Rhett tried to engage him in conversation, Santa moved on.

"Well, that was odd," Rhett said, rejoining us. "I'm not sure if he couldn't or wouldn't speak."

"Could *he* have been a *she*?" Flora asked.

"With those glasses and that nose, how would I know?" Rhett chuckled.

I watched Groucho Santa weave through the crowd to the cookie table and linger near Jake for a minute. He appeared to be sniffing him. Seconds later, he shuffled away and I lost track of him. As long as he didn't cause a scene, I'd let him be.

By now, all the entries lay on the table. The contestants were asked to mingle until the judging was concluded.

Methodically, Tito and Jake began tasting cookies and jotting their thoughts on notepads.

I joined them. "How's it going, fellas?"

"Not bad," Tito said. "The Russian tea cakes are my favorite so far."

Jake tugged at the neck of his Santa suit. "Is it hot in here?"

"There are lots of people," I said. "Want me to fetch some water or punch?"

"Already had the punch." He worked his tongue around the inside of his mouth.

"Come to think of it, it is hot," Tito said. "How do Santas do this day in and day out?"

"You're sort of pale, Jake," I said. "Want to sit down?"

"I'm fine. Which cookie is next?"

"Here." Tito picked up two fruitcake-type cookies and handed one to Jake. Tito took a bite of his. "Yum."

Jake ate half. "It tastes familiar."

"It's got cherries and nuts and something else," Tito said. "Orange zest?"

"No, that's not it. It's cardamom. I know because—" Jake stumbled backward.

I clasped his elbow. "Are you okay?"

"Yeah . . . no . . ." He shook his head. "Hot. Really hot."

Tito staggered to his right and gripped the edge of the table. "Whoa. Is the room spinning?"

Bailey broke through the crowd and threw an arm around him. "Babe, what's going on?"

Tito's face was pasty and beaded with perspiration. "I think I'm going to be sick."

I eyeballed the array of cookies. Were Tito and Jake suffering from food poisoning? Which ones had the two men eaten so far? Did the fruitcake-type cookies cause this reaction?

Over the hubbub, I yelled, "Rhett! Detective Appleby!" To Bailey I said, "Get some water."

Guests cried: "What happened?" "Is someone sick?" "What's going on?"

Rhett and Appleby appeared. Rhett propped up Jake. Appleby helped Tito.

Bailey returned with two glasses of water and shoved them at the men.

Tina and my aunt joined us. "Oh, my," they said in unison.

"I think they're suffering from food poisoning," I said. "Aunt Vera, don't let the guests eat any cookies. Tina, call 911."

Out of the corner of my eye, I saw a streak of red heading toward the front door. Groucho Santa dashed through the doorway.

At the same time, Jake wrestled free of Rhett, clutched his stomach, and whispered, "Olivia."

Chapter 16

The EMTs arrived in minutes and quickly determined Tito and Jake had been poisoned. By what, they weren't sure. They placed them onto stretchers, and with sirens blazing, they whisked them off to Mercy Urgent Care, one of two decent-sized clinics in the area.

Bailey and I fetched our purses. Rhett hugged me and apologized that he couldn't accompany me to the clinic. He had to return to work. I kissed him and said I totally understood.

To be on the safe side, my aunt and Tina would throw out all the cookies and provide gift certificates to the remaining guests.

"No one was to blame," Aunt Vera assured me. "Things happen."

I, however, did think someone was to blame. Groucho Santa. Flora had suggested Groucho could have been a man or a woman. Could it have been Emmett or Raquel? Had one of them tainted the cookies to hurt Jake? Why risk injuring Tito?

As I hurried to the door, Aunt Vera offered to take Tigger to the cottage and told me not to worry about the Sunday family dinner. She would see to Whitney, Lacy, and Spencer. I thanked her. In my panic, I had forgotten about our weekly gathering as well as my cat. *Bad Jenna.*

Bailey and I, still in our elves' outfits, drove in separate cars. Deputy Appleby, who had magically changed into his uniform, was waiting at reception when we arrived. The place smelled Lysol clean. Doctors and nurses strode purposefully along the halls. Apparently there were a number of emergency cases that afternoon. A toddler had eaten a dime-sized battery, another child thought he could climb his Christmas tree, and a woman had cut her hands to shreds arranging angel hair. For some, Christmas was not the happiest time of the year and definitely not the safest.

After a nurse advised us that we couldn't see Tito or Jake yet, we settled in the waiting room. Wood-framed vinyl chairs and tables set with magazines lined two of the walls. A muted television with closed captioning was airing CNN. Vending machines peddling snacks and hot beverages stood against the far wall. A dozen people lingered in the room. Bright overhead lighting made each of them look ghastly in spite of the soothing pastel décor. A Muzak-style version of "The Little Drummer Boy" played softly through a speaker. Conversations were hushed.

Appleby settled across the room from us. In the two chairs next to him sat the husband and wife whose child had swallowed the battery. She wept openly. My heart ached for her.

As I purchased a cup of coffee—it would have been smarter to drink water, but I craved something warm—a nurse with a stylish pixie cut stepped into the room. She informed the couple that their child was going to be fine. Relieved, they raced out. Then she approached Bailey and me. Appleby joined us. The nurse stated that the doctors still hadn't determined which poison had been used. Tito was holding down fluids, but Jake wasn't faring as well. The doctors were doing all they could.

When she departed, I tossed my cup of coffee and sat in silence, as if speaking might jinx any possibility of recovery. After an announcement was broadcast over a speaker that a doctor was needed in emergency, I leaped to my feet and began to pace.

Bailey joined me. "Who did this?"

"I don't know."

"Do you think it's related to Geoffrey's murder?"

"Maybe."

"Who do you suspect?"

I filled her in about the Groucho Santa who'd fled while the two men were suffering. "I think it might have been Emmett Atwater." I explained his motive.

She said, "A long-held grudge can fester."

I added that it could have been Raquel Adagio. "She desperately wanted to own the rare stamp Jake showed her, and she and Emmett are about the same size. If Jake dies, the stamp might be put up for sale, and she could make a bid for it."

"That's cold. Is there any other suspect on your—"

"Mrs. Martinez?" The pixie-haired nurse beckoned Bailey. "Your husband is alert. Please follow me."

Tears of joy sprang into Bailey's eyes.

"What about Jake Chapman?" I asked.

"He's being monitored. He must have received a stronger dose of whatever poison was used."

Bailey turned to me. "Jenna . . ."

"Go. Give your husband a kiss for me."

As they left, energy fizzled out of me. I slumped into a chair and stared at Appleby, who was resting his head against the wall, eyes closed.

Within minutes of Bailey's departure, Cinnamon arrived. Her eyes were at half-mast. She had chewed off any hint of lip gloss.

"Long day?" I asked.

"Christmas is not an easy time for law enforcement. Break-ins, holiday party drunkenness, bitter family disputes." She pointed toward the hallway. "How are Tito and Jake doing?"

"Tito is going to be fine. Jake is struggling. The poison—"

"What poison?"

"Didn't Appleby contact you?"

She unlocked her phone and scrolled through messages. "Okay, poison. Go on."

"I want to know whether it was deliberate or accidental. If it was deliberate . . ." I told her my theory about Groucho Santa and who might have donned the costume.

"Don't start a rumor."

"Sorry." I held up a hand, begging forgiveness. "All I'm saying is this might have been a second attempt on Jake's life."

"Why poison Tito?"

"So it wouldn't seem like the killer was going after Jake."

Cinnamon nodded then called, "Appleby!"

He jolted awake, hopped to his feet, and crossed the room in four long strides. "Chief. Sorry, I—"

"No worries. We could all do with a nap. Please set up a twenty-four-hour watch on Mr. Chapman. If you get the toxicology results before I do, call me." Cinnamon's cell phone chimed. She checked the message. "I've got to go."

Deputy Appleby saluted.

During the next hour, the nurse with the pixie cut returned twice with updates. Jake was on fluids but vomiting less. His face was covered with a rash. When Bailey reappeared, she was ebullient. Tito was being discharged. She asked about Jake.

I summarized his situation. "Time will tell."

She kissed my cheek and hurried off to collect her husband.

Around six thirty, Rhett showed up with two boxed dinners

from the Nook Café as well as the clothes I'd worn to work. I slipped into the restroom and put on the slacks, sweater, and sandals. After returning to the waiting room, I dined with Rhett on Katie's version of Christmas fish—tilapia with chopped zucchini, tomatoes, basil, and *beurre blanc* sauce. Even though the meal was excellent, worry tamped down my appetite. I ate half. Water in a paper cup served as our beverage. A large glass of wine would have been better.

After tossing our containers, I yawned.

"You should go home," Rhett said.

"Dad would want me to stay by Jake's side." I hadn't called my father yet. I wanted to wait until I had a prognosis. "You split. You've got a business to run. Aunt Vera and Tina have ours under control." I kissed him and gave him a push. "I'll be fine."

"Liar."

"I'll touch base when I know something."

He drew me into a hug. After a long moment, he pecked me on the forehead and said goodbye.

The mayor swept into the room as he was leaving and plowed toward me. "Jenna." She'd changed out of her Santa costume into a charcoal gray pantsuit and silk shirt. A silver angel-shaped broach graced her lapel. She clutched my elbow, guided me into a chair, and sat beside me. "Has Chief Pritchett stopped by? I can't reach her on her cell phone."

"A while ago. She had an emergency."

"I did a little digging." She drummed her fingers on the arm of the chair. "I don't think it's a coincidence that Jake's friend died and then Jake was poisoned."

"I agree."

"So I drove around his neighborhood to get the skinny, and I ran into the neighborhood mailman. They're like bartenders. They know everything about their customers."

"What was he doing there this late at night?"

"They work longer hours during the holidays. So many packages to deliver. He's a *she*, by the way." Z.Z.'s forehead pinched. "Why don't we call them mailpersons?"

"I'll bet somebody does."

"Anyway, she dislikes Emmett Atwater with a passion. She says he's been so rude since his wife died that she wouldn't put it past him to have tried to kill Jake. She said he often receives catalogues from gardening stores and such."

I shook my head. "I'm not following."

"All those garden catalogues offer easy access to poisons and to seeds like oleander, ricinus, you name it." She ticked the items off on her fingertips. "Tito and Jake were poisoned, weren't they?"

"Yes. The doctors don't know which poison was used, though. They're doing tests. Tox screens."

"This is so maddening." She shook her head in frustration. "Can I see him? Is he awake?"

"They're not letting anyone see him yet. Jake isn't lucid."

She stood and patted her thighs nervously. "Then I'll leave and see if I can wrangle up a friend who can speed up the tox screen process."

"The police are doing that."

"Of course. Well. Hmm . . ." She seemed eager to do some-thing — *anything*.

"If he wakes, I'll tell him you came by."

"Thank you."

As she left, I was surprised to see Jake's sister Olivia lingering in the hall. She had fastened her hair with a clip at the nape of her neck and was wearing a pair of jeans with stylishly frayed pockets, a blue-and-white plaid shirt under a pea coat, and navy blue Van's tennis shoes. Other than her tattered shoulder purse, she didn't look homeless, but she struck me as desolate. She was carrying a bouquet, the heads of the flowers aimed toward the floor. A nurse directed her into the waiting room.

I rose to greet her. "Hello, Olivia." I extended my arm.

"You're Jenna." She shook my hand and released it quickly.

"That's right." Now that I knew she and Jake were related, I saw more similarities. The eyes, the noble chin. "You're Jake's sister."

"That's right." Restlessly, she centered her St. Jude necklace and tightened each of her silver stud earrings. "I hated seeing the EMTs take him away from the party."

"You were there?"

She retreated a step. "Yes. I thought if I . . ." She hesitated. "It was how I knew he lived in Crystal Cove. I saw his picture in the newspaper. I read about him being a judge. So I came to the party. I thought if I reconnected with him in a public setting, he might talk to me."

"You believed he'd snub you otherwise?"

She rubbed her jaw. "He walked out on our family. He was angry and hated me for . . ." Her voice cracked. She staggered.

Worried she might faint, I guided her to a chair. "Come. Sit. Would you like some coffee? It's not good, but it's hot. I think there's tea, too. And some cookies."

"Tea would be lovely. One sugar. Nothing to eat."

I fetched the tea and returned. Olivia set the flowers on the neighboring chair and held the cup with both hands. She blew on the tea to cool it.

"Why search for him now?" I asked.

"I've been searching for him for years. He left when I was a freshman in high school. We . . ." Her lower lip trembled. "We lost touch."

"He told me he wrote to you often. Postcards."

"I never got one. Ever." Her face spasmed with pain as realization hit her. Her parents must have destroyed them.

"Olivia"—I took the chair beside her—"did you hear that a friend of Jake's was murdered on the night I met you?"

"Someone mentioned it. How horrible. But Jake isn't guilty, is he? He couldn't be if he's not in jail."

"No, he had an alibi. He was buying pizza."

"Thank heavens." She took a sip of tea. "I intended to see Jake that night, after the festival. I started for his house—Gracie told me where he lived—but when I got to his street, I chickened out. I wanted to see him when I was fresher. In the morning. If I'd gone there . . ." She licked her lips. "I suppose it's possible the murderer might have killed me, too. Luckily, I went back to my hotel room to think things through."

I cocked my head. "Which hotel are you staying at?"

She worried the St. Jude charm on her necklace. "The Crystal Cove Inn."

I studied her placid face. She was a good liar.

"What's wrong?" she asked.

"Gracie told me you were staying there, so I went to the inn to find you. I hoped to reunite you with Jake, but the clerk—"

"Told you I wasn't a guest." She lowered her chin and peered into her cup.

"Later that evening, my fiancé—" I paused, needing to get used to the word tripping off my tongue. "My fiancé and I were hiking in the woods. We ran into some homeless people." I described the area near the lake.

Olivia's shoulders sagged. A low moan escaped her lips. "So you know."

I nodded.

"I live out of my car. I'm not broke, but I don't have enough to afford car insurance and an apartment, too. I need my car to drive back and forth from work and—"

"What do you do?"

"Right now, I'm a seamstress for a wedding boutique. I need to drive to a lot of appointments. Over the years, I've had a number of jobs, but I can't retire because I never put away a dime. I never married, so I don't have alimony, and my social security is peanuts. Before this gig, I worked at a dry cleaner doing alterations. Before that, I was a costumer."

The idea of her as a costumer made me catch my breath. "Olivia, you said you came to the cookie swap party today."

"Dressed as Groucho Santa."

"You were Groucho?"

A smile tugged at the corners of her mouth. "It was a silly idea. Jake and I used to watch the Marx Brothers as kids, and I thought he'd pick up on the joke and we'd bond, but he didn't."

I replayed the scene in my head. "When you drew near to him, you *sniffed* him. Why?"

"He smelled like our father. He wears the same cologne, Old Spice. It was the one thing I liked about my father."

Jake, too, apparently.

"Jake and the other judge were deliberately poisoned," I said.

She gasped. "I thought it was food poisoning. Who would do such a thing?"

I recalled Jake's last word before he collapsed on the floor of the Cookbook Nook—*Olivia*—and a horrid thought sailed through my mind. Among the bouquet of flowers on the chair were lily of the valley flowers. I remembered from a previous near-fatal encounter that those flowers were so deadly even the water they stood in could be used as a poison. Was Olivia clueless, or had she come to the hospital to try again?

"Olivia, what cookie did you bring to the party?"

"Fruitcake bars. I used my—"

"Yours was the last cookie he ate."

She shot to her feet. "I didn't poison him."

"You ran out of the shop about the same time. Why?"

"Because I had to answer a call from my boss. I'm in charge of all the alterations for a wedding in January. Bridezilla wants changes." She worried her necklace harder, and I flashed on a guy I'd worked with at Taylor & Squibb who had worn a similar necklace. His sponsor at Alcoholics Anonymous had given it to him because St. Jude was the saint of impossible causes. Was Olivia an alcoholic like her parents? Was she craving a drink right now because she was lying?

"Jake uttered your name as he collapsed to the ground. Why would he do that unless he blamed you?"

"He must have realized I'd used our mother's recipe to make the cookies. She used a special spice."

"Cardamom."

"Yes. She made them every Christmas. It was the one nice thing she would do for us all year. She . . . Our father . . ." Olivia stammered. "They're dead. The ugly past is over. I thought Jake and I could build . . ." Tears pressed at the corners of her eyes. She used a pinky to wipe them away. Her fingernails were neatly trimmed, but they were yellow and cigarette-stained. "Build some good memories."

"Jake beat up your boyfriend. You must have hated him for that."

"No. I hated my boyfriend. He put a wedge—" Sobs wracked her body. "Jake and I had each other's backs."

Her keening sounds stirred me. I released the breath I was holding and wrapped an arm around her shoulders.

"I want to see him, but if it's not a good time—" She broke free of me and rose to her feet.

I tried to convince myself she was innocent and incapable of hurting her brother, but another notion occurred to me. Jake said she was a science whiz in high school. Had she been good at chemistry? Had she dosed her cookies with an untraceable poison? "Why are you a seamstress, Olivia?"

"Huh?"

"Jake said you wanted a career at NASA."

"That never panned out. I didn't have enough money to go to college. Not even junior college. Our parents were broke. They spent every dime on booze. I needed to make a living for all of us after Jake left."

"You must have resented him for abandoning you."

"Never. He had to go. Dad would have . . ." She licked her lips. "They never beat me. After they realized I could earn a living sewing, they were almost kind."

Cinnamon walked into the room and crossed to me. Olivia stiffened and tucked her chin to her chest. I understood why. How many times had a policeman armed with a gun questioned her because she lived out of her car?

"I need to use the restroom," Olivia said. "I'll be right back." She stole out the door and turned left.

"Where's Deputy Appleby?" Cinnamon asked as she approached.

"With Jake. I'm hoping for a positive update soon."

"I have toxicology results." She pulled her cell phone from her pocket and read from notes. "Jake was poisoned by an alkaloid that is easy to test for. Nicotine. Liquid nicotine, to be precise. The lethal dose is about fifteen to thirty milligrams. The higher the dose, the shorter the onset of action. Any kind of tobacco product can be used to make it."

I pictured Olivia's nicotine-stained fingernails and raced to the door. I peered down the hallway. She was gone.

Chapter 17

"What's wrong?" Cinnamon asked.

I swiveled to face her. The conversation between others in the waiting room grew quiet. "Jake's sister was just here. You must have scared her off." I summed up our conversation, pointing out that Olivia had a science background. "She seemed nice and sincere, but she's a smoker. If Jake was poisoned by nicotine—"

"Jenna." Appleby strode into the room. "Jake is asking for you."

"Is he alert?"

"He's groggy, but he's going to survive. Chief, do you want to see him?"

"Absolutely."

Appleby led the way. Cinnamon kept pace.

I trailed them. "Chief, does the lab know how the killer administered the liquid nicotine? Was it mixed in with cookie dough?"

"The technician isn't sure about the source," she said. "The effects at this dosage manifest between thirty minutes to an hour later."

"Tito and Jake didn't start taste testing cookies until after Olivia arrived," I said, "so cookies might not have been the source. Maybe Olivia isn't the killer, after all."

Cinnamon asked Appleby to hold up. She turned to me. "Did Tito and Jake drink anything?"

"Punch," I said, "but lots of people drank punch."

"I drank it," Appleby said. "But the punch was served in individual glasses. I suppose the killer could have dosed Tito and Jake's drinks separately."

"Using a syringe." Cinnamon mimed the action.

Appleby agreed.

"It must taste gross," I said. "How would the killer have doctored it so the taste wouldn't be noticed?"

"What color was your punch?" Cinnamon asked.

"Red."

"Cherry-flavored nicotine like you'd find at a vape store would probably do the trick."

I said, "Tina was handing out the punch. The killer would have needed to know which glasses Tito and Jake would take. Wait! That's not true." I recounted the scene of the Santa with the sequined collar taking the tray of punch from Tina. "Santa signaled that someone needed Tina in the storage room. I figured my aunt had requested her. Tina handed the tray to Santa, who then made the rounds."

"Did this Santa approach the victims and hand them specific glasses?" Cinnamon asked.

"I don't recall."

She turned to her deputy. "Appleby?"

"Sorry, Chief, I don't remember, either."

"Emmett Atwater smokes cigarettes," I said. "Plus, Z.Z. said he gets all sorts of garden manuals. What if he dabbles in chemistry and figured out how to extract the nicotine?" At that instant, another image came to me, of Raquel's cluttered SUV. "One other possibility." I described Raquel's dashboard to Cinnamon. "I presumed the aerosol cans were atomizers, but now I'm thinking they could have been e-cigarettes, like the ones you purchase at a vape store."

"The fact that nicotine was used doesn't mean a smoker did the deed," Appleby said.

Cinnamon arched her eyebrow. "Why were you snooping in her vehicle, Jenna?"

"I wasn't. I was helping her transport boxes from her stall at the festival. FYI, she says she told the police she went to church that night after the festival, but I'm not sure I believe her."

Appleby shifted feet. "No matter what, slipping nicotine into the punch using a syringe or other applicator is going to be hard to prove. Each Santa was wearing gloves, which means you won't find the killer's fingerprints on any of the shot glasses."

"Flora might be able to help," I said. "She was in charge of renting most of the costumes. I'll bet she knows who that particular Santa was."

"Good call. If we could get hold of the gloves, there might be traces of nicotine on them or in the costume's pockets."

The policeman stationed outside Jake's hospital room door saluted Cinnamon. "Nothing untoward, Chief."

Cinnamon thanked him and went inside. Appleby and I followed.

The attending nurse, a stout woman with a kind face, held a finger to her lips. Jake had drifted to sleep in the time it had taken Appleby to fetch me. Given that Jake was out for the count, Cinnamon decided to forgo sticking around. Appleby, too.

Seeing the arterial line needle inserted into Jake's arm and the IV fluid feeding into a vein in his hand made me queasy, but I tiptoed closer. He looked so vulnerable lying on the bed with the blanket tucked beneath his armpits. His breathing was ragged. His face was, indeed, covered with a rash.

"Can I hold his free hand?" I asked the nurse.

She nodded.

His eyelids fluttered when I touched his fingertips. Whispering, I said, "You're going to be fine, Jake. Just fine." Over the course of the next hour, I must have chanted those words fifty times.

When the nurse returned, she caught me mid-yawn and advised me to go home. She promised that someone from the hospital would keep me apprised of Jake's status.

As I drove home, I called my father. I didn't reach him and was forced to leave a message. I couldn't explain everything before our connection fizzled.

When I got home, Tigger darted to me. He circled my legs, his tail curling around my ankles. I picked him up and kissed his nose. "Yes, I'm back, but all is not right with the world." I set him down, hung my purse on the kitchen chair, and plugged in my cell phone to recharge.

The moment I did, it jangled. Rhett's name appeared on the screen. I swiped the screen to answer. "Hey." I couldn't feign energy. I was beat.

"How's Jake?" he asked.

"Out of trouble and resting." I told him about the nicotine poison. "He didn't rouse so I wasn't able to speak to him. I'm home."

"Would you like company?"

"I'd love it."

I freshened up—fear and fretting were not good for one's scent—and changed into an ecru draped-collar blouse and jeans. Padding barefoot, I threw together a plate of sliced manchego and crackers and fetched a bottle of Chalone chardonnay from the refrigerator.

When Rhett arrived, he swept me into his arms and held me tightly for a long time. I couldn't imagine anywhere I'd rather be.

"How are you holding up?" he asked when he released me.

"Frustrated. Angry. What vile person would do this?"

"Inserting the poison right under everyone's noses was bold. I'm not sure Emmett Atwater is capable of doing something like that. He seems pretty mousy."

"Weasels might look cute and cuddly, but they are bloodthirsty. Do you know what other creature in the wild kills by biting the back of the neck? The jaguar."

Rhett chucked my chin. "Aren't you the wilderness expert."

"Isn't it funny the trivia we remember?" I skirted around him to fetch a wine opener. When I turned back, we bumped into each other. "Sorry."

"Me, too. Small spaces." He took the opener from me and expertly carved off the foil on the wine bottle. "What about Raquel Adagio? Has anyone figured out whether she was at the party dressed as Santa?"

"No clue." I edged around him, nabbed a couple of cocktail napkins, and took the plate of cheese and crackers to the coffee table. Rhett brought the wine and glasses. We nestled on the sofa. In three shakes of a cat's tail, Tigger joined us. "Raquel claims she has an alibi for the night Geoffrey was killed." I took a bite of cheese and savored the flavor and nutty texture.

"How did you wheedle that out of her?"

"I don't wheedle."

He elbowed me. "Don't be so sensitive. I'm teasing."

"She was closing up at the festival and heading to the Nook for a family dinner. I helped her to her car and we got to talking. Because I was a friend of Jake's, she decided to share what she'd told the police. She was at church Wednesday night listening to the choir." I took a sip of wine. "You know, Flora Fairchild might be a valuable source of insider knowledge about this crime. She provided the costumes for the cookie swap, sold Jake's wife the tree topper the killer used to stab Geoffrey, although Flora couldn't remember seeing Raquel at church."

"So she's not a corroborating witness."

I took another sip of wine. "Cinnamon intends to go through

Flora's inventory to search for the offending Santa's costume."

"Then it's not your problem." He raised a glass to toast mine. "Let's table the discussion. For now."

I clinked his glass, took a sip of wine, and set the glass on the coffee table. I leaned back and rested my head against the sofa. My eyes closed upon impact.

Rhett kissed my cheek and ran a hand along my shoulder. "Care to talk about us, sleepyhead?"

I opened my eyes, my curiosity piqued. "What about us?"

"About when, where, and how we're getting married. You did say *yes*, if I'm not mistaken."

"I did." I wiggled my ring finger and swiveled to face him. "So . . ."

"Where will we have the wedding? How many people? Where'll we live? This place —"

"Is too small and your cabin is too remote."

"You love the beach."

"Finding someplace on the water will be way out of our budget."

"There are a few homes near Azure Park that might be manageable. From there, we can use the public access to the beach. And being that close to the park might be good for —"

"Whoa!" Adrenaline mixed with panic whooshed through me. I leaped to my feet and wrapped my arms around my rib cage. "Were you going to say kids?"

He jammed his lips together, his eyes twinkling with mischief.

"You were, weren't you?" I headed to the kitchen. The *tiny* kitchen.

Tigger followed me. So did Rhett.

"Don't you want a family?" he asked.

"I'm not sure," I said, sounding like Bailey not long ago.

Rhett slipped up behind me and encircled me with his arms. He nuzzled my neck. "You're so good with Lacy."

"Because I can give her back to her parents. And she's a teenager. She can talk and walk —"

"And chew gum all at the same time."

"Ha-ha." I twisted in his arms and gazed into his eyes. "How many?"

"I was thinking two."

"Who would take care of them? We both have full-time jobs."

"I thought you'd—"

"Give up my job? No."

"I was going to say hire a nanny." He grinned. That dimple I adored carved his cheek.

I ran my index finger along it. "A nanny?"

He took hold of my finger and kissed the tip. "We'll figure it out. We can—"

Tigger yowled and dashed to the front door. He stood facing it and hissed. He never hissed.

Rhett and I broke apart and in a few strides flanked Tigger.

"What is it, fella?" I knelt beside him and rubbed his back. He was stiff with alarm. "Rhett, he's really spooked. Is someone outside?"

Rhett peeked out the peephole. "I don't see anyone." He put his hand on the doorknob.

"Don't. Wait." I tore to the fireplace, fetched the poker, and ran back.

Rhett took it from me, opened the door, and stepped onto the porch. He peered right and left. "I don't see anyone running. No cars nearby." He turned to move inside and drew up short. "Jenna." He pointed at the front door. "That wasn't here when I arrived."

My berry and celosia wreath was gone. A black wreath made of rose lace and adorned with black beads hung in its place. The wind was whisking it to and fro. Tigger must have heard the lace scratching the door.

Heart racing, I jerked the thing off the hook and tossed it into the trash.

Rhett closed and locked the door and hurried to me. He laid the poker on the kitchen counter. "What's going on?" He gripped my shoulders. "You're shivering."

"Lacy and I saw something similar at the festival. She called it a funeral wreath."

"Who would have put it there?"

"I don't know." I broke free and paced the floor. "Olivia and Gran were checking out black wreaths the night Geoffrey was killed."

"You think Olivia did this?"

"I suppose if Raquel realized I saw her e-cigarettes on the dashboard of her car, she could have done this." I justified my reasoning. "Emmett Atwater was at the festival the other night, too.

He might have learned that Z.Z. told me what she'd discovered about him. Hanging a creepy wreath is a passive-aggressive thing to do."

"Does Flora sell these in her shop?"

"She might."

"So anyone in town could have purchased it."

Someone knocked. My insides jolted. I ran to the door and squinted through the peephole. My aunt, Whitney, Lacy, and Spencer were standing outside. I whisked open the door and invited them in.

"Dear, is everything okay?" Aunt Vera caught sight of Rhett and her hand flew to her mouth. "Oh, my. I'm sorry to intrude. I didn't notice your truck, Rhett. Turn around, everyone. Out. March."

"Stop," Rhett said. "You're not intruding, Vera. We were just chatting."

"You slammed the front door," she said. "Is everything all right, Jenna?"

"Yes. No." I pointed at the trash. The wreath was clearly visible. "Someone hung that on my door."

Lacy pounced upon the wreath and held it up by her forefinger. "Ew, Aunt Jenna. It's exactly like the one we saw." Tigger did a little jig around her ankles, as if she might play keep away with him. "It's a warning."

"A warning?" Whitney stared at me. "Why would someone need to warn you, Jenna?"

"I'll do a perimeter search." Rhett whipped open the door.

Spencer said, "I'll go with you."

Whitney hugged me. "You poor thing. You're shaking."

"No, I'm not. You're holding me too tightly." I pressed away and slapped on a courageous smile. "We heard something scratching the door. Actually, Tigger heard it. We investigated but didn't see anyone running away. No car. It had to be Emmett Atwater. Easy access."

Aunt Vera said, "You don't honestly think he killed Jake's friend, do you?"

"He's got it in for Jake. He hates him. He hates Christmas."

"No, he doesn't." She wagged a finger. "He's just sad and a tad jealous. His wife loved the holidays. She adored decorating and went over the top every year. Like Jake." Keller had said the same thing. "Now that she's gone, Emmett is bitter that Jake celebrates even though his wife died, too. Some people can't move on. I fear Emmett might be one of them."

Whitney said, "Lacy and I saw him at the bank earlier today, isn't that right, sweetheart?"

Lacy nodded. "I pointed him out because, you know." She flicked her hands by her face. "Those beady eyes."

"He looked pitiful," Whitney said.

"Maybe he's in financial trouble," my aunt suggested. "He might have been trying to get a loan, and someone turned him down."

My sister nodded. "That could be the reason he doesn't put up decorations. I don't know about you guys, but the cost of electricity in Southern California has soared."

"That gives him an even better motive," I said. "What if he broke into Jake's house hoping to steal the Blue Mauritius so he could cash it in?"

"The what?" Aunt Vera's eyes widened.

"A very rare stamp," Lacy said. "But the killer didn't steal that one."

"No, he didn't," I said. "He took Geoffrey's stamp by mistake. Maybe his intent was to take the Blue Mauritius so he could get out of the hole, but he veered into the wrong room."

Rhett returned. "I didn't see anything out there."

Spencer followed him inside. "No one on the beach, either."

"What if a ghost brought the wreath?" Lacy howled like a banshee.

Whitney swatted her. "Stop."

"Why? I believe in otherworldly spirits, don't you?"

My aunt said, "All right, you three. Back to my place for dessert, after which we'll call it a night." She said to me, "They're craving dessert since they couldn't eat any of the cookies at the swap."

"How is Jake feeling?" Lacy asked.

"He's out of the woods."

My aunt released a sigh of relief. "That's wonderful news. Do you two want to join us for dessert?"

We declined.

"Will you stay the night, Rhett?" Whitney asked.

Lacy clapped her hands over her ears and sang, "La-la-la-la."

Rhett smiled at me. I felt my cheeks warm.

"That's not what I meant," my sister said. "I simply meant that if he's *not* staying, then maybe Jenna would like to bunk with us."

"La-la-la," Lacy repeated.

"Very funny. Go." Whitney prodded her daughter through the door. Spencer chuckled.

Seeing them as a happy family made my heart swell with joy. "I'll be fine," I assured her.

My aunt stopped at the door and turned back. "What do you know about the man Gracie's dating?"

"He seems nice."

"Z.Z. told me he's adamant about buying Jake's house."

"It's a pipe dream."

"What if he thought that by killing Jake he'd have a better chance at acquiring ownership?"

A shiver ran up my neck. "Are you picking up on my vibes?"

"You've felt the same? The timing does seem quite coincidental."

Rhett looped an arm over my shoulder. "I can't see the guy setting his sights on Jake's house as a motive for murder. A lot of red tape goes into buying a house in probate."

"Good point," I said. "Plus, Adam Kittridge wasn't in town today. He went to San Francisco to spend time with his granddaughter, so he couldn't have had anything to do with poisoning Tito and Jake."

"That settles that," my aunt said. "Call if you need me."

As I closed the door, I eyed the black wreath again. If the killer's intent was to unnerve me, it had worked.

Chapter 18

Rhett and I didn't talk further about our future. We both needed sleep. At dawn, after assuring him I was fine—and *safe*—he left for work. In less than thirty minutes, I took Tigger on a walk, dressed in a cute red skirt and scalloped sweater, and ate breakfast—a piece of toast topped with a sliced hard-boiled egg, chives, and a dollop of mustard. Before heading to the shop, I called the hospital to check on Jake. He was sleeping. A guard was in place. The nurse suggested I visit later.

When I arrived at the Cookbook Nook, Pepper was setting up her children-only holiday beading class. She was going to teach her young wards how to bead strings for Christmas trees. Why was she doing so at our shop and not hers? Because she hoped to find new customers. Cross-promotion, she confided, was vital in building a business. Didn't I know it!

An hour into Pepper's class, when Katie brought in a tray of darling Rudolph the Red-nosed Reindeer treats, the children lit into them. Each treat was a frosted triangle-shaped brownie decorated with candy canes for antlers, Tootsie Rolls for ears, marshmallows and chocolate chips for eyes, and a vanilla wafer and red M&M for the nose.

During the break, Pepper drew me to one side and said, "It's done."

"What's done?"

"I secured the venue for my daughter's wedding."

"Where?"

"In a barn."

I bit back a snort. "Um, does Cinnamon know?"

"I showed her pictures. She's delighted."

I'll bet.

"You don't believe me?" Pepper pulled out her cell phone, opened her Internet browser, and clicked on a bookmarked link. Quickly, she scrolled through a dozen photographs.

To say I was astounded was an understatement. Each picture was more beautiful than the one before. The main venue was, indeed, a barn. During a nighttime wedding, little pinpoint holes in the walls allowed light from outside to filter in and create a starry atmosphere. In addition, the barn was located atop a vast vineyard with 360-degree views of the Central Valley.

"I'm thinking a daytime into evening affair," Pepper said.

"Excellent." My heart did a happy dance for Cinnamon. Her wedding would be truly memorable. "Congratulations."

"You know"—Pepper ran a finger along the collar of her beaded sweater—"if you and Rhett want my help, I'll be glad to pitch in."

"I'm pretty sure Aunt Vera will want that honor. Or Dad. But we'll talk."

Content with my answer, she returned to her class.

While I broke down the current holiday display, I assessed what more we needed for the antique cars holiday extravaganza. A box of adorable antique car salt and pepper shakers had arrived earlier. The car-themed aprons I'd ordered from Cafe Press were due to be delivered later in the afternoon.

Around eleven, as I was adding a stack of miniature presents and an Advent calendar to the display, Whitney waltzed in with Lacy. Both were beaming.

"Jenna, you won't believe what I did this morning. I taught my daughter to knit."

"A scarf," Lacy said.

"Using knit-purl stitches," Whitney went on. "Nothing fancy yet. No seed or cable stitches."

She was talking Greek to me. "That's wonderful," I said, offering a wide smile. "Aren't you heading home today?"

Lacy said, "I told Mom we couldn't go until we knew Jake was better. Is he?"

I abandoned the display and stood up. "He's on the mend, but it could be a few days before he's up and about."

"Then we're staying," Lacy announced.

Whitney held up a finger. "One more day. That's it."

"Are you going to see him, Aunt Jenna?" Lacy asked.

"Later. After work."

"Meanwhile"—Whitney looped a hand around her daughter's arm—"since we're sticking around, we're going to buy a few trinkets. Do you have an hour to join us? Spencer is off creating."

"I think I could make time."

I checked on Tina and Bailey, who were busy unpacking books. They assured me they could cover the store.

On my way out, I passed Aunt Vera, who was doing a tarot reading for the plump man who owned the toy shop. I rolled my eyes at her. The man didn't believe in anything mystical. Why was she wasting her time? She gave me a cautionary look. She believed she could convert the staunchest nonbelievers.

"Good luck," I whispered in her ear.

She batted me away.

For a short while, my sister, my niece, and I walked in silence enjoying the sunshine and cool breeze.

As we neared Artiste Arcade, Whitney said, "By the way, Sis, I've been meaning to tell you how much I like the painting you did for Dad of the three of us kids. It's perfectly placed above his fireplace."

"Thanks." I blushed, unable to remember my sister ever giving me a compliment. Who was this woman?

"You've got real talent and a keen eye for color and movement. Mom would be so proud of you."

I blinked back tears. Our mother—how I missed her.

"Ooh, look." Lacy pointed. "There's that guy we were talking about last night."

Emmett Atwater disappeared inside Home Sweet Home.

"Let's follow him." Lacy tugged my hand.

"Why?" I asked.

"Aren't you curious what he's up to?"

"He's probably buying a gift."

It dawned on me that I didn't know a thing about Emmett Atwater other than he'd lost his wife. Did he have children? Did he have a brother or sister? Was he innocently buying someone he loved a gift, or was he—my insides knotted—on the hunt for another black wreath so he could give me another scare?

"Come on." Lacy gave me another tug. "Let's do a little reconnaissance."

"I'm game." Whitney winked. "Show me how to be a sleuth. Don't you need something for that new display window?"

I grumbled. "Honestly, you two."

Laughing merrily, Whitney went in before me. Once inside, she exhaled appreciatively. "What a beautiful shop. Maybe I should open one like this in Los Angeles."

"Aunt Jenna, there he is." Lacy pointed. "Go." She shooed me. Emmett was standing near a large Christmas tree, fingering each of the ornaments. "Mom, come see where I helped Jenna pick out the star for her display. They're so beautiful. Almost every one is packed with glitter. Do we need a new one?" The two of them ventured deeper into the shop.

"Jenna." Flora intercepted me before I could move in Emmett's direction. "What are you doing here? Isn't the Cookbook Nook swamped? I sure am." She adjusted the strap of the Christmas apron she wore over her dress. "I've never seen such crowds."

"My sister and niece"—I gestured to them—"asked me to go shopping with them. They're leaving town soon. Tina and Bailey can manage without me."

"If you're browsing, you might be interested in"—Flora steered me to a display of quilts that was hanging on a curved hardwood stand at the rear of the store—"a handmade quilt. Olivia Chapman brought in three lovely ones to sell on consignment. Aren't they beautiful?"

"They sure are." One featured a woodsy Christmas theme including pine trees and reindeer. Another was done in the colors of the desert.

"My favorite is this one." Flora touched an ocean-toned quilt. "She's utilized the bargello style, which means the strips are sewn together to create movement."

"It's gorgeous." I checked the price tag: reasonable for such stunning work. "Okay, I'm sold. It would go perfectly in my bedroom."

"Sorry, you're out of luck. Maureen Adagio beat you to it. She put it on layaway." She hooked her thumb in the direction of Raquel's sister, who was on the opposite side of the store dressed jauntily in green hat and red bolero jacket over black capris. Hearing her name, she jiggled a Santa doll in greeting.

I waved back.

"She and Olivia hit it off at the Santa party," Flora said.

"Maureen was there?"

"Honey, everyone was."

I regretted having come up with the idea for the Santa costume party, given that the killer had found the perfect opportunity to strike again.

"By the way," Flora went on, "I believe Olivia would like to give up her seamstress job and stay in Crystal Cove if she could find similar work here or a bigger market for her wares. She said she would make a few more quilts on consignment. Hint, hint."

"I get it," I said, grinning. "Let me think about it. By the way, have you seen her lately?" I wondered if Cinnamon had been able to track her down.

"Not today." Flora nudged the price tags on a display of vintage cast-iron nutcrackers to the back. "Why?"

"She came to see Jake, but he was sedated and under observation. No visitors allowed. I'd like to contact her and let her know he's okay."

"I have a cell phone number for her." She picked up a loose strand of tinsel off the floor and stuffed it into the pocket of her apron. "Chief Pritchett asked for it, too. She came in this morning and asked me a ton of questions."

"Then I won't need it. The chief will bring Olivia up to speed." *And hopefully bring her in for questioning,* I mused. "Did Cinnamon find the costume gloves she was searching for?"

Flora tinged pink. "Stupid me, I'd dumped them all in a pile. I couldn't tell her which pair belonged to which costume."

I felt Emmett's gaze on me and waved to him. He turned around without acknowledging me. I refocused on Flora. "Did the chief find a syringe of any kind?"

"She did, but you're not going to like where." Flora made a ghoulish frown.

My stomach knotted. "Where?"

"In the pocket of your sweet Tina's elf costume."

"Oh, no." Heat rushed through me.

"Don't worry. Chief Pritchett doesn't suspect Tina of any wrongdoing."

"That's a relief."

"By the way, I tasted Tina's entry in the cookie swap. It was delicious!"

"Flora, how could you? I asked my aunt and Tina to throw them all out."

"Well, Tina didn't toss hers, silly. She knew they weren't poisoned. They were meringues. Adorable puffs of air. Culinary school is teaching her well. *C'est bon.*" Flora kissed her fingertips with appreciation. "FYI, Cinnamon thinks the killer was quite crafty in ditching the syringe without anyone noticing."

"You mean slipping it into Tina's pocket and implicating her." I flashed on Tina and the tray of drinks she'd handed to the ruddy-cheeked Santa, and said, "Flora, did the police ask who wore the Santa costume with the sequined lapel?"

"They did." Flora tapped her chin. "I rented three or four of those. One for a private party. Another for the guy who owns the toy store. I believe the one who came to your shindig was Charlene from Say Cheese, although it could have been—" She glanced in Emmett's direction.

"Flora," her sales clerk called. "Come quickly. Problem!"

Flora said, "Hold that thought, Jenna," and excused herself.

Was Emmett's the name she was about to utter?

I drifted toward him and reached for a glass star ornament. "Finding anything pretty, Mr. Atwater?"

His lips drew back, making him appear quite feral. "What do you want?"

"I'm hunting for antique car-style ornaments. Have you seen any?"

"No." A sleet storm would have felt warmer.

"Did you happen to join us at the Santa party yesterday?" I asked as congenially as possible, hoping to melt the iceberg. "I couldn't tell who everyone was."

"Yeah, I was there. I had a right."

"Of course you did. The more the merrier."

"I brought lace cookies. My wife's recipe."

"Was she a good cook?"

"The best." His eyes clouded over, and my heart softened slightly. Obviously he missed her, but I reminded myself not to be fooled. Men who loved their wives could be killers.

"Which Santa were you?"

"The one in the red suit." He coughed out a laugh.

"Did you have rosy cheeks and a glitzy lapel?"

"No way. Never did go in for that sort of thing, or the belly or fat cheeks. I was skinny and wearing black-rimmed glasses."

Hmm. I couldn't remember seeing a Santa by that description.

He strolled toward a wall filled with wreaths. I followed.

"I received the oddest gift last night." I pointed to the wreaths. "Someone hung a black one of those on my door."

"Black is for Halloween. Does someone think you're a witch? Heh-heh."

"Funny." I shot my finger at him and smiled.

"Yeah, I'm a real jokester."

Was he admitting to the prank?

"See you," he said and made a hasty beeline for the door.

I caught Lacy staring at me with disappointment. *So much for being good at reconnaissance.*

I noticed a display of nostalgic snow globes and moseyed toward it. I lifted one that held a snow-dusted classic truck within, a pine tree strapped in its bed, and felt a moment of childlike wonder. The globe was sitting on top of an antique car radio base and would be perfect in our new window display. Nearby, I discovered a few car-themed ornaments, including a classic purple woodie and a red tractor with a stack of wrapped presents. Perfect.

While standing in line at the checkout counter, someone tapped my shoulder. I turned to see my blue-haired neighbor grinning at me. She was dressed in flowing pants and a tunic top. Around her neck she wore a beautiful crystal necklace, no doubt to ward off evil spirits. I'd bet her chakras were flawlessly balanced.

"Hello, sweetie. Exactly the person I wanted to see. The other night when we were chatting, I forgot to tell you something. It came to me around two in the morning. Don't you hate when that happens? If you don't write it down, the thought vanishes, *poof!*" She flicked her fingers. "So I said to myself, 'Crusibella, write it down.'"

Crusibella. The name fit her.

"Seeing Emmett Atwater just now," she went on, "I remembered that I absolutely had to tell you what I'd jotted on the pad by my bed, and, *voilà*, here you are. It's Kismet."

"What did you write?"

She lowered her voice. "I saw Emmett ranting to a distinguished gentleman a couple of weeks ago about Jake's decorations.

I was walking my dog and pretended to ignore them. I considered telling the police. I don't know the man's name, but I've seen him about town. With Gracie. I hear he wants to buy Jake's place."

"Could it have been Adam Kittridge? Older with a hook nose?"

"That's the one. Emmett was telling him how much he hated Jake's lights. This Adam person commiserated, and I got to thinking what if he and Emmett conspired together? You know, kill two birds with one stone." She tapped her chin. "Or would that be vice versa? Whatever the saying is, it's bad karma. Christmas is the season to be loving and filled with light." She opened her arms to drink in good vibrations then lowered them. "I should tell the authorities my theory, don't you think?"

I nodded.

"One more thing." She tapped my wrist and lowered her voice. "Beware of dark emanations. Death will come to those who foster the darkness." Without waiting for a response, she left the shop, the train of her gown wafting behind her.

As the door swung closed, a breeze swept inside and chilled me to the bone.

Chapter 19

"Aunt Jenna, look at these!" Lacy joined me and showed me a variety of musical note ornaments in silver, gold, and glass. "Mom's buying them for our Christmas tree because I sing. Aren't they to die for?"

"Absolutely."

"When we leave here," Lacy continued, bubbling with excitement, "we're going to get something to eat at Latte Luck Café. Want to come?"

Though I needed lunch, I begged off. Thoughts of death and conspiracy were running roughshod through my mind. Should I contact Cinnamon? No, Crusibella said she would. I purchased the snow globe and the car-themed ornaments and headed back to the Cookbook Nook.

When I arrived, I noticed my aunt walking along the boardwalk with Mayor Zeller, who had a Gucci briefcase slung over her shoulder and a hefty manila folder in hand. Adam Kittridge, carrying a Cookbook Nook gift bag over one arm, accompanied them. Seeing him made me flash on what Crusibella had just told me. Had he and Emmett conspired to kill Jake?

I approached and drew up short when I realized Aunt Vera was miffed. The myriad beads she was wearing were snarled, as if she'd been worrying them for a while. I gave her a kiss and gently untangled her beads. "Is everything okay?"

"Yes." She was lying, but I didn't press. Sometimes she was like a teapot. She needed time to let off steam.

I addressed Adam Kittridge. "Hello again. How was your visit with your granddaughter in San Francisco?"

"We had a delightful time."

"Her name is Amy, right?"

"Good memory. After the recital, we went to Ghirardelli Square and devoured ice cream and took selfies. She wanted her friends to see how much caramel and whipped cream I allowed her to have on her sundae."

"Caramel." I made a swooning sound. "A girl after my own heart."

"But I'm back, and I'm a man on a mission."

"To find a vacation home."

"Actually, I'm thinking about moving here full-time. The weather is superb."

"We get our foggy days," Aunt Vera said. "Quite a few of them."

Adam grinned. "Not like San Francisco."

"True," Z.Z. said. "Most of the time it's like this." The sun gleamed in a blue, cloudless sky. A gentle breeze stirred the air.

"Rain is in the forecast," Aunt Vera stated.

"I like rain."

I watched the two of them like a tennis match. Why the tension?

Z.Z. addressed me, "In addition to purchasing a home, Adam is interested in acquiring a variety of strip malls."

Aha! So that was what was bugging my aunt.

"Surely not this one," I said judiciously.

"We're writing up an offer," Z.Z. said.

"No!" I cried.

"That's what I told them" — my aunt's jaw ticked with irritation — "but the mayor appears to be deaf."

Z.Z. clucked her tongue. "I have a resolute client, Vera. In California, realtors must always submit an offer. It's the law."

"Law-schmaw."

Adam said to me, "I'm thinking of retiring and investing in property for myself. No more buying for an LLC. No more worrying about someone else's cash flow. There are some lovely places here. I've inspected Artiste Arcade and a few others."

"Changing ownership of too many properties might alter the face and tenor of Crystal Cove," I warned.

"*Pfft.*" Z.Z. waved a hand dismissively. Was the financial strain of putting her son through school blurring her vision? She of all people knew that locals as well as tourists cared about preserving Crystal Cove's quaintness. "Adam will keep them exactly as they are."

"Absolutely," he said.

Aunt Vera slipped her hand around my elbow and guided me toward the shop. Whispering, she said, "Don't worry. The answer is no."

"But will everyone else say no, too?"

She sighed. "We can't stop evolution."

"Jenna, hold up." Z.Z. hurried to me. Adam kept pace. "How is Jake doing? The hospital won't let me talk to him."

"I haven't talked to him either. He was sleeping. But he's out of the woods, and the doctors are keeping a close eye on him."

Adam said, "Z.Z. told me what happened. How horrible. Poison? Have the police figured out who did it?"

"Not yet."

Z.Z. tapped Adam's arm. "I have another appointment."

"Go. I'm good. I think I'll do a bit more shopping."

I eyed the gift bag he was carrying. "What did you purchase already?"

"I found a couple of fabulous cookbooks for my daughter-in-law. One is a country-something Christmas book. The name will come to me." He peered into the bag, but tissue paper obscured the titles.

I said, "Is it *A Relaxing Country Christmas Cookbook: Holiday Recipes You Should Have Got from your Grandmother*!?"

"Yes."

"It's delightful. Great photographs and recipes from every kind of Christmas drink to entrées, including pheasant under glass. She'll enjoy it. Did you find any others?"

"A cookie cookbook she can share with Amy. *Cute Christmas Cookies*."

"Great choice. The cover alone, with the white mittens and star cookies dusted with powdered sugar, is worth the price."

"Amy wants to learn to bake."

"I wish I had at her age."

"Vera," Adam turned toward her, "I should pick up a few more books for my son to give his wife. Care to help me? Z.Z. says you know every title on the shelves."

She pursed her lips.

Undaunted, Adam strolled into the shop while popping a piece of gum in his mouth. Did he believe he could cajole my aunt into selling if he purchased all the books in the store? Was there no limit to his cheekiness?

Aunt Vera squinted, clearly onto him. "Forgive me," she said as she followed him inside. "I have a tarot card reading to do." She sat at the vintage table and started fiddling with the thousand-piece jigsaw puzzle featuring extremely detailed artwork of a Ford Model T and news articles about its release.

Adam said to her, "Perhaps someday you will do my reading."

"Make an appointment at the sales desk." She couldn't have sounded icier.

"Will do." Adam beckoned me. "Jenna, if you don't mind, I could use a few suggestions."

I followed him as he meandered along the aisles. "What does your son do?"

"He started out as a stockbroker but worked his way up. He's a broker-dealer now and runs his own company. He has a knack for knowing exactly which stock to buy and when and is quite prosperous, but he's busier than all get-out. As a real estate investor, I have more flexibility."

"Obviously you're good at what you do."

"Yes."

"And yet you're ready to retire."

"My wife died last year from a grueling illness. I need . . ." He exhaled. "A change."

"Won't you miss seeing your granddaughter on a regular basis?"

"I'm hoping to convince my son and his family to move here. He can do his work via the Internet. All investment brokers can nowadays. Between you and me, a small town is where I'd like to see my grandchild grow up." Adam selected a cookbook called *Love Real Food: More Than 100 Feel-Good Vegetarian Favorites to Delight the Senses and Nourish the Body* and flipped the pages back to front like my father did. "Is this good?"

"It was one of the top-rated books in 2017. Written by the woman who runs the *Cookie and Kate* blog. A key feature is most recipes have a section at the bottom sharing how to make it gluten-free, dairy-free/vegan, egg/nut-free and soy-free, which makes it very versatile to every kind of eater."

He tucked it under his arm and moved ahead.

I followed, thinking about what Crusibella had said. "Adam, one of my neighbors mentioned that you and Emmett Atwater had a conversation outside Jake's place a few weeks ago."

"Yep. That was the first day I came to town to scope it out. A friend in San Francisco was touting Crystal Cove's charms." Adam shook his head. "Poor Atwater was apoplectic about the amount of decorations Jake was putting up. What a shame to live with that kind of anger brewing, always wishing the other guy dead."

My mouth fell open. "Did he say that?"

"What? No. Of course he didn't. I'm sorry. It was a turn of phrase. He—" Adam lifted another book, fanned through it, and returned it to the shelf. "He was upset. Leave it at that."

"After that exchange, why would you want to purchase the property directly next to him? Weren't you concerned he'd be on your case, too?"

"I can deal with disgruntled property owners. It's part and parcel of my business." He leaned in. "Not to mention, in addition to wanting to learn to bake, my granddaughter wants to learn to surf. She's a real daredevil. The location of Jake's house is ideal." Adam strolled to another bookshelf, this one featuring children's books. "Ah, I love these books. I read them to my son." He picked up a copy of *James and the Giant Peach* and *Charlie and the Chocolate Factory* by Roald Dahl and added them to his stash. "Emmett and I will do fine. I promised him I wouldn't decorate to the hilt. Don't worry."

I wasn't worried in the least. Jake wouldn't sell. I caught my aunt staring at me. No client had arrived yet. She jerked her chin in Adam's direction. What was she signaling? Did she want me to question him about the theory we'd come up with? She repeated the gesture.

Certain that she wouldn't let up unless I did her bidding, I said, "Adam, Z.Z. mentioned that you studied up on Jake. Why?"

"That Z.Z. She's a card." He nodded. "I like to know what makes my competition tick. I've closed many a deal by offering the right incentive."

More gestures from my aunt.

"Um, Adam, last Wednesday"—I flitted a hand, at a loss as to how to broach the next question.

He titled his head. "You're wondering whether I killed Jake's friend, mistaking him for Jake, so I could get my hands on the property, aren't you?"

I blanched. Could he read my mind?

Adam chuckled. "Keller warned me that rumor was picking up traction."

"Keller?"

"I love that boy's ice cream. He and I have had quite a few discussions. He said the police were working the angle that someone had it in for Jake, not Jake's pal. Between you and me, seeing as the killer has obviously made another attempt on Jake's life, they should." He waved a friendly hand. "Relax. I understand why you'd question me. Jake is like family. Family protects family. I assure you, I'm after his property, not his life." He browsed titles in the next aisle and selected one of my all-time favorite cookbooks, *The Perfect Peach*. "I adore peaches. Is this a good choice?"

"Absolutely. If you buy it, try the stuffed French toast. It's to die for, and the recipe is easy enough for me to make."

"You're not a cook?"

"I'm learning."

"You're being modest."

"Trust me, I'm not."

"Me, either." Adam smiled genially, and I could see why Gran found him attractive. He was a reasonable and self-assured man. He added the book to his stack. "Where were we? Oh, yes, the night Jake's friend was killed. You probably want to know where I was."

"No, I . . . You don't have to—"

"I was at the festival. I hadn't met Gracie yet so I was on my own. What a charming event, by the way. Another of the many reasons to move here." He sauntered to another section and picked up a copy of *Culinary Reactions: The Everyday Chemistry of Cooking*. "This looks fascinating. Would this be good for an eight-year-old? Amy is into science. My fault, I fear. I wanted to be an inventor like Thomas Edison and change the world when I was growing up, but I went into business to satisfy my father. 'A man must make a decent living and not dwell with his head in the clouds,' he said." Adam *tsked*. "*Dwell*. What an archaic word, don't you think? I told Amy that she'll have no such tethers on her. If she wants to prevent global warming—and she does—she may do so."

"This book might be a little advanced," I said, "but it has clear, easy language about how the chemicals in our foods react."

"Perfect, whatever she can't figure out, I'm sure I can explain." He moved toward the checkout counter. "Anyway, back to what we were discussing . . . that night . . . I was at the festival listening to a capella groups practice. They must have done so for two hours. What great names they're coming up with nowadays. Nothing but Treble and the Tonic Fifths. I think if I were in a group, I'd name us the Ring Tones."

"Do you sing?"

"I used to. I'm a baritone. Chorus only. Never the lead. My nickname as a teenager was Croak. My voice didn't change until I was sixteen." He chuckled and approached the sales counter. "Your niece was in the group that stomped, right? Talk about a talented group, although I think the Ransom Notes' 'This Is My Wish' was my favorite song." As he handed Tina his selections and credit card, he used his chin to gesture toward my aunt and said, "Please talk to Vera about my offer. I could be an effective silent partner."

After he departed, I turned to Tina. "I have a question for you. At the party yesterday, do you remember the Santa who took the tray of punch shots from you?" I didn't have the heart to tell her that the syringe was found in her costume pocket. If Cinnamon didn't consider her a suspect, I'd let that tidbit slide.

"Sure, but I don't know who it was, if that's what you're asking."

"Was it a he or she?"

"I'm not sure. The voice was gravelly, like the person was suffering from a cold."

"Santa sent you on an errand. What was it?"

"Supposedly your aunt needed me, but when I went into the storage room, she wasn't there, so I came out and found the tray sitting on the kids' table. Weird, right?"

"The police think the killer dosed two of the punch glasses with liquid nicotine."

"They don't think that I . . ." She started to tremble and placed a palm on her chest. "I swear I didn't."

"You're in the clear."

"The person was about my height. With older eyes." She fluttered her fingers beside her own. "Though I suppose that could have been makeup. And—"

I skirted the counter and gripped her by the shoulders. "Breathe. Why don't you take a break? Visit Katie. Watch her cook."

"Yes, okay, I'll do that." Tina fled down the breezeway.

I joined my aunt. As I'd expected, no client had shown up. She'd fabricated the story.

"Well?" she asked. "What did you learn?"

"He's not the killer. He has no motive. And he has an alibi for the night Geoffrey was killed. He was watching Lacy and the others rehearse. I'm ruling him out."

"Then who is your primary suspect?"

"Whomever Cinnamon has on her radar."

"Tosh." She thwacked my arm with a deck of cards. "Out with it."

"Okay, fine. Emmett, Raquel, or Olivia." Although Olivia hadn't dressed as the ruddy-cheeked Santa. Emmett hadn't either, if he could be believed. I told her about Cinnamon finding the syringe in Tina's elf costume.

"Oh, my." She tapped her chin, thinking. "What if none of the guest Santas dosed the drinks?"

"What do you mean? Someone did."

Aunt Vera raised an eyebrow. "Have you completely ruled out Jake?"

"Why would he poison himself?"

"To remove himself as a suspect for killing his friend."

Chapter 20

I hated that my aunt had put a negative thought in my head about Jake. Why would he have killed Geoffrey? Plus, he was caught on camera at the grocery store. Did the time of death match his alibi?

My stomach grumbled. I needed food. I hurried to the café, and after making sure Tina was calmer, I chose the daily sandwich combo Katie was featuring on the menu—a hoagie with salami, provolone, and peppers with a side of shoestring fries. I returned to the shop and disappeared into the storage room to call my father.

After spreading out my meal on the desk and opening the sandwich so I could eat the insides first—my favorite part—I tapped in Dad's number on my cell phone.

When I reached him, he informed me that he and Lola were having a nightcap at the bar on the boat. The charming city of Würzburg was their view.

"Are you jealous?" he asked.

"You bet I am." How I craved a vacation.

"What's up? How's Jake coping? I tried calling him at home. He didn't pick up."

I filled my father in about the nicotine poisoning but assured him Jake was on the mend. Then I launched into the doubt my aunt had stirred in me.

"Jake would never kill anyone," my father said. "Never."

"He hit someone when he was younger. Beat him to a pulp."

"That was ages ago."

"You knew about it?"

"Yes."

Bailey slipped into the storage room. She mimed asking if I wanted her to leave. I twirled a finger, signaling she could stay, and pressed *Speaker* on the phone.

"Bailey has joined me. I'm letting her listen in."

"Hey, Bailey," my father said. "Your mother is having the time of her life."

"Good to hear. Give her my love, but don't let me interrupt."

"Will do. Moving on, Jenna, what motives do you have for each of your primary suspects?"

Bailey snatched some of my fries. Usually, I'd swat her fingers. This time I let her have them.

"Jake's sister Olivia might believe she'll inherit his money, being his only remaining family, but he's written a will that gives everything he has to charity."

"Does she know that?" Dad asked.

"I don't have a clue."

"Does she have an alibi?"

"She gave me one, but I called her out on it, knowing it was false. She fled before providing another."

"Next suspect?"

I loved how black and white Dad could be at times. "Raquel Adagio, who owns Forget Me Not Collectibles — "

"I knew her father."

I spelled out the significance of the Blue Mauritius stamp and how Gran had overheard Raquel crowing about it. "Jake showed it to Raquel on the first night of the festival, the night Geoffrey died. It's possible she stole into Jake's house, took the wrong stamp from Geoffrey's room because the guest room and master bedroom look the same, and as she was running out, Geoffrey accosted her."

"Is she strong enough to kill someone his size?"

"He wasn't that big, Dad. Skin and bones, like Jake. And Raquel regularly lifts large boxes. The Christmas items the killer used to stab him and strangle him were right by the kitchen door, too, which makes me think this could have been a spur-of-the-moment act, not premeditated."

"Does she have an alibi?"

"She claims she was at church. I don't know if Cinnamon has corroborated that."

"Make a note," he said.

Bailey fetched a notepad and pen and scribbled his command.

I launched into my third suspect, Emmett Atwater. "My biggest problem with Emmett is he would've recognized Jake, so why kill Geoffrey?"

"Was it dark?"

"No. Jake's house is lit up like a Christmas palace."

"Maybe Emmett has a sight issue or photophobia," Dad suggested.

"What's that?" Bailey asked.

"Sensitivity to light," I said. A colleague at Taylor & Squibb had the hardest time whenever she was on a set and flash photography was being used. She couldn't handle the strobing effect. "I'd mentioned to Cinnamon that anger might have blurred his vision, Dad."

"That's a good possibility."

Bailey jotted another note.

My father said, "Go to Cinnamon and review all that you have. See what else she will share."

"She won't—"

"Do it."

"Yes, sir."

"Tell her I asked her to do *me* the favor of looping me in on this one. I owe Jake."

We ended the call, and I turned to Bailey. "Hungry?" My fries and the meat on my hoagie were gone.

Her cheeks reddened. "Guess I was. Sorry. I could use a latte, couldn't you? My treat." She tucked the notes she'd written in the pocket of her capris and grabbed her purse.

When we emerged from the storage room, Tina was at the checkout counter, Aunt Vera was aligning books on shelves, and three customers were browsing Christmas-themed kitchen items.

"Back in a few," I said.

On the way to Latte Luck Café, I realized Bailey must have come into the storage room to chat, but now she wasn't saying a word. I nudged her elbow. "Are you going to tell me what's going on?"

"No."

I pulled her to a stop. "Bailey . . ."

"I *am* pregnant."

"I knew it! Congratulations." I clutched her shoulders. "Hold it. Your lower lip is trembling. What's wrong? Are you nervous? Afraid of getting fat? Worried about being a mother?"

"All of the above. What if I cry all the time, or my brain becomes mush or—"

"Mothers don't lose their ability to think."

"I'll have to take time off from work."

"Of course. We'll manage. What else?" I gazed into her worried eyes. "There's something else. I feel it down to my toes. Spill."

"You'd make a good detective." She shimmied free of me and rubbed between her eyebrows to de-stress. "Tito thinks I should become a full-time mother."

"Uh-uh. You've been working since you were sixteen. You like to work. It stimulates those little gray cells. Tell him we'll accommodate whatever schedule you need. Besides . . ." I knuckled her arm.

"Besides what?"

"Don't forget about your new role as a limited partner."

"Yipes! I did forget. My mind *is* mush. Come on. Let's really celebrate. My treat." Bailey clasped my hand and rushed forward to the café. She pushed through the doors, pulling me inside with her. "I'm also in the mood for ice cream."

"And pickles?"

"As a matter of fact, yes."

I scrunched my nose. "Ew."

As per usual in the afternoon, Cinnamon was at the café, too. She often came in to pick up local gossip. Anything to help solve a case. She was at the counter paying for an iced coffee.

When she caught sight of Bailey and me, she raised an eyebrow. She popped a straw into her drink and sidled up to us. "Looking for me?"

"No, we're celebrating," Bailey said. "I'm pregnant." The news instantly defused the tension.

"How wonderful." Cinnamon gave her a hug. "Are you excited? When are you due?"

"Late May, early June."

"You're three months pregnant?" Cinnamon gaped. "But you don't show."

"The doctor tells me I will around five months." Bailey's eyes gleamed with happiness, and I breathed easier. Our little chat had done wonders to relieve her stress about making such a big life decision. She pulled the notes she'd written from her pocket and handed them to me. "Here you go."

"What are those?" Cinnamon asked.

I said, "I spoke with my father, and he wanted me to ask you a few questions."

"Swell, now he's joining the Jenna Hart Detective Agency?"

"Cut it out."

"Sorry. Feeling snarky and a bit flummoxed by this case. Go on."

"He'd like you to do him the favor of looping him in on this. He owes Jake." *And you owe him,* I thought, but I kept my mouth shut.

Cinnamon took a sip of her drink. "What does he want to know?"

Reading from the list, I said, "Do you know if Emmett Atwater has photophobia, which would explain how he mistook Geoffrey for Jake?"

"I don't. I'll follow up."

"Did he confess to lying about my brother-in-law returning to the scene?"

Cinnamon wriggled her mouth.

"Forget that. You know he did. How about verifying Raquel Adagio's alibi?"

"I told you I don't believe Raquel—"

I shook the notes. "Don't shoot the messenger."

She grunted. "You and your father. Man, oh, man. Okay, I asked her. She seemed cagey. Appleby's checking out her alibi. In the meantime, I ordered a search warrant for her house and shop. We didn't find anything in either. What else?"

"Did you track down Olivia Chapman? Flora gave you her cell phone number."

"How do you—"

"I happened to be in Home Sweet Home earlier with my sister and niece, and Flora mentioned the mix-up with the costume gloves."

Cinnamon frowned. "She shouldn't have."

"I think she confided in me because the poisoning happened at my shop, and Jake is my friend. She said you found the syringe in Tina's costume pocket, but there's not a chance she did it."

"I agree."

Phew. I let out the breath I was holding. "Did you find fingerprints on the syringe?"

"No. Wiped clean."

"If you can't reach Olivia by cell phone, you might check the area near the lake by Rhett's cabin for her car. A few homeless people saw her in the vicinity."

"Aren't you a wealth of information." She took another sip of her drink, making a loud slurp. On purpose. "Listen, Jenna, my people have been questioning everyone who attended the party. Flora provided a list of all the people to whom she rented costumes. We will get to the bottom of this. Promise your father that. And when I come up with more data, I'll fill you in so you can *loop* him in, okay?" After miming the twirling of a rope, she made a U-turn and strode out of the shop.

Bailey and I purchased our drinks—she'd been kidding about craving ice cream and pickles—and we headed back to the Cookbook Nook. Right before reaching Fisherman's Village, I saw Olivia feeding a meter for her car. She had slung three wreaths of varying colors on her forearm.

"There she is," I said to Bailey.

"Who?"

"Jake's sister. I'd like to speak to her."

"Go. I'll make sure everything runs smoothly at the shop."

"No heavy lifting," I warned.

"Don't baby me." Bailey gave me a quick hug followed by a gentle push.

I hastened my pace to catch up to Olivia. "Hey there," I said.

She whirled around. The flaps of her pea coat flew open, revealing a navy blue turtleneck. The blue jeans were the same pair she'd worn to the hospital. Her hair was brushed and wet. She smoothed her hair with a hand. "Forgive my appearance. I'm coming from the gym."

Was that where she took showers since she didn't have an apartment?

She closed her jacket and adjusted the wreaths she was carrying.

"Those are pretty," I said. "Did you make them?"

"No. I bought them at the festival. For coworkers." She fingered the berries on the red-toned wreath. "Each has a color preference. One likes cream. Another likes green."

"Did you purchase a black one?"

"Black? Heavens. Do they make those? How horrid." She wrinkled her nose.

161

At the hospital, she'd proven to be a good liar. Was she lying now?

"Sorry to say goodbye"—she lowered her chin the way she had the other day when Cinnamon had shown up in the hospital waiting room; she was getting ready to ditch me—"but I'm in a rush." She strode north on Buena Vista.

I charged after her. For an older woman, she was fast.

"Where are you off to?" I asked.

"Home Sweet Home. Flora has sold one of my quilts."

"Olivia, your brother was poisoned."

"So you said."

"Don't you want to know how?"

"Of course."

"By liquid nicotine."

"Never heard of such a thing." She hesitated. "You think I did it because I'm a smoker, don't you?"

"You were a budding scientist in high school."

"I didn't poison my brother. I love him."

"Why didn't you stick around the hospital the other night, then, and wait to find out if he was okay?"

"Because . . ." She pressed her lips together.

"Because the chief of police appeared."

"Yes."

"Why did you lie about going to a hotel the night Jake's friend was killed?"

Olivia exhaled. Her shoulders sagged. "You or the police are bound to find out. I'm an alcoholic, like our parents."

As I'd suspected.

She sucked back a sob. "Coming here to see my brother, being nervous about meeting him, I fell off the wagon. What if he rejected me? Or he learned how low I'd sunk? That night, I went to buy more booze, but when I got to the store, I didn't go in. I . . ." She plucked holly leaves on the cream wreath. "I went to an AA meeting."

I put a consoling hand on her shoulder. "Is there anyone who could corroborate you being there?"

"Yes, but I couldn't ask her to. They call it *anonymous* for a reason." Tears flooded her eyes.

"Tell the police. I'm sure they'll be able to keep their inquiry discreet."

She lifted her chin and blinked with hope.

Chapter 21

The rest of the afternoon passed in a nanosecond. While I worked on the window display, setting out the snow globe along with the classic car ornaments and a few of the specialty books, Bailey and Tina racked up sales. My aunt did a reading for Pepper, of all people; she'd never shown any interest in the past. Did she want to know about her love life or the prospects for her daughter's wedding? I half expected Cinnamon to read me the riot act after Olivia contacted her, but she didn't. Had Olivia failed to follow through, or was Cinnamon tolerating my intervention because my father's request held sway? I hoped the second and not the first.

When the day was over, I dropped Tigger at home and headed to the hospital to visit Jake. A policeman stood guard outside. I introduced myself; he checked a list and allowed me to go in.

To my surprise, Jake was on his feet and dressed in jeans and a tan T-shirt. Zoey Zeller was helping him shrug into his jacket. His face was still rashy and daubed with some kind of ointment. A middle-aged nurse with an implacable face toured the room making notations on a chart attached to a clipboard.

"Now the other arm," Z.Z. said.

"What are you doing?" I asked.

"Leaving," Jake grunted.

Z.Z. smiled. "He's weak but determined."

I said, "Stubborn, you mean."

Jake made a face at me and nudged Z.Z. away. "I can't laze around here forever. I've got work to do."

"You're not going to clean the beach, you old fool," Z.Z. said.

"Who else is going to do it?"

"Crystal Cove has a fully employed crew."

"Not as good as me." He began to gather his personal belongings, which were lying on the bed: a watch, a wallet, a spanking new cell phone, and a set of keys. "Besides, I need to organize Geoffrey's funeral."

"What's the rush?" Z.Z. asked. "He's not going anywhere."

Jake glowered at her. "That was cruel."

"You appreciate honesty."

Jake rubbed the back of his neck. "Yeah, I do."

"Now, I've arranged for a bodyguard—"

"I don't need one," Jake countered.

"Whether you do or not, I've arranged for one. Don't fight me."

To diffuse their stare-down, I said, "Jake, my dad says hello. He left you a message at home. Also, I had a conversation with your sister. She came by to see you here yesterday, but you were in bad shape, and she couldn't stay. She had a work emergency that she needed to handle." I faltered, not wishing to reveal that she'd ducked out on Cinnamon. So much for being *honest*.

"I thought you said she was homeless."

"She is, but she's employed. She works as a seamstress for a bridal company."

"A seamstress?" He moaned. "Oh, man, that's on me. She had so much potential. It's my fault she didn't realize her dreams."

"She's not upset about what happened between you and her," I assured him. "She doesn't blame you. And she's using her talents well. On her own time, she makes beautiful quilts. If she could, I think that's what she'd like to do full-time."

Z.Z. said, "Maybe you could help her get established here."

Jake's face flinched. "Not if she—"

"She didn't kill Geoffrey," I said. "That's what I wanted to tell you. She has an alibi." I didn't elaborate. He didn't need to hear the details from me.

"I'd like to see her. Does she have a cell phone?" he asked as he pocketed his new one.

"I imagine so. Flora or the police could give you her number."

"Okay." He fumbled with his wallet, trying to stuff it into his other pocket. It fell to the floor. A couple of photographs spilled out of it.

I picked up the items and started to offer them to him but held off. "Who's this?" I displayed a photograph of a young Jake with his arm around an attractive brunette. He tried to snatch it away.

"That's not your wife," Z.Z. said.

"No, it's Am—" He cleared his throat; his face flushed pink. "Her name was Amelia."

I wagged the photograph teasingly. "Is she the one that got away?"

"The one that got away?" Z.Z. echoed.

"Long story," Jake said.

Z.Z. peered at the picture. "Her eyes are incredible."

"Just like Elizabeth Taylor's," he said dreamily.

"Should I be jealous?"

"Mr. Chapman." The nurse rapped on the door and jerked her thumb toward the bed. "Why are you dallying? Care to climb back in?"

"No, ma'am. Thank you, ma'am. We're leaving, ma'am. Adios." Jake saluted and started to leave, saying over his shoulder, "I'd tell you more about Amelia, ladies, but I'd better make tracks before this tyrant decides to strap me to the bed against my will."

The nurse's mouth quirked up on one side. Obviously she and Jake had bonded.

At the door, Jake held out his hand to me. "My personals, please."

"What's your cell phone number?" I asked in negotiation. "I'm sure my dad will want it."

He rattled it off. "Now, give me . . ." He opened his palm, demanding his wallet and photos.

Reluctantly, I turned over the items, even though the romantic in me was craving to know more about Amelia.

• • •

When I arrived home, my front door was standing wide open. A frisson of fear skittered up my spine but vanished when I saw my sister's car parked in the driveway near my aunt's vintage red Mustang.

I dashed into the cottage, while noting that a new wreath made with fresh greenery, red berries, miniature pinecones, and a gorgeous burgundy bow was hanging on my door. Whitney was in my kitchen pulling a tray of sugar cookies out of the oven. Lacy, dressed in her blood-red dress, her hair spiked with gel and her face made up, was kneeling on the floor taunting Tigger with the tail end of a ball of red yarn.

"Wow, Lacy, nice getup," I said.

"Thanks." She blew me a kiss.

To my sister, I said, "Why is my door wide open? And all my windows?"

"We're airing out your place."

"It wasn't stuffy."

"It needed airing. Where have you been?"

"Why does it matter?" I asked, a teensy bite in my tone. Her imperious nature brought out the worst in me.

"Jenna," she coaxed.

Quickly I tamped down a huffy retort, either because the cookies smelled heavenly and I wanted one, or because I was growing up. I wasn't sure which. "I was at the hospital seeing Jake."

"How's he doing?" Lacy asked.

"On his way home."

She clapped with glee.

I said to my sister, "Why are you here?"

"Spencer is working and —"

"Dad is, like, really psyched about this project," Lacy cut in, "so he dropped us here and took off." She trilled, "Fa-la-la."

Who was this girl? Definitely not the dour child who had arrived here a few days ago.

Whitney grinned. "Since we're free and it's our last night, Lacy wants you to take us on a walking tour so she can see all the wreaths in town before the winner is announced. That's why she dressed up for you."

"For me?"

"We brought you a new wreath, too," Lacy chimed. "I picked it out. Say, did you find out who left the black one on the door?"

"No." The notion made me shiver. I hated that it had happened. I hated even more that I didn't know who did it.

Whitney said, "It was probably a wayward teenager."

"Mo-o-om." Lacy rolled her eyes.

"What? Some teenagers are wayward." Whitney threw her a dismissive look. "Come with us on our walk, Jenna. You don't have plans with Rhett, do you?"

"No." Right as I was leaving work, he had texted me saying he missed me and was sorry he couldn't see me because the staff holiday party was tonight. I'd texted back that I missed him, too, and would call once I got home.

"Please say yes, Aunt Jenna." Lacy scrambled to her feet and tossed the ball of yarn across the room so Tigger would chase it.

"Cute." I pointed. She was wearing the darling sandals we'd purchased at the Gossip Parlor.

"Mom likes them, too. Please say yes," she repeated.

"We can grab a bite to eat at the Pelican Brief first if you're hungry," Whitney suggested. "You haven't eaten, have you?"

I picked up a cookie and took a bite. "Now I have."

"Very funny."

"Yum. These aren't plain old sugar cookies." I wiggled the remaining portion at her. "What did you add, raspberry?"

"Good guess. Chopped fine. And a hint of nutmeg."

"Love them. They'll make a perfect holiday treat at the café. Are they a bribe?"

Whitney batted her eyelashes. "If you need them to be."

"I *need* to change shoes." I liked to wear sandals, but for a three-mile hike—that was the approximate distance from one end of town to the other—I preferred Keds.

• • •

In the daytime, Crystal Cove was charming. At night, during the holidays, it was stunning. Strands of lights arced across Buena Vista Boulevard. Tracers outlined many of the shop windows. Artiste Arcade had woven Christmas lights through its arched arbor of morning glories. Mini San Francisco, a grouping of six shops that bore a resemblance to classic structures in the city, had painted its windows to look like stained glass.

As I was texting Rhett about how my sister had sweet-talked me into accompanying them, Lacy asked, "Which wreath do you like best so far, Aunt Jenna?" Her eyes were glowing with good vibes.

"The cheese-themed one on Say Cheese's door is darling." It was made up of cubes of cheese and olives woven onto a wreath of rosemary.

Rhett texted back: *Want company later?*

I was no fool. I responded: *You bet I do.*

Whitney said, "I like this one." She pointed to the wreath on the entrance to Nuts and Bolts. Our father had used wrenches, screwdrivers, and oilcans for his arrangement.

"It's cool," Lacy said, taking a second to admire it.

"Psst!" Whitney whispered. "There's your father. Keep moving. I don't want him to think we're spying on him."

Spencer didn't look up, enraptured with his work near the sales counter.

Lacy scooted forward. "I liked the wreath on the pet store with the little bones and chew toys. Did you see the miniature doghouse ornament on it? So cute. Ooh-ooh!" She pointed. "Carolers! Let's cross the street."

Outside the Play Room Toy Store, three carolers were singing "Come Rest Ye Merry Gentlemen." The store owner stood among the crowd, slyly guiding a few of them inside.

We listened through one song before heading to the Pelican Brief Diner next door.

"Hey, Jenna!" Bailey hustled toward us. She was carrying a to-go cup from Latte Luck Café. "What are you up to?"

"We're grabbing a bite to eat. Then we're viewing wreaths."

"May I join? I'm solo. Tito's trying to get the scoop about the oldest antique car in town."

I turned to my sister. "Is it okay?"

"Sure." She grinned. "The more the merrier."

The Pelican Brief Diner's aqua blue wreath featured an ocean theme: miniature dolphins, pelicans, seagulls, and seashells. The restaurant was pretty jammed, but the hostess seated us within ten minutes. I ordered my usual: fish and chips. Bailey and Lacy opted for fish burgers, and Whitney went for the fish tacos.

After dinner, we set off on our hunt to view the remaining wreaths. Near Spellbinder's Book Store, we ran into Adam Kittridge, Gran, and her two youngest granddaughters. The girls, dressed identically in red dresses and ballet shoes, were carrying sturdy bags from the shop, each filled with books. Gran's arm was looped through Adam's.

"Good evening, ladies," she said. "Blissful night, isn't it?" She was the one who appeared to be over the moon. Was she falling in love? Suddenly, I felt as protective as Bailey had the other day. I wasn't sure why. Maybe my aunt's vibes about Adam were tickling my worry antennae. He seemed like a perfectly nice man, and he hadn't made an offer to purchase Fisherman's Village. Yet.

"Any new prospects for property to purchase?" I asked him.

"Jake Chapman's house." He winked.

"Not for sale." I winked back. "My aunt heard of a place that's going on the market not far from us."

"Dear me." Gran placed a hand on her chest. "You must think I'm horrible, Jenna. How is Jake? Have you seen him? The last I heard he was on the mend, but that isn't saying much." She turned to Adam. "Jake was poisoned. Can you imagine?"

"He's heading home."

"That's wonderful news. Will he be all right alone?"

I nodded. "Z.Z. arranged for a bodyguard."

Adam laughed. "I'll bet he loved that."

"Not a whit," I said.

Gran addressed Bailey. "How is your darling Tito feeling?"

"Fine, thanks, Gran. Off drumming up a new story."

"Gran," the taller of the girls said, "can we show Miss Jenna what we bought?"

"Of course."

Both girls opened the handles of their bags. "Mysteries," they said in unison.

The shorter girl said, "Gran says they're a great way to get young minds to solve puzzles. We love puzzles. Do you?"

"I'm a huge mystery fan."

"I've read every Nancy Drew Mystery," the taller girl said.

"And I love Trixie Belden," her sister chimed.

"All right, girls, that's enough." Gran gathered the collar of her cranberry red sweater to ward off a slight breeze. "Jenna, we're planning to hear Z.Z. announce the wreath winner at the dolphins." At the crossroads where Crystal Cove Road met Buena Vista Boulevard stood a pair of intertwined dancing dolphin statues, a great lure for picture-taking tourists. "Will we see you there?"

"If all goes according to plan."

Chapter 22

Taking our time, we sauntered to the far end of town, commenting on each wreath we saw. After crossing the road to make the return trip, we passed a number of shops. The wreath for Die Hard Fan, a collectibles store for sports aficionados, was made up of trading cards. Sweet Success had fashioned its tasty wreath using hard candies.

Outside Forget Me Not, Raquel Adagio's official shop, Whitney pulled to a stop and pointed. "How clever!" On the door hung a wreath decorated with laminated one- and five-cent stamps as well as miniature antique postal boxes and postal trucks. My sister fingered the boxes, opening and closing their doors.

Through the picture window, I spotted Raquel dusting counters. Her cheeks were bright red. Either she was flush from exertion or she'd been outdoors all day and was suffering a wind- and sunburn.

"Aunt Jenna, is this the same shop that was at the festival?" Lacy asked. "With the stamps and such?"

"It is."

"Can we go inside? We could sneakily search for the missing stamp."

I rolled my eyes at her.

Bailey stifled a grin and whispered, "Uh-oh, it appears you have another amateur sleuth in the family."

"Ha-ha."

Like the shop's display cases at the festival, each in the main shop was rimmed with twinkling lights and contained stamps and other curios. A few self-supporting bookshelves stood against the right wall. Two held leather-bound books. One featured antique postal paraphernalia, like a date stamp, a brass letter scale, and a variety of ornate letter openers.

Lacy crossed to a collection of framed stamps hanging on the wall beyond the bookshelves and began examining each one. Whitney joined her and wrapped an arm around her. How I enjoyed seeing them bond.

"Hi, Jenna. Hey, Bailey." Raquel moved behind the sales counter and stowed her feather duster. "What brings you in?"

"We're wreath viewing. Yours is nice."

"Made it myself. I'm quite handy with a glue gun." She twisted the fragrance oil burner at the edge of the counter.

With the movement, the flame flickered. I flinched as an image of the burner tipping over and its flame lighting her wares on fire zipped through my mind. Raquel didn't seem concerned. Pushing the hazardous notion away, I said, "Did you have a successful festival?"

"Sure did."

"Did you sell or buy any unique stamps?"

"Other than Jake's?"

"I didn't mean—"

"I'm messing with you." She flapped a hand. "How are Jake and Tito doing, by the way? I was worried when I saw the EMTs cart them away from the party."

"You were there?"

"Wouldn't have missed it. I love a good cookie swap."

"What were you dressed as?" I asked, wondering if she would admit that she was the ruddy-cheeked Santa with the sequined lapel.

"An elf with lots of glitter on my face. Boy"—she made a chuffing sound—"is that stuff difficult to get off. There's glitter everywhere in my house. And look what the glue did to my face. See how chapped my cheeks are?"

Guess I'd been wrong about her being outside all day. "Ouch."

"Never again. I have a facial scheduled for tomorrow. Do I ever need one."

Whitney and Lacy joined us. Lacy pitched forward, elbows on the sales counter. "My mom is in love with your collection of knitting stamps. She likes the ones from Finland the best."

Raquel grinned. "They're fun, aren't they? Like little works of art."

"To answer your earlier question, Raquel," I said, "Tito is fine and Jake is on the mend. He's heading home from the hospital."

"That's good to hear," Raquel said. "Did they get the flu, or were they poisoned?"

"Why would you ask if they were poisoned?" Lacy asked, her eyes narrowing with suspicion.

"Because . . ." Raquel sputtered. "Because what else could it have been?"

"They *were* poisoned," I said. "With liquid nicotine."

"Ew." Raquel wrinkled her nose.

"It turns out nicotine can be boiled down from cigarettes. It's also found in vape stores."

"And someone did that on purpose? Ick."

Whitney said, "Isn't vaping the most ridiculous thing? For years, we've been trying to get young people not to start smoking. Then this comes along, and it's considered cool." She skewered Lacy with a look. "You don't vape, do you?"

"Get real, Mother. I'm a singer." Lacy squared her shoulders, as if being a *singer* said it all.

"Raquel," I said, "I believe I saw a vape atomizer in your SUV. On the dashboard."

"A what?"

"An e-cigarette."

"Oh, *that*. It was my sister's."

"Ms. Adagio," a woman called as she strolled into the store.

Raquel waved. "I'll be right there." To us, she added, "I have an appointment." She seemed eager to end the conversation.

Not so fast. I said, "The vape atomizer was your sister's?"

"Yeah, she's a bit of a slob. She tossed all her junk on my dash the other night when she was helping me. She—" Raquel's eyes widened. "For the love of Pete, Jenna, you don't think I poisoned Jake and Tito, do you? Why would I do such a thing?"

Bailey said, "Because if Jake died, you'd get a chance to bid for his Blue Mauritius stamp at an estate sale."

"Don't be ridiculous."

I said, "Gracie Goldsmith overheard you talking to another vendor at the festival about how much you wanted the stamp."

Bailey added, "Apparently, your father searched for it his whole life."

Raquel gripped the edge of the counter with her fingers. "Now, wait a second. I was nowhere near the cookies at the Santa party. I couldn't have poisoned Jake and Tito. I've been watching my weight." She patted her abdomen.

"Then why did you come?" Bailey countered.

Raquel balked. "To get ideas for recipes. For when I can eat them again."

"FYI," Bailey went on, "the poison wasn't in the cookies."

"It wasn't?" Raquel blinked.

Her mistake either meant she was telling the truth or adept at covering a lie.

I said, "I want to believe you, Raquel, but Flora and I were chatting about the night Jake's friend was killed, and she doesn't remember seeing you in the congregation." Raquel didn't need to know that Flora couldn't see long distances.

Tears pressed at the corners of Raquel's eyes. "I've got to meet with my customer."

I reached out to her. She retreated a step and mewled like a wounded animal.

I withdrew my hand and softened my tone, so as not to scare her. "Tell me the truth. Where were you that night?"

Her shoulders sagged. In a quavering voice, she said, "I . . . I went to Jake's. You're right. But I didn't kill his friend. I had to see the stamp again. All I wanted to do was hold it."

"She's lying," Lacy murmured.

"No, I'm not. I closed the shop at the festival early and I really did go there," Raquel continued. "I noticed the kitchen door was open, and adrenaline whooshed through me."

"You wanted to steal the stamp," Lacy said. "Admit it."

"No, I—" She looked from Lacy to me. "I stepped inside. No alarm went off. But then I heard men's voices in a room toward the front of the house. They were loud. One yodeled."

"What time was this?" I asked.

"Around eight thirty."

That must have been when Emmett heard my brother-in-law telling Geoffrey the joke.

"I peeked around the corner and glimpsed Jake in white shirt and jeans pacing the room—no jacket."

"It wasn't Jake," I said. "It was Geoffrey."

She blinked. "I didn't know that."

"Go on."

"I thought if I could locate his jacket—*Jake's* jacket—I could view the stamp."

"Steal it," Lacy said.

"I dashed upstairs, peeked into the bedroom on the left, and saw the jacket hanging on a chair. I tiptoed inside and pulled out the envelope, but then I heard footsteps and someone yelling, 'Cheese or Pepperoni?'"

That had to have been Jake, leaving for the store.

"I panicked. If I went downstairs, I was certain I'd get caught—"

"For stealing," Lacy cut in.

"So I darted out of the room and up the stairs to the third floor, which turned out to be an attic. It was dark, and I didn't switch on a light, but I could tell it was filled with toys and a rocking chair and an old wardrobe-style closet."

That fell in line with how Jake had described it.

"When I heard footsteps retreat and the house went silent, I decided to escape. But I couldn't. The lock on the attic door had jammed, trapping me inside. The attic window was painted shut, too. Distraught, I sat in the rocker and tried to figure out my next move." She licked her lips. "I must have lost track of time, because the next thing I knew I heard the shriek of sirens, and not long after that I heard policemen scouring the house. Their voices were harsh. Their radios crackled. If they caught me, I was toast."

"For stealing," Lacy inserted.

"Yes. For stealing," Raquel huffed. "So I ducked into the wardrobe. It was filled with fur coats."

"The police had to have searched the attic," I said.

"They did, hastily. They left the attic door ajar. I waited until they completed their investigation to run away. When I heard Geoffrey had been killed, I knew I couldn't tell anyone what I'd done." She thumped the counter. "You've got to believe me. Call Jake. Ask him about the wardrobe."

I punched in Jake's cell phone number. He answered after the first ring.

"What's up?" he asked. I heard Z.Z. talking in the background. He hushed her.

"What's in the wardrobe in your attic?"

"Fur coats. Why?"

I explained quickly. He whistled. I told him to give my best to Z.Z. and ended the call.

"You see?" Raquel sighed with relief. "I'm not a murderer."

"Do you still have Geoffrey's envelope?"

She paled. "Yes."

"Go to the precinct and bring the envelope and stamp. Tell them Jake will vouch for your description of the attic. I don't think he'll press charges."

"I will. Thank you." Her eyes brimmed with tears. "Please don't tell anyone until I do."

"I'll give you twenty-four hours."

"Twelve," Bailey said.

"Four," my sister and Lacy chimed.

"I'm going there right now," Raquel said. "After this appointment, I'll close up. Promise."

As Whitney, Lacy, Bailey, and I were leaving, Raquel's sister Maureen arrived, vape cigarette in hand. She switched it off with five quick clicks and stowed it in her tote.

"Hello, Jenna." She tugged down the hem of her snug black sweater so her midriff didn't show.

Before I could respond, Raquel nabbed her sister by the elbow and whisked her into the storage room, no doubt to explain her dilemma.

On the walk to the twin dolphins, a niggling suspicion about Maureen snaked its way into my psyche. Had she, like Raquel, known about their father's lifelong mission to find a Blue Mauritius stamp? She had seen Jake and Geoffrey discussing the stamps with her sister. Had she hoped she could do what I'd mistakenly theorized Raquel had wanted to do, kill Jake and obtain the Blue Mauritius at an estate sale? I recalled my initial meeting with her. She had been wearing an outfit similar to tonight's, one that a cat burglar would crave. Did she follow Raquel to Jake's and wait to see if her sister was successful? I pictured the rest of the scenario. When Raquel didn't reappear, Maureen headed inside. Geoffrey caught her sneaking in and accosted her. She reached for the first thing she could—the star. She stabbed him, but Geoffrey didn't go down. They tussled. She hoisted the brick and struck him in the head. That time, he toppled. Out of her mind with fear, unsure he would stay down, she strangled and bound him with the Christmas lights and fled. A few days later, feeling emboldened and once again believing she could acquire the stamp at an estate sale, she appeared at the Cookbook Nook dressed as Santa and poisoned Jake.

Chapter 23

After the ceremony, I dropped Whitney and Lacy at my father's house. I told them how great it was having them in town, we exchanged hugs, and I hurried home.

Rhett hadn't arrived yet, so, *call me crazy,* I made a quick tour around the outside of my cottage. No opened windows. No lurking strangers. No black wreaths.

When I slipped inside, Tigger glanced up from a pillow but didn't budge. The ball of yarn that Lacy had given him was completely unfurled. "Tired?" I said as I rubbed him under the chin. "Me, too." But not too tired to see my fiancé.

After removing my jacket and Keds, I padded barefoot to the kitchen still thinking about Maureen and the e-cigarettes and whether Cinnamon would want my head on a platter if I called her with my latest theory.

I opened a bottle of pinot grigio and poured some into two glasses. As I returned the corkscrew to the drawer, I spotted a stack of blank recipe cards and pulled out a few. When I'd worked at Taylor & Squibb, we often storyboarded our ad campaigns using notecards, filling them with graphic images or dialogue to visualize our media plan.

On the topmost card I jotted *Emmett Atwater: anger,* sketched a string of Christmas lights, and attached it to my refrigerator with a starfish-shaped magnet. On the next card I scrawled Olivia's name, as well as *inheritance* and *alibi verified yet?* I added a rough drawing of the quilt I'd liked at Home Sweet Home. On the third, I half-heartedly wrote *Adam Kittridge.* Was he a suspect merely because he wanted Jake's house and no other would do? Gran said he'd *studied* Jake. Perhaps that was a lie. What if they'd known each other when they were younger, and Adam held a long-standing grudge? He couldn't have poisoned Jake and Tito because he was in the city visiting his granddaughter, but maybe he'd persuaded Emmett to abet him. I made a note to ask Jake about Adam. I made an additional note to prompt Aunt Vera to do a third-party tarot reading so we could learn more about him. Though she'd be reluctant to do so, she would be the first to say niggling suspicions had to be put to rest.

On a fourth card, I scribbled *Raquel Adagio: money*. Then I drew a picture of the Blue Mauritius and added the question: *Innocent?* Cinnamon would have to make that determination, although Raquel's alibi did sound ridiculously naïve and, therefore, believable.

On a fifth card, I wrote *Maureen Adagio: same motive*. I added a different image: a black wreath. Was it significant that I'd attributed that to her? What was her alibi?

As I reached for my wine, my cell phone rang. "Please don't cancel, Rhett," I murmured, but it wasn't him. It was an unknown local number. I answered cautiously. "Hello?"

"Jenna, it's Raquel."

"Hey, what's up?" I glimpsed the card I'd written for her and a quiver of fear skittered up my neck. Did she have ESP or was she peeking through a break in my drapes?

"I saw you staring at my sister as you were leaving."

"No, I wasn't."

"Yes, you were, and I'm warning you, don't even go there."

Her tone was so accusatory that I eyed the front door to make sure I'd locked it. I had. "Go where?"

"Thinking the same thing you thought about me, that she killed Jake's friend so she could get her hands on Jake's stamp. We both know she was there the night he showed it to me, so she heard all about it, but I'm telling you, she didn't do it."

"She's working two jobs, Raquel. The Blue Mauritius would bring a hefty fee and pay off a lot of debts."

"She doesn't need money. She makes over three hundred thousand dollars a year."

I gasped. "Are you kidding? That's a lot of money."

"San Francisco socialites pay well to keep healthy."

"Even well-paid people can wrack up debt," I countered.

"She doesn't. Ever. She's a fanatic about paying cash."

"A dietician knows science," I said. "She could have figured out how to make nicotine poison."

"Ha! That's where you're wrong. Reenie failed chemistry. Oh, sure, she knows how to calorie count and assemble nutritious meals, but that's the extent of her expertise. Heck, she can't even make a decent salad dressing, and that's a simple ratio of two to one."

I had to admit Raquel was making a good case for her sister. Even so, I said, "She vapes. That's pure nicotine."

"When she became a dietician, she vowed to rid herself of all vices. Smoking was her biggest one. She tried the gum and the patch, but neither worked. Vaping cuts the edge, she says. She's given herself until January first to quit that. Please believe me, Jenna. Neither of us is guilty." Raquel clicked her tongue. "If it makes you feel better, I'll bring her along when I talk to the police and she'll give her alibi, too, okay? FYI, at the time of Geoffrey's death, she was tripping the light fandango with her main squeeze, a district court judge. He was an Eagle Scout. He won't lie."

A split second after I ended the call, Rhett knocked on the door. I whipped it open and threw my arms around him. My senses did a happy dance. How I adored the Pierre Cardin cologne he'd dabbed on his neck.

"Missed me, huh?" He offered a cockeyed smile.

"Like crazy."

He sauntered inside, looking handsome in a light blue sweater over blue jeans. "Did you have fun with your sister?"

"I did. This was a positive trip for both of us."

"No more sisterly rivalry?"

"I think we've outgrown it." I hoped I had.

I fetched our wine, and we sat on the couch holding hands, being content with silence. Tigger hopped up and wedged between us.

After a long while, Rhett said, "I think we should elope."

"As if. Aunt Vera would never allow it."

"We've both been married before."

"To the wrong people. And you eloped the first time. You're not getting out of an official ceremony. Let's do this right. Invite friends and family. We can make it small. Intimate. A day to remember." I didn't want to get married in a barn, but I wanted something magical. "Okay?"

He released my hand and ran his fingers along my collarbone. "Okay."

We kissed for a long time. Around midnight, he rose to his feet, prepared to head home. He stopped when he caught sight of the storyboard cards on the refrigerator. "Ahem." He raised an eyebrow. "Does Cinnamon know you're, as your father would say, *postulating*?"

Dad used the term to tease me.

"She does."

"And she approves?"

"My father wants me in on this. She consented to his wishes."

"Promise you'll be careful."

"Always."

After he left, I closed the door and a goofy smile graced my face. I couldn't wait until we would wake up in the same house every day. My future with him was going to be everything it wasn't with David, open and honest and loving.

• • •

Tuesday morning, I awoke to the sound of thunder, which surprised me. I didn't think the storm was due until tomorrow. Dressed in my pajamas, I opened the front door to make sure I'd heard right. I had. The sky was dark gray and filled with bloated clouds. Tigger huddled apprehensively by my ankle.

"Don't worry, boy," I cooed. "I won't let you get wet."

My aunt walked out of her house looking sunny in a yellow caftan. "Good morning, dear." She was carrying a stack of caftans as well as turbans.

"Good morning," I shouted over a second rumble. "What are you doing?"

"Errands. I'm like the postal worker. Rain or shine. I'm taking these to the dry cleaner before everyone is delivering their last-minute pre-holiday items, and then I'm off to the grocery. I have some serious baking to do." Aunt Vera liked to give home-baked goods to a number of volunteer organizations during the holidays.

She opened the trunk of her Mustang and started shoving her things inside. At the same time, one of the turbans fell to the ground, and the purse that she'd slung over her shoulder slid down her arm.

I jogged over, picked up the turban, and handed it to her. "Why don't I take everything in for you?"

"Don't be silly." She adjusted her purse strap. "I'm not feeble and I'm not a witch. I won't melt in rain." She shoved the errant turban in with the others and closed the trunk.

"Then let me come with you. I don't have a thing to do at the shop. The window display is done. Books were delivered yesterday. It would do me good to take a real day off."

Her forehead pinched with concern. "Why aren't you spending it with Rhett? You two haven't—"

"Don't worry. We're as happy as clams. He has a private fishing tour today, even if it rains." I knuckled her arm. "Come on, say yes."

"Fine. You'll drive." She pulled her car keys from her purse and dangled them in front of my face.

"Your car?" She never let anyone drive the Mustang.

"Yes. I have a terrible cramp in my calf from standing too long yesterday. I should rest it." She gave me a nudge. "Go. Get dressed."

Twenty minutes later, as we drove along Buena Vista Boulevard, a procession of antique cars was making its way into town.

"Aren't they handsome?" my aunt exclaimed. "I particularly like the 1936 Ford with its smooth lines. See it?"

"I'm partial to the Ford Town Sedan. Did you see the elves peeking out the windows?"

"Phooey. I missed that." She fluttered her hand. "Dear, stop! There's the dry cleaner."

I pulled in to a nearby parking spot and hopped out. My aunt took a bit longer than I to climb out of the car. When we had all of her clothes and turbans in tow, we headed into the facility.

Crystal Cove Cleaners was quite large. There were three counters to receive or deliver clothing. Moving racks of clothing soared into the upper rafters of the building. A full-time alterationist sat in a cubby behind a glass partition.

A sprite of a clerk in her uniform of blue blouse and black leggings approached Emmett Atwater, who was standing at the far right counter. She handed him a navy jacket covered in plastic wrap. "Here you are." To Adam Kittridge, who was standing at the far left counter removing items from a suede jacket, she said, "Be right with you, sir. No need to empty the pockets. I'll get it for you." She acknowledged my aunt with a nod. "Hi, Vera."

Seeing both men in one place made me flash on the cards that

I'd affixed to my refrigerator. Were either of them guilty of murder? They seemed so . . . *normal.* I set my aunt's clothing on the center counter.

"Hello, Emmett," my aunt said.

"Good day, ma'am." He was wearing a crisp white shirt, sea blue tie, and pressed navy pants. His hair was neatly combed. He offered money to the clerk, but she waved him off and pointed to the sign over her head: *One free cleaning if it's for an interview.*

"Why are you looking for a job, Emmett?" my aunt asked. "You're retired."

"I was, but I can't remain so. I'm . . ." He drew into himself as if protecting his core. "I'm bankrupt. Coughing up money for my mother's hospice and paying the legal bills after my wife's accidental death wiped out our savings. I can't make ends meet on what I receive from social security."

My aunt petted his shoulder. "I'm sorry to hear you're struggling."

"I tried to get a loan at the bank—"

"But they turned you down," I said.

"All the banks did." He licked his lips. "That's where I was last Wednesday night."

"Wait a sec." I held up a warning hand. "That was the night Jake's friend was killed. Did you lie to the police when you said you were at the movies? You told them you saw *It's a Wonderful Life.* You showed them a ticket."

"Yes."

"Yes, you *did* see the movie or *yes* you lied?"

"Both."

"Did you lie about seeing my brother-in-law return?"

He muttered, "Yes."

"To make someone other than you look guilty."

"I'm not proud of what I did."

I regarded him skeptically. "Which bank were you at? All of them would have been closed."

"I . . . I wasn't at a bank, exactly. I was arranging a loan from"— the color drained from his face—"a private lender."

"A loan shark."

"I had to. I had nowhere else to turn. You play the cards you're dealt. That's what my wife used to say." He pressed his lips together. "After I met with him, I went to see the movie. Did I ever identify with George Bailey. I was ready to kill myself. But when the movie ended and I thought about my brother and nephews and how my suicide might affect them, I changed my mind."

So he did have family.

A single tear slipped down his cheek. He swiped it with the back of his hand. "My wife would be heartbroken if she knew I'd lost everything. I tried to make do as long as I could, but I'm living too long."

"What about tapping the equity in your house?" I asked.

"We did a reverse mortgage. What a crock. It's all gone."

Aunt Vera said, "You need to tell the police everything, Emmett. Have the private lender vouch for you. Clear your name."

He bobbed his head.

"And then you need to nail this job," she added. "What is it?"

"Night manager at a grocery store. I was a manager before."

"Of a major corporation," she stated.

"Once a manager, always a manager. I'm old. Not a lot of jobs for folks my age." He offered a pained smile and left.

As the door swung closed, Adam Kittridge made a sorrowful *tsk*ing sound. "It's a shame to see a man humiliated, isn't it?" He smoothed the front of his black shirt, adjusted the collar of his jacket, and donned his leather gloves. "Such a shame."

My aunt nodded. "Yes, indeed."

The clerk pulled a green and pink envelope plus a few other items from the pockets of Adam's winter coat. She brushed lint and something sparkly off of everything and withdrew a photograph from the items. "Aww. Is this your granddaughter with your wife?" She shook the photo.

"Yes," he muttered.

"She looks exactly like her." The clerk displayed the photograph to my aunt and me. "Isn't she a darling girl?" Adam's granddaughter and wife were bundled in skiing outfits. "What are their names?"

"Amy and Amy."

"How sweet is that, naming her after her grandma." The clerk handed Adam a receipt for his clothing.

"Amy was my wife's nickname. Her real name was Amelia."

My heart snagged in my chest. Did he say *Amelia*? I peered at the photograph again. "She had beautiful eyes," I said. "Like Elizabeth Taylor's."

Adam nodded. "They were the light to her wonderful soul."

"How long were you married?" my aunt asked.

"Fifty-two years."

"That's a milestone."

I viewed the photograph again and noticed something new. Young Amy's jaw was strong and noble, like Jake's and his sister's. Was it a trick of light? "Where did you take this photo, Adam, at Lake Tahoe?"

"Squaw Valley. For Amy's fifth birthday." He retrieved the photograph. "That reminds me. I promised I'd buy her a snow globe."

"They have beautiful ones at Home Sweet Home," my aunt said.

"Good suggestion. See you around."

As he left, I remembered Crusibella's warning: *Beware of dark emanations.* Adam was dressed all in black—darker than dark.

To the clerk who was sorting through my aunt's items, I said, "Quick. Give us our chit." She did, and I tore to the Mustang.

Chapter 24

My aunt hustled after me and climbed into the passenger seat. "What's going on with you?"

I turned on the ignition and pulled into traffic. Adam, on foot, was moving in the direction of Flora's shop.

"Jenna, speak to me. You're perspiring."

"I could be wrong, but I think Adam's granddaughter might actually be Jake's granddaughter."

While searching for a parking spot, I told the story about Jake and Amelia and how she'd run out on him after he'd beaten up his sister's boyfriend. "What if Amelia was pregnant with Jake's child at the time?"

"Why wouldn't she tell him?"

"Because she didn't want her child to have a felon as a father."

"Except Jake didn't go to prison for assault," my aunt reasoned.

"She didn't know that, and by the time she had resettled, in San Francisco I imagine, she'd met a man who was well established with a bright future ahead of him."

"Adam Kittridge." My aunt nodded. "Yes, that makes sense and would justify why she kept silent all that time, if that's what she did."

"What if Adam found out the truth recently? It's possible his wife revealed something on her deathbed. A dying person might confess an age-old secret. What if he meant to kill Jake to keep that secret?" I drummed the steering wheel. "Did you hear what Adam said at the cleaner's as Emmett was leaving? He said it was a shame to see a man humiliated. What if he didn't mean Emmett? What if he meant himself?"

"Questioning the paternity of his child might explain the 23 and Me search he was doing."

"How do you know he was doing a search?"

My aunt swiveled in the passenger seat. "The envelope that the clerk pulled from Adam's jacket had the company's distinctive pink-and-green logo on it. I noticed because I've been interested in learning more about our ancestors."

"That gives Adam a clear motive to want Jake dead. If he were eliminated, there would be no evidence. Who would think to do a

DNA test? Adam definitely could have mistaken Geoffrey for Jake, since they'd never —" I gasped. "The glitter."

"What about it?"

"The star the killer used on Geoffrey was covered with glitter. Raquel said glitter is everywhere in her house, and Tina said glitter sticks to everything. Glitter was clinging to the items the clerk removed from Adam's pockets at the cleaner's. If the police could match the star's glitter to what might have stuck to his things —"

"Have the police asked him his alibi for that night?"

"Probably not. He has no overt reason to be a person of interest. But, curiously, he told me it the other day."

"Why?"

"I asked him a question. One thing led to another."

"You take too many risks."

"I didn't ask him about his alibi. Keller told him about a rumor and . . ." I flapped a hand. "It'll take too long to explain. Looking back at that encounter, however, something had sounded off about it, like he'd rehearsed it. Why did he feel the need to tell me?" A notion hit me. "Aha! I get why he suggested Gran go to the police with evidence about Raquel."

"I'm not following."

"Gran was chatting with Adam and told him I had a *sensibility* about previous murders. He suggested she tell the police about Raquel wanting the stamp to divert suspicion from himself."

My aunt shook her head, still not comprehending. "Wasn't he out of town when Jake was poisoned?"

"He could have lied about that."

On the opposite side of the street, a green MG, circa the late 1930s, was pulling out of a parking spot. I made a U-turn and veered into it. Thunder rumbled overhead. Mild rain splattered the windshield — not enough to scare a bird, but enough to put everyone in town on alert for the storm that was about to come.

"Aunt Vera, call the police while I delay Adam."

"Jenna, sweetheart" — she reached over the console and gripped my wrist — "please don't put yourself in harm's way. Let's call the police together. Adam will be shopping for a bit. A policeman will arrive before he leaves."

I pulled free. "What if he changes his mind and doesn't make a purchase? Or he realizes we saw those items from his jacket and, knowing we're on to him, decides to kidnap his granddaughter and disappear?"

"Jenna—"

"I've got to keep him in sight until the police show up."

"Dear, if you go in, he'll figure out you followed him."

"I'll come up with a good cover story. Promise."

Aunt Vera released me, knowing there was no stopping me.

I slipped inside Home Sweet Home and spotted Adam where I'd expected, at the rear of the store near the snow globes. Drawing in a deep calming breath—there were plenty of people browsing the holiday wares who could help if Adam chose to run—I ambled in that direction. I passed Flora, whose cheeks were glowing with excitement from the activity in the shop, and weaved between a fake Christmas tree decked out with miniature antique vehicles and another dripping with crystal icicles. I sidled around the display of Olivia's quilts and a baker's rack filled with a number of vintage cast-iron nutcrackers.

"That's beautiful," I said to Adam as I drew near, indicating the globe he was holding that featured a little girl kneeling in a red dress. She was blowing snow off her hands. "She reminds me of your granddaughter."

Adam's eyes narrowed. "What are you doing here?"

Better to get out in front of this one, I thought, and forced a genial laugh. "Before you think I'm following you, I'm not. You inspired me to buy a snow globe for our display window. I'm looking for an antique car one. Flora must have ordered a few. You know about the antique car parade that will occur the day before Christmas, don't you?" To convince him of my quest, I began to inspect the snow globes. "We have lots of festivals in Crystal Cove, as you must be learning by now. You went to the a cappella festival last Wednesday night. You listened to my niece sing."

"And stomp. What was the song they sang?" He snapped his fingers. "Oh, right. 'Same Old Lang Syne.' One of my wife's favorites."

The notion that had bothered me before ticked at the back of my mind. His answers sounded pat and practiced. I recalled how Raquel had recited hymns she'd supposedly heard the choir sing at church. Was Adam doing the same? He could have gleaned the information from a festival program, or he could have heard others chatting about Lacy's group stomping to the Fogelberg song. It had been unique.

Testing him, I said, "The clogs and Irish outfits Nothing but Treble wore were really something, weren't they?"

"Yes, they were."

I cheered inwardly. He didn't have a clue that they'd worn black getups and boots. His alibi was bogus.

He set down the snow globe with the girl and picked up a second one filled with penguins. "This is perfect. Amy loves these little guys."

"Because she wants to protect them from global warming?"

"Good memory."

I picked up a globe similar to the one I'd previously purchased with the snow-dusted classic truck inside. "What do you think of this one?"

"Nice." Adam reached into his pocket, pulled out an orange packet of gum, and popped a piece into his mouth.

My insides lurched. It was Nicorette, a nicotine-based gum, typically chewed to help a person stop smoking. Adam had told me that he'd wanted to become an inventor until his father steered him in another direction. Most likely, an inventor couldn't extract nicotine from gum, but he might know how to do so with cigarettes.

"I'd better get going," he said, pivoting to leave.

"Adam, wait. Do you have a picture of you and your granddaughter when you went for ice cream in the city? You said you took selfies. I'd love to see the two of you together."

He hesitated. "I accidentally erased it."

Exactly as I'd expected. He'd lied about going to the city that day. He must have been the ruddy-cheeked Santa who helped Tina distribute the punch.

"What's going on, Jenna?" His voice could have cut diamonds. "Why the twenty questions?"

Flora scurried to us. "Is everything okay?" She must have sensed conflict because she was all smiles — the ultimate peacemaker. "Adam, don't tell me you want the snow globe Jenna's holding. I have more."

He threw her a caustic look. She recoiled, clearly thrown by his aggression.

Adam turned back to me. "Why don't you tell Flora what you're doing?"

"I'm admiring a snow globe." I jiggled it. Snow billowed up and fell to the surface.

"No, you're grilling me." He aimed a finger at me. "As if you're trying to solve a crime."

I flashed on the night I'd run into Adam and Gran at the festival. Had he worried that I was close to solving Geoffrey's murder and tried to scare me off by hanging a black wreath on my door?

Adam heaved the penguin snow globe into his other hand like a pitcher trying to get the feel of a baseball. Would he bash me upside the head like he had Geoffrey? I held a globe, as well, but I was no baseball player. Frisbee was my forte.

I glanced at the door of the shop. No police yet. Dang. I set the snow globe down and seized a cast-iron nutcracker from a shelf. When playing baseball, carry a bat.

"What do you think you know, Jenna?" Adam asked with silver-tongued ease.

"I don't think you went to San Francisco the day we had the Santa party. I think you came dressed as Santa, and you poisoned Jake and Tito."

"Oh, dear," Flora sputtered.

"I also think you lied about being at the festival the night Geoffrey died. My niece and her group were wearing black jeans and boots; no clogs, no Irish costumes."

Adam shifted feet.

"I believe you went to Jake Chapman's house with the intention of killing Jake but you mistakenly killed his friend. When you realized your error, you tried again. At the party. You created a concoction of nicotine and, using a syringe, inserted the poison into the shot glasses. You took the tray of drinks from my assistant and gave one to Tito as well as Jake."

"That's ridiculous."

"Tina is talking to the police sketch artist right now," I lied. "I'm sure your eyes will give you away." I held his gaze. My ability to remain neutral had made me a good negotiator at Taylor & Squibb.

Adam squared his shoulders. "Honestly, Jenna, why would I want Jake dead? Purchasing a house in probate can be messy."

"Out of rage. Your son isn't yours, is he? He's Jake's son. That's why you initiated a 23 and Me search."

"Heavens." Flora placed a hand on her chest.

"Your granddaughter has many of the same physical traits as Jake," I went on. "Did your wife confess as she lay dying? Did you feel humiliated?"

Adams eyes grew steely, which I took as a *yes*.

"Did your wife threaten to tell him? Did you intend to kill Jake so you could erase all trace of him, and then, to gloat, occupy his home?"

Adam growled and hurled the penguin-themed snow globe at me.

In the nick of time, I raised the nutcracker. The snow globe smacked into it and fell into a basket of crystal ornaments. My hand vibrated from the impact.

Customers gasped.

Adam turned to flee.

"Jenna!" Flora yelled.

She threw me one end of a quilt. I dropped the nutcracker and caught a corner. Together we raced after Adam, hurled the quilt over him, and yanked him to the floor. He struggled to get free. We pinned the quilt with our knees.

Seconds later, my aunt appeared with Cinnamon and Deputy Appleby. The crowd backed away.

"What's going on, Jenna?" Cinnamon demanded.

Adam's head shot free of the quilt. "Don't believe a thing she says, Chief Pritchett."

Cinnamon gave me the evil eye.

I didn't flinch. I was getting accustomed to her ominous looks. Quickly, I explained my theory. "Check his pockets. You'll find the 23 and Me letter. And now, if it's all right with you, I'd like to touch base with Dad and bring him up to speed."

Chapter 25

Dad and Lola arrived home around six in the morning on Christmas Eve. He checked in with me first thing to make sure we were still celebrating that evening. I responded with a resounding *yes*. Aunt Vera was opening her home to the family as well as Jake, our chief of police, her fiancé, and a few others.

"I'm making Yorkshire pudding," I said.

"You?"

"One of the easiest dishes in the world. I won't fail." At least I hoped I wouldn't.

At seven that evening, Dad and Lola arrived carrying flowers for my aunt, two bottles of expensive wine, and tokens from their trip. My particular favorite was a kitchen magnet of the Danube.

Aunt Vera had decorated her living room to the hilt: a beautiful blue-themed tree, a crèche on a bed of angel hair, and numerous snow globes. A pair of old-fashioned stockings with my aunt and father's knitted names hung from the mantel over the fireplace. An array of nutcrackers that she had collected over the years adorned the mantel, as well. On the coffee table sat a cheese display that was designed like a wreath. A basket of crackers accompanied it.

I was the official wine pourer.

After filling my father's glass with chardonnay, he said, "How are you?"

Before I could reach him by telephone to tell him about the fracas with Adam Kittridge, Bailey had gotten hold of her mother. As a result, Dad had barraged me with emails: *who, what, when,* and *was I all right?*

"Cinnamon is giving me the cold shoulder."

"She'll thaw."

I glanced at her standing across the living room, looking quite chic in a winter white sheath as she chatted with Deputy Appleby and her fiancé, Bucky. My comment that she looked nice had fallen on deaf ears. "In the next millennia," I quipped.

My father scoffed. "You helped her solve the case."

"She doesn't want me to get involved in another investigation." Four emails from her had echoed that refrain. "Between you and me, I think she's worried I'm vying for her job."

He roared with laughter.

Cinnamon turned and gave us a searing look, as if she knew what we were talking about. Dad, totally out of character, gave her the shaka sign—three middle fingers folded down against the palm, thumb and pinky extended. In Hawaii it meant *Be cool.*

"So fill me in." My father slipped an arm around my waist and steered me to the French doors leading to the lanai. The night was chilly, so we weren't eating outside, but the doors were slightly ajar to allow in fresh air. The sound of waves hitting the shore soothed me. "Give me a quick recap. How is Jake doing? He looks good." He jerked his head to the right.

Jake was standing by the fireplace with his sister Olivia. He wore his standard leather jacket, white shirt, and jeans. His hair was combed, his smile relaxed. Olivia seemed at ease, too. She was wearing a cream silk blouse tucked into a red pencil skirt, and her hairdo was new and stylish. She was sipping a cup of tea and nodding at something Jake was saying.

"Jake is the ultimate Santa Claus," I said. "He's helping his sister get on her feet by paying rent on a shop in town where she can sell her wares. Also, he heard what happened to Emmett, and despite his dispute with the guy, has offered to loan him money so Emmett won't be obligated to a private lender."

Dad smiled. "Grandpa taught him well, didn't he?"

I nodded. I hadn't known my grandfather. He'd died before I was born, but the stories I'd heard from so many made him out to be a saint. "Jake reached out to his son," I said, "but he hasn't heard from him."

"I imagine this past week has been quite a shock to the boy."

"He's not a boy. He's in his fifties."

"Even so, learning that the man who raised you was capable of murder and discovering you had a father you'd never known has to be shocking. He'll come around."

"Jake isn't so sure."

"Is Adam Kittridge in prison?"

"Pending bail. Needless to say, Gran was surprised beyond compare."

Rhett strode through the front door and raised both hands, each holding a bottle of wine. "I come bearing gifts."

My aunt, who was decked out in a green caftan and copious strands of red beads, took the wine. Rhett hung up his pea coat on a rack in the foyer, adjusted the hem and sleeves of his cable-knit sweater, and followed my aunt into the kitchen. He blew me a kiss over his shoulder before disappearing.

"Ahem," my father said. "As for Rhett, there's something you haven't told me."

"I'm sure Bailey has."

"What did I do?" she said, stealing into our conversation. Tito had yet to arrive. She had been helping my aunt make biscuits. She wore a reindeer-themed apron over her red dress.

"Told my father about Rhett and me."

"No, I didn't."

"Yeah, you did." I shot a finger at her. "I can see you blushing even under a layer of flour dust."

"I told my mother. She was supposed to keep it quiet."

"Ha! I knew it." I broke free of my father and glowered at my pal. "Did you also tell her you're pregnant?"

"What?" Lola burst from the kitchen, wiping her hands on an apron that matched her daughter's. "Bailey Bird Martinez, how could you not have told me?"

"I told Cary." Bailey pointed at my father.

He grinned. "Apparently I can keep a secret when asked to." He joined his beloved and gave her a peck on the cheek.

Lola pushed him away, looped her arm through her daughter's, and drew her to one side. I overheard the initial questions: *When is the due date? What's the sex? Have you picked a name?* Mom stuff. Soon, I hoped I would get the pertinent information, too. For a chatterbox, Bailey was keeping the details close to the vest.

Dad turned to me. "Back to you and Rhett."

"Yes, we're engaged. We have not set a date. We don't know where we're getting married. But we're going to start looking for somewhere in town to live. That's as much as I know."

Rhett stole up behind me and kissed me on the neck. "I know a little bit more than that."

I whirled around. "What are you talking about?"

His eyes gleamed with impishness. "I went looking with Z.Z. today and I found a house. It's a one-story ranch house with a bit of a view. Easy access to the beach. I think it's perfect, but you're the boss, so I need your approval. We'll go the day after Christmas to see it, okay? In the meantime, did you know Z.Z. found your brother-in-law a patent attorney to work with in Los Angeles? He's the son of one of her college friends. Young guy. Eager for new clients."

"That's great."

"Spencer is stoked."

Clang, clang.

Katie appeared in the archway leading to the dining room carrying a cowbell and baton. She looked adorable in a pretty floral dress sans chef's coat and toque. "Dinner is served!" She clanged the bell again.

Aunt Vera had closed the café for the night and had asked Katie and three of her staff plus her fiancé, Keller, to fix our dinner — other than the Yorkshire pudding — after which they'd all join us for the meal. One big happy family. I was looking forward to Keller's eggnog ice cream with churro-style cookies.

After making my Yorkshire pudding — Katie said she'd set it in the oven at the appropriate time — I'd helped my aunt set the table. A trio of candles surrounded by green foliage glimmered as the centerpiece. Gold-rimmed charger plates, topped with red-and-gold napkins and bordered by my aunt's favorite sterling silver, sat on a tablecloth featuring the Twelve Days of Christmas. Baccarat crystal wineglasses and water glasses finished each place setting.

As we were taking our places at the table, Tito appeared in the archway. "Ahem, excuse me. I have an announcement."

"We know you're pregnant," Dad said wryly. "Come. Sit."

"Sorry, sir. That isn't my announcement. We have, um, a few extras guests."

"The more the merrier," my aunt said. "Bring them in."

Tito motioned for the people to come in.

A gaunt middle-aged man in a tweed jacket, white shirt, and jeans moved into the archway alongside Tito. He was holding the hand of a little girl with eyes like Elizabeth Taylor's.

Recipes

Brownies (Gluten-free)
Brownie Frosting
Brownie Reindeer
Brownie Christmas Trees
Cheese Wreath
Christmas Wreath with Pecans
Crystal Cove Succotash
Jenna's Breakfast Casserole
Strawberry Santas
Popovers with Parmesan (Gluten-free)
Squash Apple Soup
White Chocolate Crackle
Yorkshire Pudding
Yule Log
Yule Log (Gluten-free)

Brownies (Gluten-free)

From Katie:

This is the best brownie recipe I've ever concocted, and it's gluten-free!! So chocolate-y, so moist. By the way, "whey" powder helps keep gluten-free baked goods stay moist longer. Also, check out the recipes following this for Brownie Reindeer and Brownie Christmas Trees. I saw pictures on Pinterest and knew I had to serve these to children who visited during the holidays.

(Makes 12–16)

1/2 cup unsalted butter plus 1 tablespoon
1-1/2 cups sugar
1/2 teaspoon salt
1 teaspoon gluten-free vanilla extract
3/4 cup Dutch-process cocoa (I like Penzey's)
3 large eggs
3/4 cup gluten-free flour (I like a combo of sweet rice flour and tapioca flour)
1 teaspoon baking powder
1 teaspoon whey powder
1 cup chocolate chips

Preheat oven to 350 degrees F, rub a round 9-inch pan with one tablespoon of butter and then line with parchment paper.

In a medium saucepan, melt the 1/2 cup unsalted butter over medium-high heat. Add sugar and salt and stir until the mixture lightens in color. A pale yellow is fine.

Transfer the mixture to a large mixing bowl. Blend in the vanilla and cocoa, and then add the eggs. Mix until shiny, about 1 minute.

Add in the flour, baking powder, and whey powder. Stir in the chocolate chips.

Pour the batter into the prepared pan. Make sure you spread it to the edges.

Bake for 32–36 minutes until the top of the brownie is set. Insert a toothpick in the center to make sure it's cooked through. A tad of chocolate at the tip is fine.

Remove from oven and cool 15–20 minutes before cutting. For the prettiest brownies, wait until they are completely cool, then slice. That way, no crumbs!

Once cool, cover any that you're not eating tightly with plastic wrap or store in sealed glass containers.

Brownie Frosting

(Yield: 1 to 1-1/2 cups)

6 tablespoons butter, softened
2-2/3 cups confectioners' sugar
1/2 cup baking cocoa
1 teaspoon vanilla extract
1/8 to 1/4 cup milk

In a large bowl, cream butter and confectioners' sugar until combined. Beat in cocoa and vanilla. Add 1/8 cup milk, adding more if necessary, until the frosting achieves spreading consistency. If you add too much milk at first, it will be runny, so remember, *less is more.*

Reindeer Brownies

Use the brownie recipe, but bake it in two 9-inch cake pans so they are ultra thin for 10–15 minutes.

(Makes 12–16)

For decoration:

Peppermint candy canes with hooked tops
Brownie frosting (see recipe above)
Tootsie Rolls
Small marshmallows
Tiny chocolate chips
Vanilla wafers (not gluten-free; see below)
Red M&Ms

How to construct:

Cut brownies into wedge shapes (6–8 per cake pan). Set on decorative flat plate.

Carefully insert candy canes for antlers at the top of the long edge of the wedge.

Paint the brownie with a thin coat of brownie frosting.

Cut Tootsie Roll on a diagonal. Set a Tootsie Roll on each side of long edge of the wedge for ears.

Snip marshmallows in half and set in the upper middle of the brownie face. Using a teensy amount of icing, affix tiny chocolate chips to the marshmallows for eyes.

Add a vanilla wafer to the pointed end of the wedge. Then, using a small amount of icing, affix a red M&M on top for the nose. (Note: Vanilla wafers are not gluten-free. If you need to eat gluten-free – the brownie recipe *is* – then omit this cookie and only use the M&M.)

Brownie Christmas Trees

Use the brownie recipe, but bake it in two 9-inch cake pans so they are ultra thin for 10–15 minutes.

(Makes 12–16)

For decoration:

Peppermint sticks cut to 2-inch length
Green gel icing or green frosting
White or silver ball-shaped sprinkles
Sno-Caps candies

How to construct:

Cut brownies into wedge shapes (6–8 per cake pan). Set on decorative flat platter.

Carefully insert peppermint stick for tree trunk.

Ice with green swirls, on an angle. (If using green frosting instead of gel, you might want to use a piping tool fitted with a very small tip.)

Sprinkle with white or silver sprinkles.

Using gel or icing, "glue" one Sno-Caps candy at top of tree for the star.

Cheese Wreath

From Aunt Vera:

I love serving appetizers to my guests. During the holidays, a party made up entirely of appetizers is often preferred. Enjoy the ease of this beautiful wreath.

(Serves 12–16)

8–12 sprigs rosemary, rinsed
3 different cheeses cubed, about 2–3 cups
8–12 green and black olives
2 strips of red bell pepper
Crackers

On a pretty platter (square or round), lay out the rosemary in a circular fashion.

Leaving the center empty, create a ring of cheese, standing the cubes on top of each other.

Balance the olives at various intervals on the cheese, like ornaments.

At the top or bottom of your wreath, add the 2 strips of red bell pepper to resemble a bow.

Christmas Wreath with Pecans

From Katie:

I love this bread. It's so soft and it's beautiful to serve. You might want to use a piping tool to add the icing. It's a lovely bread all by itself, but if you serve it warm, your guests might like it served with butter or even apple butter. My one tip: use the parchment paper to roll out the dough, and use a sizeable cutting board or even do the rolling directly on a clean counter so you get the most evenly shaped rectangle you can muster.

(Serves 12–16)

Bread:

2 packages (1/4 ounce each) active dry yeast
1-1/2 cups warm water (110° to 115°)
6 tablespoons butter, melted
1/3 cup nonfat dry milk powder
1/4 cup light brown sugar, packed
1 egg
3/4 teaspoon salt
4-1/2 to 5-1/2 cups all-purpose flour, divided
2 tablespoons butter, melted
1/2 cup chopped pecans, if desired
1-1/2 teaspoons ground cinnamon

Icing:

1 cup powdered sugar
1 tablespoon water
1/4 teaspoon vanilla extract

In a large bowl, dissolve yeast in warm water (you can use a candy thermometer to gauge the temperature). When the yeast is frothy, add the melted butter, milk powder, brown sugar, egg, salt, and 4 cups of flour. Beat on medium speed for 3 minutes. Stir in enough remaining flour to form a soft but not "runny" dough. If it's too runny, you won't be able to knead it.

Turn onto a well-floured surface; knead until smooth and elastic, about 6–8 minutes.

Place in a greased bowl, turning once to grease the top. Cover and let rise in a warm place until doubled, about 1 hour.

Punch down dough. On a lightly floured surface, roll the dough into a large rectangle, 18 inches x 12 inches. I like to cover the dough with parchment paper so the rolling pin doesn't stick. The rectangle might not be perfectly even, but that's okay. Remove the parchment paper. Brush dough with melted butter. Sprinkle with chopped pecans (if desired) and cinnamon, leaving 1/2 inch of edge free.

Roll up jelly roll style, starting with the long side. Pinch the seam to seal.

Again, I like to use parchment paper to pick up the roll so it doesn't smoosh. Place the roll, seam-side down, on a greased baking sheet. Form a ring and pinch the ends together. (Tip: if you want, you can reserve a small portion of dough and decorate this section with a dough "bow" before serving.) Using kitchen shears, snip the dough from the outside edge to about two-thirds of the way toward the center of ring. Yes, the whole dough, not just the top. Do this every inch. Then separate the sections slightly and twist the dough to let the filling show. It's amazing how elastic dough is!

Cover and let rise until doubled, about 45 minutes.

Bake at 375° for 20–25 minutes. The ring should be golden brown. Remove from oven.

To make the icing, combine powdered sugar, water, and extract. Drizzle over the warm bread. Serve warm.

Crystal Cove Succotash

From Katie:

You need an army of sous chefs to make fresh lima beans. Luckily, I have a very talented crew. For those of you making this at home, it's okay to use frozen lima beans. Because of the lovely green and red colors in this recipe, it makes a perfect side dish for the Christmas table.

(Serves 2–4)

2 tablespoons butter
2 tablespoons white wine
1 bunch scallions, white and green parts thinly sliced
1 teaspoon salt
1 teaspoon fresh ground pepper
1 cup fresh corn (cut off the cob)
1 cup fresh cooked lima beans (see below)
1 cup heavy cream
2-1/2 cups shredded white chicken breast, cooked (about 2 large chicken breasts)
1 tomato, chopped fine

In a large skillet, melt the butter over medium heat. Add the wine and then the scallions. Season with salt and pepper and cook, stirring, for 2 minutes.

Add the corn, lima beans, and cream, and bring to a boil. Stir in the chicken and cook, stirring occasionally, until the sauce is thickened, 4–5 minutes. Stir in the tomato right before serving.

To pre-cook chicken breast:

Wrap chicken breast in foil and bake at 300 degrees F for 45 minutes. Remove from oven and let cool. Shred when cool enough to pull apart.

To Make Fresh Lima Beans:

2 pounds baby lima beans, fresh in the shell
1/2 teaspoon salt

Shell the beans, pulling the string, and wash thoroughly. Soak overnight in enough water to cover by an inch.

When ready, put 2 cups of fresh water and salt into a medium saucepan and add the beans. Cook the beans until tender, about 30 minutes. Drain the liquid.

Jenna's Breakfast Casserole

From Jenna:

This casserole is so easy that even I can make it, and the beautiful colors of red and green shine through, making it a perfect holiday breakfast or brunch item. Enjoy.

(Serves 8–12)

3 yellow potatoes, shredded
6 green onions, shredded
3 zucchinis, shredded
1 large tomato, chopped
1/2 large Vidalia onion, chopped
12 eggs
1-1/2 cups grated Cheddar cheese
1/4 cup grated Parmesan cheese

Preheat oven to 350 degrees F and oil a 9 x 13 pan.

Using a food processor, shred the potatoes then set them in a small bowl and douse them with boiling hot water for about 5–6 minutes to partially cook. Pour off water and arrange the potatoes in pre-oiled pan.

Using a food processor, shred the green onions and zucchini.

Spread them on top of the potatoes and top with chopped tomato and chopped Vidalia onion.

In a large bowl, beat the eggs and stir in the Cheddar. Pour over the veggies. If necessary, with clean hands or a spoon, mix the eggs, potatoes, and vegetables so everything is incorporated.

Top with Parmesan cheese.

Bake for 40–50 minutes. You want the potatoes tender.

Strawberry Santas

From Jenna:

I love these adorable desserts. They're like little bites of crust-less strawberry cheesecake. Perfect for kids' parties as well as adult parties. I saw it on Pinterest, thanks to Katie, who told me she gets lots of ideas for new foods on that site. Enjoy.

(Makes 12–20)

12–20 strawberries
Cream cheese frosting (recipe below)
24–40 miniature chocolate chips

Wash and slice off bottoms of strawberries to create Santa's "hat and body." (Proportion about 1/3 for hat and 2/3 for body.)

Set the largest side of the body on plate. Using a piping tube with a star tip, swirl frosting on top to create Santa's face and beard.

Put strawberry "hat" on and add a touch of frosting for the hat's "pompom."

Insert two chocolate chips into the frosting "face" for eyes.

Cream Cheese Frosting:

1 cup powdered sugar
1/4 cup butter, softened
1 8-ounce package of cream cheese, softened
1 teaspoon vanilla extract

Put all the ingredients into a medium bowl. Blend until smooth.

Note: leftovers may be placed in sealed container and refrigerated. Bring to room temperature to reuse.

Popovers with Parmesan (Gluten-free)

From Katie:

For those who have to follow a gluten-free diet, these are a great substitute for Yorkshire pudding. They pop up nicely. You will need a popover pan.

(Serves 6)

3 tablespoons unsalted butter, melted and divided
1/4 cup milk
1/4 cup water
2 large eggs
3/4 cup plus 2 tablespoons gluten-free flour
1/2 teaspoon xanthan gum
1/2 teaspoon salt
1/2 teaspoon ground black pepper
1/2 teaspoon garlic salt
1/2 teaspoon dried rosemary
1/2 teaspoon dried thyme
1/4 cup finely grated Parmesan cheese

Preheat oven to 375 degrees F.

Divide 2 tablespoons melted butter among the wells of a 6-cup popover pan, brushing each to coat. Place popover pan in oven to preheat.

In a large bowl, whisk together the milk, water, and eggs. Gradually whisk in remaining tablespoon melted butter.

Add the gluten-free flour, xanthan gum, salt, pepper, garlic salt, rosemary, and thyme. Whisk until batter is well combined. Carefully remove hot popover pan from the oven and ladle the batter evenly among the popover cups (they'll be about half full).

Sprinkle each with Parmesan cheese.

Bake for 25 minutes until puffed and golden. Do not open the oven during baking time. Run a knife around each popover and remove popover from pan. Using a small knife, make a small slit in the side of each popover to release the steam. Serve immediately.

Squash Apple Soup

From Katie:

If Jenna hadn't hired me to run the Nook Café, I might have become a soup chef. I adore soup and I love making it. There's something about the savory aromas and the variety of textures that call to me. This soup is perfect for a winter's night. The bacon adds exactly the right zing.

(Serves 4)

8 slices bacon, cut into 1/4-inch strips
2-1/2 pounds butternut squash, peeled, seeded, and cut into 1/2-inch cubes
1/2 Vidalia or sweet onion, finely diced
1 Granny Smith apple, peeled, cored, and diced
1-1/2 tablespoons finely chopped fresh thyme or rosemary
1/2 teaspoon white pepper
4 cups chicken broth
2 green onions, green ends only, diced

In a large stockpot set over medium heat, cook the bacon, stirring occasionally, until crisp and golden, 8–10 minutes. Transfer the bacon to a plate lined with paper towels.

Increase the heat to medium high. Add the butternut squash to the pot with the bacon fat and cook until lightly browned, 8–10 minutes. Don't stir too often or it won't brown. You *want* it to brown. FYI, the bottom of the pot will start turning brown. This is okay.

Stir in the diced onion, apple, thyme (or rosemary), and white pepper, and cook for 4 minutes.

Add the broth, scraping up the browned bits in the pot with a spoon. Bring to a boil over high heat and then reduce the heat to simmer, and cook until the squash, onions, and apples are very soft, 8–10 minutes. Remove from the heat and let cool about 5 minutes.

Add *half* the bacon to the soup and stir.

Purée the soup using a standing blender or immersion blender. You'll have to do small batches if you use the standing blender.

Pour the soup into bowls and garnish each serving with remaining bacon and diced green onions.

White Chocolate Crackle

From Jenna:

I remember having this crackle at a Christmas party when I worked at Taylor & Squibb. One of the assistants made it and gave me the recipe. Until now, I'd never felt comfortable making it, but I'm getting pretty good with candy recipes. I'm a demon with fudge. This doesn't require a candy thermometer, just good eyeballing to know when something is ready to go. Enjoy!

(Serves 12–24)

40 salted saltine crackers (or gluten-free matzo, if you need to eat gluten-free)
1 cup unsalted butter
1 cup packed dark brown sugar
2 4-ounce bars white chocolate, chopped into bits
Toppings including pistachio pieces and dried cranberries

Preheat oven to 350 degrees F. Line a baking sheet with foil. Spread the crackers on the foil in a single layer and fold up the edges of the foil to contain the crackers.

In a small saucepan, melt the butter and brown sugar over medium heat. Simmer for 5 minutes. Stir constantly. It will turn a nice brown toffee color. Pour the mixture over the crackers and spread to cover.

Bake the cracker and toffee mixture in the oven for 5 minutes. Remove from oven and sprinkle the chopped white chocolate over the toffee.

Let stand for 2–4 minutes until the white chocolate melts, then spread evenly over the toffee.

Top with chopped pistachio pieces and dried cranberries for a nice Christmas color.

Chill in the refrigerator for about 2 hours. Peel away the foil and break the crackle into pieces.

Store in an airtight container and refrigerate for up to 2 weeks. This may be frozen for 1 month if you like to prepare ahead. Makes great gifts wrapped in decorative cellophane bags.

Yorkshire Pudding

From Jenna:

Even I can make this and never fail. Four ingredients. Perfect! My grandmother handed down the recipe to my mother. I love Yorkshire pudding by itself, but it's especially wonderful topped with butter and served with roast beef. Enjoy! PS: If you want to make a gluten-free version, substitute gluten-free flour for the flour. It won't "puff" like regular Yorkshire pudding, it'll be flat, but it's quite tasty.

(Serves 4–6)

4 tablespoons meat fat (from roast) or canola oil
1 cup milk
1 cup flour
4 eggs

Preheat oven to 450 degrees F.

Rub meat fat or canola oil on the bottom and sides of 9 x 13 pan. Make sure you coat the corners.

In a medium bowl, mix milk, flour, and eggs with blender.

Pour mixture into the 9 x 13 pan.

Bake at 450 degrees for 15 minutes. Turn heat down to 350 degrees. Bake 10–15 minutes longer, until golden brown. The pudding will rise up the sides of the pan.

Serve hot with butter.

Yule Log

From Katie:

This Yule log is intense to make. It's not for the faint of heart, but it's delicious. I'm going to provide a gluten-free version as well, so check out the recipe below. If you're feeling very creative, make meringue mushrooms to decorate the log.

(Serves 8–12)

Chocolate Jelly Roll:

3-1/2 ounces dark semi-sweet chocolate
4 egg yolks
3/4 cup sugar
1 teaspoon vanilla
3/4 cup flour
1 teaspoon baking powder
1/2 teaspoon salt
up to 1/2 cup boiling water
4 egg whites
3 tablespoons powdered sugar

Whipped Cream Filling:

1 pint heavy whipping cream
3 teaspoons sugar

Chocolate Butter Cream Frosting:

1/2 cup butter
1/2 cup cocoa powder
dash salt
4 tablespoons cream
4 cups powdered sugar
1 ounce espresso

Chocolate Jelly Roll:

Preheat oven to 375 degrees F. Make sure rack is in the middle of the oven. Grease and line a jelly roll pan with parchment paper.

In a small bowl, microwave the chocolate until melted, about 15 seconds at a time. Do not overcook.

In a large bowl, beat yolks, add sugar, and vanilla. Add cooled chocolate.

In a separate bowl, mix flour, baking powder, and salt. Add to egg and chocolate mixture and stir. Add up to 1/2 cup boiling water to make a stiff batter.

In another bowl, whip egg whites to stiff peaks. Add a large spoonful of the whipped whites to the batter to lighten before lightly folding in the remaining egg whites.

Spread the batter on the parchment paper in the jelly roll pan, making sure you get the batter all the way to the corners.

Bake 13–15 minutes.

Remove cake from the oven and loosen the corners right away with a spatula. Let the cake rest for about 10 minutes. Sprinkle with 3 tablespoons powdered sugar. Place a clean (thin) kitchen towel over the cake and carefully flip out of the pan onto a clean counter. Carefully remove the parchment paper. Starting with a short end, roll the cake *and* towel together. Wrap and chill for about 1 hour.

Whipped Cream Filling:

Whip cream in a deep bowl. As the cream starts to hold its shape in soft peaks, add the sugar, 1 teaspoon at a time. Beat until thick. Stop before it becomes BUTTER! About 3–4 minutes.

Unroll the cake on a clean surface. Spread the cream to the edges, leaving 1 inch of space on the outer edge, where the cake will come together. Roll the cake back up, *without* the towel this time. Only cake and cream. Place the cake seam-side down on your serving platter. Chill again, for 1 hour, before frosting.

Chocolate Butter Cream Frosting:

Melt butter in a saucepan over medium-low heat. Add cocoa and salt and stir until smooth. Add cream and stir. Then add powdered sugar 1 cup at a time, stirring until smooth each time. When the frosting gets too hard to stir, add the espresso a little at a time until you get a nice, satiny consistency. Cool the mixture!

Frost the log. After frosting, use a knife or fork to make rough edges and stripes to give the look of natural bark. Because it's a thick frosting, you might have to "saw" back and forth through the frosting. It's fun!

Yule Log (Gluten-free)

(Serves 8–12)

Chocolate Jelly Roll:

3-1/2 ounces dark semi-sweet chocolate
4 egg yolks
3/4 cup sugar
1 teaspoon gluten-free vanilla
3/4 cup sweet rice flour (or a mixture of your favorite gluten-free flour)
1 teaspoon baking powder
1/2 teaspoon xanthan gum
1/2 teaspoon salt
up to 1/2 cup boiling water
4 egg whites
3 tablespoons powdered sugar

Whipped Cream Filling:

1 pint heavy whipping cream
3 teaspoons sugar

Chocolate Butter Cream Frosting:

1/2 cup butter
1/2 cup cocoa powder
dash salt
4 tablespoons cream
4 cups powdered sugar
1 ounce espresso

Chocolate Jelly Roll:

Preheat oven to 375 degrees F. Make sure rack is in the middle of the oven. Grease and line a jelly roll pan with parchment paper.

In a small bowl, microwave the chocolate until melted, about 15 seconds at a time. Do not overcook.

In a large bowl, beat yolks, add sugar, and gluten-free vanilla. Add cooled chocolate.

In a separate bowl, mix gluten-free flour, baking powder, xanthan gum, and salt. Add to egg and chocolate mixture and stir. Add up to 1/2 cup boiling water to make a stiff batter.

In another bowl, whip egg whites to stiff peaks. Add a large spoonful of the whipped whites to the batter to lighten before lightly folding in the remaining egg whites.

Spread the batter on the parchment paper in the jelly roll pan, making sure you get the batter all the way to the corners.

Bake 13–15 minutes.

Remove cake from the oven and loosen the corners right away with a spatula. Let the cake rest for about 10 minutes. Sprinkle with 3 tablespoons powdered sugar. Place a clean (thin) kitchen towel over the cake and carefully flip out of the pan onto a clean counter. Carefully remove the parchment paper. Starting with a short end, roll the cake *and* towel together. Wrap and chill for about 1 hour.

Whipped Cream Filling:

Whip cream in a deep bowl. As the cream starts to hold its shape in soft peaks, add the sugar, 1 teaspoon at a time. Beat until thick. Stop before it becomes BUTTER! About 3–4 minutes.

Unroll the cake on a clean surface. Spread the cream to the edges, leaving 1 inch of space on the outer edge, where the cake will come together. Roll the cake back up, *without* the towel this time. Only cake and cream. Place the cake seam-side down on your serving platter. Chill again, for 1 hour, before frosting.

Chocolate Butter Cream Frosting:

Melt butter in a saucepan over medium-low heat. Add cocoa and salt and stir until smooth. Add cream and stir. Then add powdered sugar 1 cup at a time, stirring until smooth each time. When the frosting gets too hard to stir, add the espresso a little at a time until you get a nice, satiny consistency. Cool the mixture!

After frosting the log, use a knife or fork to make rough edges and stripes to give the look of natural bark. Because it's a thick frosting, you might have to "saw" back and forth through the frosting. It's fun!

About the Author

Daryl Wood Gerber is the Agatha Award–winning, nationally bestselling author of the French Bistro Mysteries, featuring a bistro owner in Napa Valley, as well as the Cookbook Nook Mysteries, featuring an admitted foodie and owner of a cookbook store in Crystal Cove, California. Under the pen name Avery Aames, Daryl writes the Cheese Shop Mysteries, featuring a cheese shop owner in Providence, Ohio.

As a girl, Daryl considered becoming a writer, but she was dissuaded by a seventh-grade teacher. It wasn't until she was in her twenties that she had the temerity to try her hand at writing again . . . for TV and screen. Why? Because she was an actress in Hollywood. A fun tidbit for mystery buffs: Daryl co-starred on *Murder, She Wrote* as well as other TV shows. As a writer, she created the format for the popular sitcom *Out of This World*. When she moved across the country with her husband, she returned to writing what she loved to read: mysteries and thrillers.

Daryl is originally from the Bay Area and graduated from Stanford University. She loves to cook, read, golf, swim, and garden. She also likes adventure and has been known to jump out of a perfectly good airplane. Here are a few of Daryl's lifelong mottos: perseverance will out; believe you can; never give up. She hopes they will become yours, as well.

To learn more about Daryl and her books, visit her website at DarylWoodGerber.com.